SHADES OF CHAOS

SARAH URQUHART

Join my newsletter to keep up to date on new releases, special events, and sneak peeks.
https://bit.ly/sarahurq

ALSO IN THE KING'S MERCENARIES SERIES

For the touch of crazy that lives in all of us. Be bold Wild Ones!

1

"WHO KILLED HIM?" HENDRICK STARED DOWN HIS
father, who sat on the buttery leather couch, leaning
comfortably back in the corner, his arm lying across the
back with a glass of scotch in his hand. The bastard's
expression lay as relaxed as his body. One thick eyebrow
arched as he tilted his head back to look up at his son.
Not that Hendrick would ever admit to being as such.

"It's already taken care of. That isn't what we need to
focus on right now."

"Who. Killed. Him?" Finding the person who killed
his brother and burning him inch by slow, torturous
inch was Hendrick's only focus. He wouldn't have ever
stepped foot in this house if Shane was still here. He
didn't have to with Shane taking his place. And that was
the only reason his Simon Pierce withheld information
about his brother's murderer. A bargaining chip to keep
Hendrick here.

"It's over. There are other matters that can't wait."

Four months. Four months since Hendrick received
the note.

For Kit. Shane is dead.

The other mercenaries didn't know his true name and hadn't realized that by reading that note aloud, they'd shattered his heart.

"And what fucking matters would those be?" Hendrick was purposely playing dumb. His father had already tried to act as if Hendrick would come home to rule the family and business. On the day of the funeral. If he hadn't needed to be as close to Shane as possible that day, his parents wouldn't have ever seen him.

"The business is floundering and there are vultures swarming without a proper leader. Alliances need to be made and you need to do your job."

"You do it."

"I'm retired." His head rolled along the back of the couch as if just the thought of work exhausted his poor old body. Hendrick inwardly snorted. The man was barely sixty and as fit as he was twenty years ago.

"Not anymore, unless you'd like to hand it all off to one of the loyal grunts that have been here for years." Some men working for his family had been there since Hendrick was born. Even their sons worked in the family business now.

"That isn't how it works. Now," His father peeled himself away from the soft cushions to lean his elbows on his knees. He started to speak, then frowned, interrupting his own thoughts. "For God's sake, Kit. Sit down and stop towering."

"No."

His father sighed. "I've set up several alliances. All that's left is your approval of the contracts. In fact, we can deal with at least one of them shortly." A sly grin lifted the corners of his lips. Hendrick learned never to trust that grin. He needed to get out of here.

"Give me the fucking name." He didn't think his father realized exactly how dangerous Hendrick had become since he left. And he let some of it show in his eyes. He'd been told on more than one occasion how crazy his eyes looked, and he'd embraced it. It was something that had always been part of him, the reason he'd never fit in here. No one considered him stable. They thought crazy meant impulsive. Impulsiveness was rare for him.

His father's lower jaw rolled as he moved his mouth around in thought. "I'll give you the name. After you finish dealing with the alliances and take your place here."

Hendrick studied the man. He'd spent enough years doing it. What every movement meant, his tells and the way he played games. It had been well over a decade since Hendrick set eyes on the man until the funeral, but as he observed him now, not much had changed besides the bastard's desire to be a lazy retiree.

"Well?"

"You don't know who killed Shane." He dropped his voice and added just the right lilt to create a threat.

His father blinked away the surprise that had slightly flared. "Do you think I would have gone this long without avenging my son's murder?" He attempted to match Hendrick's tone and stood when he finished speaking as if realizing the tone didn't hold as much power with him sitting down.

Hendrick still towered over his father and he moved toe to toe with the man who tried to claim he'd raised him. "Yes, I do. I'll find out who. I'll deal with it, leaving you out of it. And I'm never coming back here."

Hendrick turned and stalked through the house. A lot had changed over the years. Same layout, but every surface shone with the upgrade of expensive surfaces. His mother hovered in the kitchen as he passed.

"Kit! Where are you going?"

She'd been kind and had done her best, but at the end of every day, her loyalties remained with their father. She'd say what she needed to appease him and Shane, offering the sweetness more of a grandmother than a mother, then would turn her back and allow their father to do as he pleased regarding them.

Hendrick settled the same threatening glare on her, but he saved her his words. Although knowingly blind and blissful in her life, she was his mother and a woman that only aimed to please everyone in her path.

She startled and stepped back. "Please don't leave. We need you."

"No, you don't." Hendrick left, letting the door slam hard behind him. Childish satisfaction at the echoing sound filled his following sigh.

He breathed in the night air, the barely there chill, and rolled his neck. Stalking around the property, he evaded the guards and made it to his truck without being spotted. He hadn't parked directly at his parent's house, but toward the back and at the edge of the neighbor's property. The neighboring property was empty and up for sale. If there hadn't been a grieving crime family next door, it would have already sold. Prospective buyers were concerned about getting in the middle of an upcoming feud. But Hendrick's father didn't seem at all interested in revenge or feuding. He was only interested in living a comfortable retirement while still pulling strings.

A flash of white stopped his tracks. Trees still shielded him from being seen, but flowing white fabric glowed under the moon. The woman with chestnut waves had a bag slung over her shoulder, forcing her to tilt her body to keep it there while she fisted her dress to expose her feet and watch her steps. Her head swiveled after every three steps. While she wasn't yet panting, her breathing was shallow and steady.

She spotted his truck and stood straighter. Round eyes searched the area before she took off, running on her tiptoes to lessen the noise. Hendrick watched her heft her bag into the bed and take one more look around before pulling her dress up further and setting one foot on the tire to launch herself over. She ducked down in the back.

He had a stowaway.

Keeping an ear out for anyone following her or for his father's guards, Hendrick moved toward his truck on silent feet.

"Are you sure you want to get in there?" He pitched his voice low and angled toward the bed rather than out toward the trees.

Her reply started with a choked squeak until she looked up at him and she calmed with a breath. She didn't fear being found, but only found by someone specific.

Slender fingers gripped the edge, and she popped her head up over the side. "Uh." Wide eyes of someone caught red-handed made a show of looking at him, the trees, and then the bed of his truck. "Yes. I'm sure this is the way out of here." She ducked back down, hiding away against the top of the bed.

For once, the crazy part of him had nothing to say. Left speechless, Hendrick stared at the spot where her head had been seconds ago.

The same hand slapped the edge, and she pulled her head back up. "This is the part where you get in the truck and drive away, pretending you never saw me." She stared at him.

Hendrick heard the rustling in the trees. Whoever was after her was on her tail. But what was she doing on his father's property and was it his guards chasing her?

Her eyes widened as if she'd snapped at him. *Move, dumbass.* As soon as he took his first step, she tucked herself back in the bed of his truck.

Shutting the driver's door, he started the truck and pulled away seconds before guards burst through the trees. He'd help his stow away escape them. But he wouldn't let her escape him.

———————

THE NEXT BREATH that filled Kinley's lungs didn't hurt as the truck pulled away. She didn't know who the man sitting behind the wheel was, but he didn't belong to her father, and that was all that mattered. Kinley planned to wait for a slow stretch of traffic or for him to stop somewhere, anywhere, and she'd jump out and run. Entirely random and therefore harder to track. She had a change of clothes in her bag, toiletries, and her wallet. With her own money. She hadn't depended on her father's funds for a long time. It was shocking how much money one could make online these days.

The truck kept at a steady pace. Street lights flashed in and out of the truck bed, but they never seemed to get caught at a red light. What were the odds? He took turns too fast for her to make a leap for it. Not that he sped. But the man knew she was trying to run.

The announcement her father made only hours ago was the nail in Kinley's life. He'd never change his mind and see her for more than weak, and on occasion, a disappointment. For what use was a daughter?

A hell of a lot if he ever stopped rolling his eyes long enough to see what was in front of him.

White fabric flowed around her body, and she hated it. It wasn't hers or something she'd choose for herself. Her mother had floated into her bedroom with excitement carrying this dress.

"I've been holding onto this secret for months. I'm so excited." She cradled the dress and laid it out on Kinley's bed.

"A secret?" Kinley filled with dread as she frowned at the dress.

"You're engaged, Kinley." Her mother bounced and gripped Kinley's hands. "Isn't that wonderful?"

Engaged and to meet her betrothed in a few short hours. There'd been a reason they kept it a secret from her until the last minute. They thought she'd try to escape, and by giving her no time to plan, she couldn't.

Kinley could form a plan fairly quick and had a large purse packed in under five minutes. She'd followed the current set of guards to her parents and out of the house like the good girl her father expected her to be. He knew nothing about her.

While living under his nose with almost lifelong guards hovering over her shoulder, she became an entirely different person than he thought possible. To him, she was a pretty ornament that shouldn't speak. Her mother had become a silent annoyance to him. But that had been her own doing. Not that Kinley didn't sympathize with her reasons, but her mother didn't look for a way out of her current situation—what Kinley equated to servitude.

The street lights became fewer and farther between until they were non-existent. Her body cramped from the balled up position. After an easy half an hour more, the truck turned slower.

Kinley peered over the edge, and trees were the only thing in sight. She'd have to hike back into town to find a way out of it. But oh well, she'd do what she had to escape.

As the truck lurched to a stop, she braced one foot on the edge and launched herself to the ground on the passenger side of the truck. Gripping her bag tight over her shoulder, she ran. It didn't matter where just yet, as long as she was alone.

"I wouldn't go that way," the man called after her, his voice booming in the quiet darkness.

"Doesn't matter what you'd do," Kinley yelled back and kept running.

"You'll ruin that pretty dress in the heath."

That brought her to a stop. She didn't give a care in the world about this dress, but she didn't want to travel dragging a wet dress and feet. The heath was filled with soft, soggy, thick grass with patchy ponds. She'd never know where she'd step next.

Turning an exact ninety degrees, she threw a brow over her shoulder before starting her hike. He'd already seen her and wasn't chasing her—there was no need to run anymore and tire herself out.

"The coyotes up that way have settled their dens a lot closer this year." As if given a cue, a high howl echoed.

Kinley sighed and faced him. She hadn't looked at him earlier for more time than to determine he didn't belong to her father, but now she took him in. Shaggy dark blond hair that reached the bottoms of his ears. Broad square shoulders stretched the long-sleeved shirt he wore. A clean face showed the hard edges and his eyes were deep, despite not being able to see the colour from this distance. He was tall and hard, and if he didn't want her to escape him, she wouldn't. But he leaned against his truck with his hands in his pockets and one ankle crossed over the other.

He arched a brow as if to ask what her next move was.

"Well, which direction do you suggest?" She unclenched her teeth so she didn't speak through them.

"That one." He tilted his head over his left shoulder. A small house sat behind where he'd parked the truck.

"That one looks as dangerous and as disappointing as the coyotes and the heath." Kinley shook her head and decided the road was the best choice and worth the risk. "Thanks for the ride." She had to walk past him along the short driveway.

A large hand struck out and caught her elbow. "No."

"No?" If she kept her neck back this far for long, it'd ache horribly.

"You're coming inside and telling me why you're running and who you're running from." His eyes dropped down her body, taking in the dress all the way to the ground and then back up to her face. Not that he had to strain his neck.

9

"Listen, I appreciate your cooperation in my escape, but I don't owe you an explanation." The less people knew, the better.

"Yes, you do. Who could end up on my tail?"

Kinley pursed her lips. It wasn't an unfair request. But what would stop him from turning them around and delivering her back to her parents, demanding a reward?

He robbed her of her decision as he pulled her closer to his chest. His grin was an odd mix—soft but edgy, kind, but a cruelty lurked. He moved them toward the dark blue door, punching in a code on the electronic lock. Keeping her in front of him, he gently pushed her into the house and shut and locked the door behind him.

"Spill."

"I'm running away from home." Kinley announced like Dorothy to Professor Marvel, and spun herself around, letting the dress flourish around her legs. Cocking her head, she granted him a calculating smile, attempting to warn him not to fuck with her.

"Interesting statement your escape is making." A thick finger moved up and down, indicating her dress.

"The dress is lying."

His nostrils flared with the effort of holding back the twitch in his lips.

"It also wasn't my choice."

"And what would you have worn to run away from home?" Humour laced the question, but it was faint.

She narrowed her eyes. "Something practical. Like I said, the dress lies."

"Why are you running away from home?"

"My father made plans for my future and leaving the

situation is the only way to avoid it altogether." Kinley circled the open level of the house, keeping herself facing the man that still stood in front of the door. A fine layer of dust lay on most surfaces, but it wasn't enough for her to believe someone had abandoned the place. A small table sat in the centre of an L-shaped kitchen, and large furniture filled the living space. At the right, a short hallway presumably led to bedrooms, bathrooms, and whatever else the house had. Double glass doors were on the other side of the house, behind one couch.

"So it's your father that will be on your tail?" He moved closer to her, not following her, but cutting across the centre of the house.

"Whoever he sends after me, yes." Kinley shrugged. She doubted her father would do any physical searching of his own.

"What lies is that dress saying?"

When she snapped her head up, he wasn't looking at her face, but scanning the dress. "Looks like you understand perfectly." Sweet innocence had been the intention. Hoping the sight enticed her *betrothed*.

The white, bohemian lace covered fabric hugged her breasts with capped shoulders and reached the floor. *A demure sight of amicability*, her father had said as she'd walked down the stairs.

She wasn't anything like the good girl he imagined.

THERE WAS ONLY one thing keeping Hendrick from letting the woman go on her own with no explanation. And that was because he'd found her escaping his father's property. His parents had been expecting company and had wanted Hendrick to stay, not just for good, but to meet whoever was coming for dinner.

Apparently, the slight woman in front of him and her parents had been their expected company. He had to give her credit for her escape. Stowing away in the first vehicle she found hadn't been a terrible plan, even if a little risky. If he were the man his father wanted him to be, she'd be in a whole lot of trouble.

"What's your name?" He continued to stalk her around his small safe house, keeping space between them, but staying close enough to grab her if she tried to run.

Light brown eyes studied him. "Kinley. Yours?"

"Hendrick." At least that was the name he preferred and was best known by.

She nodded and her shoulders imperceptibly relaxed.

"Are you hungry?" They weren't going anywhere tonight. He might as well make them both comfortable and take his time getting her story from her.

Her lips twisted as she nodded.

Hendrick kept his safe houses stocked with non-perishables, updating them regularly. This place was one of three. King's Mercenaries had plenty of their own, but Hendrick hadn't wanted to drag this onto King and Dak's territory. They still didn't know his true name or where he came from. None of the mercenaries did.

He'd run away from home, as Kinley had described it. He didn't want his bosses to know he came from one of the most powerful crime families in town. Would it have coloured their perception of him when he started working with them? Definitely. Would it be an issue now, after years of working together? Maybe. Trust was the driving force of their group, and keeping a secret this big for so long would dent that shining trust. A catch twenty-two if he ever saw one.

"Sit." Hendrick pointed to the small table in the kitchen. If he was going to cook, he needed Kinley to stay in one place. One where if she tried to run, she'd make enough noise he'd have time to catch her.

Glaring, she pulled out a chair and sat, but kept it away from the table. She had more than enough room to leap up and run.

Hendrick leaned down behind her, pausing until the size of him towering over her back registered. Gripping the sides of the chair next to her hips, he lifted and tucked her legs under the table.

"So where were you off to this evening that you never made it to?" Hendrick opened the cupboards and pulled out a box of pasta and a jar of sauce. It wasn't anything special, but it would do. He kept garlic bread in the freezer. He let that thaw on the counter enough until the pasta was done.

"A dinner."

He set the pot down a little harder than necessary on the stove top and turned on her. He waited until she fidgeted under his stare before speaking. "I can help you."

"I don't need help." Her chin lifted and her back straightened with poised, confident strength. Maybe she didn't need help. But that didn't mean she couldn't take it.

"I didn't say you did. Just said I can." He leaned against the counter while waiting for the water to boil.

"My parents wanted me to meet someone tonight."

"This have anything to do with the future your father planned for you?"

"It had everything to do with that." Menace filled her tone, but she didn't aim it at him. Her eyes focused on the centre of the small table in front of her.

Hendrick didn't like where this was going and he was putting an end to the vague tidbits. That white dress made her look like a beach bride or a bride about to attend her engagement party. Placing one hand on the back of the chair and one on the table, he leaned down to see every twitch of her eyes, every tell in the tiny muscles in her soft face. "What did your father want that dress to say? I suggest you don't evade the question this time."

"Amiable. Soft. Sweet." She paused. "Pure." She uttered each word with disdain.

"And why would he want it to say that?" Hendrick tilted his head. Despite the hatred of those descriptions, her breath still caught after each one. She blinked rapidly the longer he stayed near. "I wonder." He moved so his breath brushed her ear. "Is that dress screaming lies or whispering truths?"

She didn't answer either question, but her breathing sped up.

"Who did they want you to meet, Kinley?" At his father's house.

"My father arranged a marriage."

Hendrick snapped. Fire burned his eyes and the flirting for the truth stopped in an instant. Wrapping a hand around her throat, he used his thumb to force her head back to look at him. His father had used the word alliances, one of which was supposed to attend dinner that night. One fucking old school way to form an alliance was through marriage.

Kinley's eyes matched his fury, but she trembled beneath him with a touch of fear. He was twice her size and had a grip on her neck.

"Who did he want you to marry?"

Her evasiveness vanished. "Kit Pierce."

His fingers tightened a fraction before he let her go with a growl that echoed in the tiny house. That growl morphed into a terrifying laughter. He barely saw the shock on Kinley's face as he doubled over at the waist.

His father was a fucking idiot.

"I don't understand why this made you angry. Or why this is funny." Her hands gripped the table, ready to bolt, but she continued to stare at him.

"What's your surname?"

"Curry."

He started laughing again. Another powerful crime family. They ran a series of restaurants and clubs that were used to arrange meetings, trades, run goods through. Without them, many of the deals of crime syndicates wouldn't be possible, or at the very least, a lot more susceptible to getting caught.

"You recognize the names and families. My father wanted me to marry so that my husband could take over the Curry business instead of his inept daughter."

"I'll tell you a secret. Both Pierce and your father are fucking idiots."

"What are you talking about?"

"Kit," his own name tasted strange on his tongue, "won't take over any business. Even his own father's. You would have been safe from marrying the guy."

"How do you know that?"

"I think you forgot where we met." The water was boiling now, so he turned his back on her to pour the pasta into the pot.

"You know the family."

He didn't need to answer that.

"What's Kit like?" Now that the threat was over, she seemed curious. Hendrick glanced over his shoulder. Anger and fear still lingered in her posture and those hazelnut eyes, but she frowned up at him.

"Crazy. Consider yourself lucky."

2

KNOWING SHE WOULDN'T HAVE TO MARRY KIT
didn't lessen the importance of her decision. If she
hadn't left, opportunities for her would have been
nonexistent. It had always been part of her plan and
hadn't been the first time she tried to escape.

The urgency of the night fled. No nuptials for her.
But who was this man and how was he connected to the
Pierce's?

"You said you could help. How?"

"Depends on what you want to do. I can help you
get out of the city, the province, even the country, if
that's what you want. Or I can set you up right under
your father's nose in a way you're untouchable." He
talked while stirring the sauce in the pot and pushing
garlic bread down in the toaster.

"And what would it cost me?"

Hendrick paused, setting the large spoon down over
the rim of the pot. He turned, his deep eyes taking her
in, from her face and down as much of her torso that

was visible above the table. His eyes were hazel most of the time, but she swore she saw green as he continued to stare. Hazel could be so unpredictable. "Nothing."

"Bullshit."

His lips quirked, but he didn't burst into laughter as he had earlier.

"My father may believe me to be inept, but he's wrong. I know more about his business and how this world runs than he does. There's always a price, a deal, a bargain. There's no need to trick one out of me. As I said, I don't need your help, but I'm curious what you're capable of."

With his lips still holding an amusing lilt, he turned back to the food. They both remained silent as he dished up two plates and set them on the table.

"Thank you." She managed the regal politeness with which her mother had raised her.

"You're right."

"You don't need to inform me of that."

He chuckled. "I'll make you a deal."

"You can suggest it. I may not agree."

"Naturally. I'll help you. I can at least make it easier and quicker for you to get away or even to taunt your father. In exchange for an answer to my earlier question."

"I answered all your questions." Despite holding the truth and details until he'd had his hand wrapped around her throat.

"No, you didn't."

She frowned, playing back their conversation. "Which question?"

"Is that dress screaming lies or whispering truths?"

The answer was both, and she didn't need the man

who kept staring at it to know that. "What would you do to help? What makes you capable of providing the things to make my escape easier and quicker?"

"Have you heard of *King Security*?"

She grinned. *King Security* was the polite legal name of the business. "You mean *King's Mercenaries*? Yes, I know who they are." Run by the man known as the king of mercenaries for almost two decades.

"I'm one of them."

Kinley lost her grin and lost her courage. *King's Mercenaries* were deadly and the best. No one crossed them, at least no one who knew what was good for them. And she was sitting across from one of them. One of the deadliest assassins and men for hire. "No deal. I'll manage on my own."

"I won't hurt you, Kinley." His voice changed, lowering in a way that made her name come out smooth.

She looked away, shutting him out while they ate. She wondered if her father was foolish enough to go against the mercenaries. It wouldn't be the first time he'd made a foolish decision and put the entire family at risk. If Kinley didn't have the ear of several of her father's men, she wouldn't have been able to get them out of that mess.

Hendrick didn't push her, even after they finished eating and he cleaned up. But she thought it might be just as foolish to align herself with the mercenaries as it would be to go against them.

"Thank you for your help tonight, Hendrick. But I think it's best if I do this on my own." She stood from the table and faced him.

"Suit yourself. Get some rest and in the morning I'll

drop you off wherever you want." His tone was all business for only a moment. It took two steps to bring him in front of her, and his face changed as soon as he towered over her. "But I still want an answer to my question."

"Sorry to disappoint you." Inwardly, she cursed the breathless whisper that responded to him.

"Have you been stuck under your father's roof your entire life?"

"Pretty much."

"Sweet and amiable are choices of your own. But soft? Yes. Pure? I have to wonder."

"You can wonder all you want. I said, no deal."

"It's late. We should get some sleep." But he didn't move away from her or give her space. His body heat warmed her front even though they didn't touch.

"I appreciate it. Which room is mine?" Kinley intended to take the kindness rather than offend the mercenary. The twice her size mercenary.

"There's only one." He delivered those three words with deep vibrations from his chest. Despite the danger this man posed, she wasn't immune to him. But she couldn't let him think he'd get anything more from her than verbal gratitude.

"That couch is going to be very uncomfortable for someone your size."

He laughed, a full bark bursting forward. A large hand landed on her shoulder and slid down her arm. "Neither of us is sleeping on the couch." He cupped her elbow and steered her down the hall. "Not when I'm positive you'd run the moment I fell asleep."

"A smart person would."

"Very true." He took her into the bedroom and let her go.

She fought the urge to rub her elbow. Not from a harsh grip, but to wipe away the tingles left from the extra blood flow his touch had caused. The bedroom was as cozy as the rest of the house. A queen sized bed with a massive headboard centred the room. Two nightstands sitting on either side were the only other furniture. Sliding doors across from the bed housed a small closet. And to the left of the bedroom door was a bathroom.

"There are clothes in the closet. Not sure what or the sizes, but you're welcome to use anything you find." Hendrick leaned against the wall beside the door and crossed his arms. With a single arched brow, he nodded toward the closet and then the bathroom.

Kinley mimicked his stance and stared back with the same arch to her own brow. She used the challenge as time for herself to decide how to handle her current situation. This was the most freedom she'd had her entire life, but the man in front of her wouldn't allow her to leave.

She had to ask if he was giving her the choice to leave or stay, wouldn't she choose to stay? It was late, dark, and she didn't know where they were. Would she willingly choose to stay with one of King's mercenaries? Fighting him now and storming out into the night would only be cutting her nose off to spite her face.

Kinley released them from whatever staring trance she'd put them in and opened the closet. T-shirts, jeans, sweats, pajamas, men's, women's all hung in an organized row.

She hated the dress, but the clothes weren't hers. Again, not using them was only childish. And sleeping in this dress would be a nightmare. She had her own change of clothes with her, but only the one and she'd need those in the morning.

A soft pajama set in mint green caught her attention. Pulling the hanger down, she draped them over her arm. His eyes hadn't left her, and Kinley met the heat of his stare the entire short stroll to the bathroom.

HENDRICK DIDN'T MOVE from his position next to the bedroom door until Kinley tucked herself under the covers. She'd walked out of the bathroom in the soft pajamas. They were far from scandalous, and if he remembered right, there were several such pieces in that closet. The sleeves stopped just below her elbows and the pants were long enough they covered her feet.

What the fuck had his father been thinking? Had he thought the innocent-looking bride would help entice him to stay? Fucking idiot.

Hendrick only had one mission that mattered right now. Find who killed his brother. And Kinley had her own mission. But that didn't mean Hendrick would allow her to run off into the night.

Once the blankets were tucked under her chin, and she pushed herself to the edge of the bed, Hendrick stripped down to his boxers. He left his clothes on the floor next to the door. The sheets were cool as he slid between them. Laying on his back, he let out a long sigh and tucked his arm behind his head.

"Goodnight, Kinley." With his eyes closed, he

counted her breaths until she answered. Two. Three. Four.

"Night."

He'd meant it when he told her he'd help her in whatever way she wanted. Helping her say fuck you to her own father would be a way for him to say the same to his.

An arranged marriage as an alliance. Hendrick inwardly shook his head. No sane woman would align themselves with him. He was unpredictable to outside eyes. It didn't matter he was always cautious. To those watching him, he came across as unhinged. Just the way he liked it.

Indulging in that insane part of him, letting it free every once in a while reminded him of who he was and who he never wanted to be.

As Kinley's breathing slowed and deepened, Hendrick turned his head to make out the silhouette of her in the dark. What would have happened to her if she hadn't gotten away when she did? Would life have just carried on as normal? Would she have been auctioned off to someone else, or would they have used her as bait for him? How the hell did she get away?

His lips twitched. He hoped he could get the story from her in the morning. In the morning, before he helped her disappear. She may have claimed she didn't want the help of one of King's mercenaries, but he was going to help her, anyway.

It took practice over the years to force a certain type of sleep. He only allowed his mind to slip into a lower level of unconsciousness to ensure if Kinley got out of bed, he'd wake instantly.

But the night passed with no attempts from the

woman next to him. She'd slept, despite tossing and turning most of the night. Dawn would creep through the windows soon and Kinley had just settled into a deep sleep again. If Hendrick was going to shower without worry of her running, he'd have to do it now.

He silently left the bed. Leaving the bathroom door open a crack, he took one of the quickest showers of his life.

Why he should care if she ran, he didn't understand. But Hendrick didn't like the image of her back in the hands of her father. Or his. Not that she wouldn't be fine on her own, but Hendrick could guarantee it.

With the towel wrapped around his hips, he leaned against the bathroom door and watched her sleep. His chest twisted at the sight of her. A pawn. That was how his father saw everyone. As a pawn. Even Shane had been a pawn in his eyes, and he expected Hendrick to step into his brother's shoes so he could do the same to him. But his father didn't know what Shane had been capable of. Shane had been winning the loyalty of every single one of their father's favourites. His power had been dwindling for years without his knowledge because he was too lazy to step out of his cushy vacation homes.

And that was how Kinley's father felt about her. Someone to use to further himself. Hendrick would make sure she was out of their reach. He needed to convince her to accept his help without letting her know who he was. Her supposed betrothed.

Holding back a sigh, Hendrick moved to the closet to find clean clothes. The moment he dropped the towel, a small gasp came from the bed. He paused and cocked his head.

"Good morning, Kinley."

She didn't answer him. He looked over his shoulder in time to see her pull the blankets over her face.

"Hmm. Interesting reaction." He murmured. The blankets muffled a feminine growl. Hendrick didn't bother holding back his chuckle as he turned around before grabbing clothes from the closet. "Why hide, Kinley? It's nothing you haven't seen before. Isn't it?" He was an ass for pushing her, but since she refused to answer his question about her dress, he was obsessed with finding out.

She slapped the blankets down on her lap and sat up, meeting his eyes and nothing else. His grin grew as he met her glare, waiting for her to break and for those round eyes to drop. He didn't want to miss a second of what crossed her features when she saw him. The amount of money sitting in his account would make an insane fortune if he bet it on that dress of hers. Those whispered truths were getting louder.

But for all that truth, he knew it wasn't her choice or doing. She'd been trapped in her father's home from what he'd gathered last night.

Her breathing quickened. Hendrick dropped his chin, making her sternly focused gaze move. Her eyes landed on his cock and her face tightened in an effort not to react, but Hendrick saw the slight twitch.

Kinley's tongue slid along her lips and she brought her face back up to his as she rose from the bed. She set her shoulders back and gripped her reaction in a figuratively tight grip, locking down the rising blush.

"Fuck you." The words escaped with a soft strength that didn't throw any hatred. Powerful and confident, she cocked her brow and strode to the bathroom.

Well, damn. But he should have expected that after how they'd met.

Hendrick dressed and busied himself with making coffee and breakfast while he listened to the shower run. He froze when Kinley walked into the kitchen. Jeans hugged her rounded hips, and a simple T-shirt covered the rest of her. She'd put her wet hair into two braids that went past her shoulders down her back. Hendrick liked this look better than the white dress. Not that he hadn't had images of tearing that dress from her to devour her. But the woman in front of him now was the complete opposite of the stow away he'd found in his truck.

KINLEY HAD SPENT way too much time catching her breath in the shower. But as soon as she did, she hadn't lingered and got herself to the kitchen as fast as possible. After seeing what he hid under those clothes, she couldn't look at him the same.

One look at his naked body and Kinley had cursed her father. She was smart and could manage her father's entire business with one hand tied behind her back. The free one was to defend herself. Kinley was more capable than anyone believed. But put her in front of the one thing she never grasped out of life and her lungs struggled.

"Where do you want me to take you?" Hendrick asked with one raised brow while he stirred something on the stove. It smelled like oatmeal.

"The airport." Kinley slid between him and the

counter to pull down a cup and pour herself a coffee. It was hard to ignore his body heat and to keep her body from touching his. Staying there, she forced down any reaction she had toward him. She closed her eyes over the first slow sip. "This is good."

"I'm picky with my coffee."

She moved out from the corner and leaned against the other end.

"Where do you plan on flying to?" He didn't move his gaze from the pot.

"That's on a need to know basis." All it would take was for one person to know her plans for her to lose any head start. She wasn't naïve enough not to think her father couldn't find out where she went once she'd boarded the plane, but she'd continue to lose him until she found the place she wanted to be.

"Fair enough." His tone suggested he understood. Being a mercenary, she imagined he was full of secrets. "But I wish you'd let me help you."

"Why?" She gripped her mug tighter and let sweet bitterness fill her tone. "Because there must be a flaw somewhere in my plan that will lead to getting caught?" She wasn't the damsel in white she'd appeared to be— that her father saw her as.

Hendrick took the pot off the burner and turned around to face her. "No." He crossed his arms and took his time looking her over from head to toe, sending shivers in his wake. "I only want to help. Why not use whatever you have at your disposal to ensure you succeed?"

"Once I'm on the plane, I'm no concern of yours, or anyone." She smiled, softening. He wasn't wrong and despite who he worked for, he'd been kind. "The airport will be more than enough help. Thank you."

Hendrick nodded. She sat at the table while he dished up two bowls. The silence stretched as they ate and sipped the coffee. Left in her thoughts, Kinley tried to imagine one of her many dreams of escape. She had the outline of a plan, just enough to put her out of her father's reach. But where she wanted to end up and what she wanted to do with her independence, Kinley wasn't sure. She'd had multiple dreams over the years. Living somewhere remote. Going to school and getting a degree or two. Starting her own competing business to her father's and becoming the sharpest thorn in his side. She had the money to do whatever she wanted. As long as she never found herself under his guard again.

To help hurry them along, Kinley cleared the table and washed the dishes. She'd already packed her bag, snatching a change of clothes from the closet. She'd send a replacement for him. Not because the closet was low on clothes, but because that was how she intended to conduct herself. And she didn't need to give Hendrick, one of King's mercenaries, a reason to hunt her down.

With everything cleared, she pulled the strap to her purse over her shoulder and faced Hendrick. "I'd like to go now. Please."

"Let's go." He slapped the table and stood, gesturing her to go ahead of him. The trill of a phone broke her stride, and she watched Hendrick pull the phone from his pocket and wince.

He answered with his name and listened for several minutes before his eyes trapped hers. She watched his eyes darken and narrow. Adrenaline spiked, a harsh zap through her system. Her fight-or-flight response kicked into overdrive.

And while she had confidence in her skills, one glance at Hendrick had her doubting her ability against him.

3

HENDRICK HAD ALREADY IGNORED ENOUGH OF Dak's and King's calls. If he was going to be on the run for even the next few hours, he should at least check in with them.

"Hendrick."

"Finally. You've answered." Dak used the low monotone meant to intimidate. Not that it did much good.

Hendrick didn't need to speak. On a normal day, he'd have all kinds of things to say to get under his boss's skin, but he'd had less and less of that since his brother died.

"I have a job for you. Missing person, and the client has requested *you* handle it."

Hendrick's eyes snapped up to Kinley. The missing person stood in front of him and he was related to the one who requested him. The mercenaries might not know who he was, but his family knew where Hendrick worked.

He caught the tightening of her grip on the strap of

her purse too late. With impressive speed, she attacked. A hard front kick to his diaphragm had him dropping his phone and the keys that had been hanging from his other hand. But he never heard the clang of them hitting the floor.

Kinley snatched them from the air and bolted toward the door. The damn woman left him speechless for a second time.

"Hendrick!" Dak boomed through the phone speaker on the floor.

"Call you back," he said to the floor and ran after Kinley, who'd already made it outside. The white flats on her feet surprisingly stayed in place as she kicked up dust behind her. She could run. But his strides gave him enough advantage to catch her.

The lock on his truck clicked, and she slowed, skidding to a stop at the door. But she didn't touch the handle before he had an arm around her waist and spun her in the air to throw her over his shoulder. He squeezed her legs to keep her from kicking him, but he had no way to stop her from lifting herself off his back and bracing her hands on his shoulders.

"Let me go." She glared down at him.

"So you can steal my truck? No. Why the fuck did you run?"

"Time was up."

She'd seen something in his stare to spook her. He stalked back toward the house. "You might want to duck." He didn't slow as he approached the door.

Kinley dropped her weight down his back. Hendrick kicked the door shut, set her down on the counter, and pried his keys from her fist. "Don't move."

Not taking his eyes from her, he picked up his phone from the floor. The call hadn't disconnected.

"I said I'd call you back. Why didn't you hang up?" He moved to stand in front of Kinley.

"I had the time to wait. What's going on?"

"Doesn't matter."

The silence said more than any words Dak could utter. Hendrick hadn't been the same since Shane died and everyone had started tiptoeing around him.

"What are the details?" He needed everything about the job request.

"You're going after Kinley Curry. Daughter of Granville Curry—I don't need to tell you who he is. He requested you. Said a friend recommended you. She's gone missing. They didn't say how, but have been searching all night. Blocked roads out of town and stationed people at all airports. They believe she's still in town."

Fuck. "Give it a day and call them back. Say we've already tracked her down. She's long gone and out of our territory." He held Kinley's gaze as he said it. He needed her to understand he wouldn't hand her over to her father. Her lips parted and those round eyes wouldn't settle in one place on his face as she searched for any insight into his thoughts.

"Why would I say that?" Caution slowed his words.

"Do you have the exact roads they're blocking? Their locations?"

"I can get them."

"Do. Fast." Hendrick hung up. He had to deal with Kinley before he could deal with Dak. It would irritate Dak, but this was bigger than Hendrick hanging up on him. Part of what made the mercenaries as good as they were was the trust they all had in each other.

He slipped his phone in his pocket and set both hands down on the counter beside Kinley.

"I won't give you back to your father."

"So I was right? He's hired *King's Mercenaries*."

"Yes."

"You say you won't, but what about the others?"

"That isn't how we work. Besides, your father requested me."

"Why?"

The truth was on the tip of his tongue, but he said only what he was willing for her to know. "A friend recommended me, I guess." That friend had to be his father. It wasn't a recommendation at all. It was a way to pull him into this without him knowing.

"Then why wouldn't you let me run?"

"Because you were about to steal my truck."

"I would have returned it."

"Your plan to hit the airport is out."

"What do you mean it's out?" She lowered her voice and shoved against his chest, but Hendrick didn't move. Space gave her an advantage, and he wouldn't let his guard down around her again.

"Your father has blocked every way out of town overnight. Roads and airports. I'm getting their locations to find out if we're already past where they've set up their blocks. We aren't in town, but we aren't far out of it."

"We should have kept driving last night. I expected road blocks. I never expected him to cover the airports."

His phone buzzed. It was a text from Roen. He'd

sent maps marking the locations on the roads out of town. "Fuck."

"No." She shook her head and took his phone from his hand. "There has to be a way to get past them." She swiped through the pictures, her breath sawing in and out of her lungs. It was like watching her fingers clinging to the edge of a cliff.

His phone buzzed again in her hand and he took it back. Reading the message, he sighed. "Sorry, Kinley."

"Why?" she asked slowly.

"Your father has put a prize on your head. And they've hired us to find you. If one of us drives past any of those locations, they'll chase us."

Her eyes moved, like thoughts chasing each other. "A decoy."

Hendrick waited for her to finish her plan.

She shut her eyes. "He has enough people to chase all the decoys."

"What's your end goal?"

"That depended on where I landed. I had so many choices once I was free of him." Her shoulders dropped with her voice.

"I can still get you away from him. But it will take a few days at least." Hendrick took a step back, giving her the choice to trust him. Giving the impression he trusted her for the moment.

Kinley eyed him from under her full lashes, suspicion rooted in the hazelnut orbs. "And in return?"

Hendrick had no price. Not when helping her helped him. But he didn't want her to know who he was. He needed to come up with an acceptable trade. Because he sure as hell wouldn't take her money either. "A kiss."

34

She snorted and jumped off the counter. She grinned, a calculating lift to her lips, and she shook her head. "Just a kiss? Are you sure you don't want to demand it all? No, get on your knees and suck me off? No, lay on your back and take it like a good girl? Just a kiss and you'll do a job that's worth a fortune? Bullshit."

The way the words slid from her lips with familiarity lit a fire in his gut. And not a good one. When he spoke, his voice sounded closer to Dak's scarred one than his own. "Who the fuck told you to do those things?"

———

INSTINCT MADE KINLEY take a step back, but she forced herself to keep it at one. She hadn't shown that kind of fear in a long time, but it had been a long time since she'd heard that level of danger echoed in words.

"No one." Not in the past three years, anyway. "Don't change the subject." She dropped her own threat in her tone, that sweet strength that she'd perfected. "That isn't an acceptable deal."

He blinked, and the danger vanished. His mouth softened, and he took slow steps to close the distance she'd put between them. "Seems like you're getting the better end of it. Unless you want me to order you to your knees. I'd make sure you're wearing that white dress first." Her suggestion of going to her knees had been filled with hatred, disdain, the echo of idiots who dared speak. But with Hendrick's anger gone, the suggestion on his lips burned like heat from the summer sun.

She shook her head through a humourless laugh.

"And you keep asking what the dress is saying. I think you're only hearing what you want. Men are too predictable."

"I'll hear what *you* tell me. Not the dress." Hendrick closed the last inch. She had to tilt her head back to look at him and he had to bend his head down to look directly at her. "But that doesn't mean I can't be creative with it."

"No. Deal." She couldn't step back from him. Not without caving to a weakness she refused to accept.

"You don't have a choice. But I'm not asking for more than a kiss as payment. I don't need your money. And neither does King."

His breath brushed over her cheek.

"Choose now, Kinley."

"Or what?"

The chuckle that escaped him was both terrifying and delicious. "I'll decide for you."

The very thing she was running from. "Fine. Put your hands behind your back."

Hendrick leaned his head back and frowned, despite the grin that still played on his lips.

"A kiss is all you're going to get. Keep your hands behind your back."

His grin widened, and he clasped his hands behind him. Kinley kept hers at her sides. She waited. Hendrick didn't need his hands. He bent his head and kept his lips just out of reach. His breath caressed her face the same way she imagined his fingers would. He tilted his head this way and that, as if taking in every inch of her before having a taste.

Kinley's breath picked up and her lips followed his. He froze for an instant above her before he touched his lips to hers. It was the only part of their bodies that touched. He kept his chest away from hers, and his hands never appeared. The only thing he used to seduce her was his lips. His damn sinful lips.

And then his tongue licked the seam of her mouth and she opened, but he didn't move in. His tongue teased her upper lip and disappeared.

No. She wanted to scream. But that would only prove her inexperience.

Hendrick did it again, sliding only slightly inside her mouth. But the moment the tip of her tongue met his, he retreated. Kinley moved too fast to stop herself. With her hands clutching his shirt, she pulled herself up on her tiptoes to take over the kiss.

He didn't let her, but he gave her what she'd been searching for. *More.* He didn't have to touch her because she was doing it for the both of them. She soaked in his hardness as her hands slid up his chest and over his shoulders. She gasped when she pressed her chest to his. What the hell had come over her?

What a stupid question. She knew what came over her. Kinley had wanted this experience for years. And only once had come close. But that seemed pathetic compared to this kiss. Just a kiss.

Hendrick broke the kiss, but didn't lift his head. "Deal." He whispered the single word, but it didn't register.

As far as she was concerned, payment wasn't complete. He needed to kiss her more.

"Can I move my hands, Kinley?" He reclaimed her lips. The kiss changed. A firm demand that bordered on begging.

His hands. He still hadn't touched her and now he

was asking. Kinley clung to him. What would happen if she said yes?

"Y..." Her eyes snapped open, and she pushed herself away from him. "No. We're done." She didn't want it to happen like this. Not when she was on the run or in hiding. She deserved more.

His eyes were hazy as they slid down her body. His chest heaved, and every muscle twitched. Clearing his throat, he stepped back. "Done."

HIS HANDS HAD long since gone numb from the tight grip he had on them. The deal was done, and that was the only thing he needed to remember and think about. He didn't need to think about how she'd clung to him. She'd taken her time to kiss him back, to make a move of her own, proving her inexperience. Hendrick may have teased her in such a way to coax that reaction from her.

Kinley's breaths sawed in and out of her chest as heavily as his own. Her hands squeezed the strap of her purse sitting across her body. Those hands felt so small around his neck.

"Do you still want to leave town?" Hendrick needed to get them moving. Seducing his own runaway bride wasn't on his wish list. Best to take the single kiss and get the job done. Dragging Kinley along with him on his mission of vengeance wasn't an option. Besides, Kinley was part of his father's plans.

"Yes." Kinley straightened her shoulders.

Hendrick turned to get the weapons he had stashed here. He hadn't taken any with him to his father's for fear of killing the man in his arrogance. Not that he needed his own weapons to do it, but they made it too easy. A shadow moved in the trees outside the living room window behind Kinley. Deer always hovered around this house, seeing it as a safe place. Hendrick froze and kept his eye on that window.

"What is it?" Kinley looked over her shoulder and back at him. She missed the second man-sized shadow.

"Fuck. We have company." He didn't have the same security set up at this safe house as some others owned by Dak or King. Something he'd have to remedy at the next one.

"How?"

"Don't know. Hide in the bathroom." She'd be trapped if they got past him, but it was a room she couldn't use to escape from him and one that someone couldn't get into from the outside.

"No." She moved closer to him and spread her feet, bracing herself with one behind her.

"What the fuck do you think you're doing?"

"Whatever the fuck I want." She kept her eyes on the front door.

Hendrick wrapped an arm around her waist and lifted her. Holding her against his side, he moved to the kitchen and reached under the sink for the gun he had stashed there. Slipping that in his waistband, he moved to the fridge and took one knife taped to the top of it. Kinley struggled against him, but without her feet on the floor, his grip didn't loosen. But she was smart enough not to make a sound.

He dropped her in the bedroom. "Stay here. They're here for you. Don't let them find you." He slammed the bedroom door at the same time someone kicked in the front door. Three men filed in, spreading out.

Hendrick rolled his shoulders and spun the knife around his wrist to get the attention of all three of them. He caught the handle of the knife and settled the back side of the blade up his forearm.

"My favourite way to start the day." Hendrick stalked closer, moving away from the bedroom door.

"Hand her over." The one standing in the centre took point, lifting his chin. The relaxed stance was all for show. Hendrick saw the muscle beneath the suit jacket. He had a thick neck and broad shoulders. The other two were dressed similarly, but didn't have the same mass. Hendrick wished he'd had that second hand to grab more knives rather than carrying Kinley to the bedroom.

"You'll have to be more specific." Each of the three carried more weapons than Hendrick, based on the lay of their clothes. Only two held a gun in their hand. Memory throbbed in his thigh. He may have recovered from his last injury, but the ghost of it always took longer to fade. He pushed it away. Trying to protect an injury that was no longer there would give them a weakness to strike. And he had three of them to go against on his own.

"Come on out, Kinley!" He didn't take his eyes off Hendrick as he raised his voice.

When the bedroom door didn't open, Hendrick shrugged. "Sorry, guess she's not here. Don't let the knife hit you on the way out." Hendrick changed his grip on the handle and spun the knife around his wrist again for show. He could take out one with the knife, possibly a second with the gun, but he'd bet all three of them moved as fast as him.

"We have hired you to find her and hand her over. This won't look good for *King's Mercenaries*." He didn't bother to wonder how they knew he worked for King. Since starting *King Security* and therefore *King's Mercenaries*, he imagined many had their faces well memorized. All three of them moved closer, hands tightening around their guns, still pointed at the floor.

"I think we're all damn good looking. At least I am. There's one fucker that could use a serious haircut."

Their quirked brows said they didn't enjoy his humour.

The bedroom door opened behind him and all three men tensed. "That's enough." Kinley's firm voice carried. "I'm not going back, Cassius." Kinley stopped just behind Hendrick's shoulder. It surprised part of him she didn't put herself in front of him. But there was still time.

Cassius sighed. "Yes, you are." He almost sounded regretful.

"You're a great liar, Cass. Tell him you didn't find me. Look the other way."

Cassius narrowed his eyes, seeming to consider her words. If Kinley had that kind of influence on her father's men, she'd have escaped long before now and would be far away from here.

The other two moved closer to Cassius, flanking him. They knew the other man wasn't taking Kinley seriously. Hendrick adjusted his grip on his knife and readied himself to grab his gun. He'd rather leave it where it was with Kinley so close.

"I've never looked the other way, kiddo. Time to come home." A sad, patronizing smile sagged on his face. The man looked to be about King's age, so had likely been in Kinley's life since she was little. The woman at his shoulder didn't look older than twenty-three, if she was even that.

He watched Kinley slip the strap of her purse over her head and drop the bag to the floor. "No." She stretched the single syllable and lowered her tone. She possessed a strength that the men working for her father didn't respect. Hendrick didn't like that.

"Either leave or make your attempt, boys. I've got things to do." Hendrick circled his free hand in a hurry-it-up gesture.

The guy on Cassius's right rushed toward Hendrick, a fist cocked back. Hendrick laughed and ducked, swiping the arm with the knife forward. The guy was quick to leap back.

Cassius flicked his finger and the third guy came at Hendrick's right. And Cassius himself walked toward Kinley.

Of course, the woman didn't stand still. She charged him. He blocked for a front kick, but she ducked around him and kicked out to hit him in the back of the knee. His leg bent, but he didn't fall to the ground.

"Not bad, kiddo."

They moved out of Hendrick's peripheral vision and he had to focus on the two still attacking him. He moved the three of them closer to a wall where one couldn't get out of reach of his knife. He sliced across the guy's ribs, feeling the metal scrape against bone.

With one groaning and slumping to the floor, Hendrick swung around to land a solid punch to the other's jaw. But he was made of sterner stuff than he looked. He came back with one of his own.

Over the guy's shoulder, Hendrick saw Kinley fighting with Cassius. While she wasn't making it easy for him, he wasn't struggling. Cassius shook his head and reached for her arm. Kinley grabbed his wrist and tried to pull him past her with his own momentum.

Cassius chuckled. "I taught you everything you know, Kinley. You can't win."

At that, Hendrick was done taking things easy.

4

A SICKENING POP CUT OFF CASSIUS'S LOW LAUGH.
The sound was loud enough to draw Cassius's attention.
Despite dreading the sound had come from Hendrick,
Kinley kept her attention on Cassius. If she didn't, she
could lose her chance at escape. A tear crowded the
corner of her eye, but Cassius still stood in front of her.

The slight distraction was enough for her to get the
upper hand. A punch to the groin bent him over
enoughto grab the back of his neck and slam his head
down on her knee. She took three large steps back and
surveyed the room.

Otto's dead form lay at Hendrick's feet and he had
his gun pointed at Jude slumped against the wall with
an arm over his ribs. But Hendrick's eyes looked like the
most dangerous thing in the room.

"You can leave alone, or grab your buddy and go."
His eyes landed on her long enough to gesture her
behind him. He moved further from the two bodies.
Kinley knew the odds still may not be in their favour
and she listened to him. Because not listening to him

meant taking her chances against Cassius again. And he'd been right. She was good, but not that good. Not against the one who taught her.

Cassius grunted and straightened, not bothering to hold a hand over his face. *Damn*. She'd missed his nose, but his eye was taking on a gorgeous purple hue that would look decadent as a silk dress.

He pulled out his gun, making a show of its reveal. "Or I shoot you and take Kinley."

Kinley moved in front of Hendrick. He would not get hurt because of her. "No, you won't. Leave, Cassius. You've lost this round. You won't shoot me."

"Don't be so sure of that, Kinley." But he moved his gaze to Jude, not following through on his threat. He moved toward the door, keeping his gun pointing at the floor. Jude pushed himself up from the wall and followed.

Kinley sagged against Hendrick behind her the moment they were out of sight.

A large hand slid around her stomach and moved up her body, between her breasts, until he clasped her throat. "Don't you ever put yourself on the wrong side of a gun again." His tone bit into her ear. A growl that carried hints of the man who'd toyed with Cassius. "But," he paused, "I'm impressed."

Kinley didn't move or say anything. She only waited for him to loosen his hold.

"Change of plans." He let her go, but urged her toward the bedroom. "Grab your bag."

"Where are we going?" She threw the strap over her head and shoulder.

"There's an escape door in the bedroom. It's only a door that comes out on that side of the house. They kept moving past my truck, but if I were them, I'd take up a position to shoot me and grab you the moment we leave."

"You're right." Cassius had given up too easily.

"Ever been on a motorcycle?"

"No." She'd begged her father to let her get one, though. That gave her too much freedom for his taste.

"I have one stored not far behind the house. Walk silently. Can you do that?"

"Yes." Kinley had used that to her advantage plenty of times in her escape attempts over the years. No one ever expected it of her.

"Good. Once we get outside, stay behind me unless I say otherwise. If you fall behind, loop your hand in my belt."

"Got it." It seemed whatever she had planned was long gone. She had to put her future in Hendrick's hands. He'd promised her he wouldn't hand her over, and he hadn't. He'd killed Otto and would have killed Jude. If her father ever got her back, he'd blame Otto's death and anyone else's on her. But she had no sympathy for them anymore.

When Cassius first burst into the house, she might have. But not after the way he'd patronized her, then threatened to shoot her. For years, she'd thought she'd had at least some respect and loyalty from Cassius and even some others. She'd been wrong. Their loyalty didn't stray from the money.

Hendrick ran his hand along the floorboards under the bedroom window. When he found what he was looking for, he pushed until the other end of the board popped up. Reaching under it, he pulled. An entire square door big enough for a man the size of Hendrick and then some opened. He held out his hand to help her down.

Pushing away her hesitation, she set her hand in his and looked into the hole in the floor. A ladder led to the ground.

"There's a tunnel. We'll have to crawl, but it's short. I'm right behind you."

She nodded and descended under the earth. Thinking of it that way didn't help, but she refused to allow her nerves to show. At the bottom, Kinley turned. He'd made the tunnel wall out of compacted dirt. This was how she was going to die. Buried alive while escaping. A married life to a man she didn't know didn't sound so bad. Maybe her future husband would be easier to escape than her father.

The small amount of light faded as Hendrick shut the hatch. The thud of the door was enough to vibrate the ground beneath her. She shrieked and lowered herself until her chin hit the dirt.

Hendrick set his hand on her ankle. "Easy. Everything's okay, Kinley."

"Yup. I'm fine." She nodded her head too fast to be convincing, not that he could see her.

"Claustrophobic?"

"Didn't think so." Kinley swallowed and took deep breaths through her nose.

"We need to hurry." He had urgency in his voice, but he didn't push.

"I know." She moved, keeping her eyes closed in a way to block out her imagination. It was pitch black in the tunnel, so her eyes wouldn't help her find her way.

"Should reach the end soon."

Kinley started counting to ten in her head and when

she hit eight, her head bumped into a piece of wood. Stretching a hand out in front of her, she felt for the ladder.

"Stop at the top."

Kinley reached above her with each rung she climbed. "There."

Hendrick continued to climb, flattening her to the ladder. Her anxiety melted away as his body surrounded hers. Warmth and safety filled her.

Light seeped in as he lifted another hatch in the ground. Hendrick climbed over her and out. After a quick look, he reached a hand down for her. He grasped his fingers around her wrist and pulled. She barely had to use her own feet to push her weight up.

When she spun around, she saw the small house behind them.

Hendrick tucked her behind him and started hiking. Kinley focused on her steps and stayed as close to him as she could. It was difficult not to let her attention search for Cassius. She had to leave that up to Hendrick.

She bumped into his back when he stopped. He shot a cocked brow over his shoulder and she mouthed an apology. A large bush sat in front of him, but he reached out and pulled at the branches. They came off like a blanket, revealing a motorcycle. He got on and passed her a helmet before sliding one over his head.

There had been a time she could have named the rugged-looking bike. When her father wouldn't let her get one of her own, she'd stopped reading about them, threw away all her magazines, and ended the dream there. She had more important things to dream about.

Kinley got on behind him and wrapped her arms around his stomach. He started the bike and wasted no time driving over the grass and brush covering the ground until they hit the gravel road. Tires kicked up rocks and dirt somewhere behind them, but Hendrick was quicker. Whatever vehicle Cassius had didn't have the power to catch up to them.

Squeezing tight, Kinley let go for the ride. She laid everything in Hendrick's hands as he swerved in and around traffic the moment they hit town. Toward the heart of her problems.

THE OPTION OF doing this alone died when Cassius barged into the safe house. It died when Kinley put herself between him and the deadly end of a gun. He'd exerted an insane amount of effort to keep the hand he'd slid up her body from squeezing too hard. The urge to pin her to the wall and fuck her into submission had punched him in the gut. It was unwanted and unwelcome. That's why he had to take her back to *King Security*.

Traffic wasn't heavy enough to prevent Hendrick from zipping in and around vehicles, getting them there faster and with less chance of anyone catching up to them or finding them in town. The bike almost felt foreign underneath him. He had three bikes and a couple of trucks. But this one stayed hidden at that safe house most of the time.

Kinley's arms tightened and Hendrick's core tensed. Irritation flared through him. He'd kissed her and hadn't wanted to stop. What the hell had he been thinking? She was his runaway bride. A bride he'd never asked for or wanted. And she was an interruption to what he was supposed to be doing. He'd put off finding Shane's killer long enough. When the note for him arrived, he'd still been healing from a stab wound in the leg.

The day his heart stopped remained frozen in his memory. Training Ember and Sophie in throwing knives while Dak read the note aloud, confusing everyone but Hendrick. They'd assumed they had delivered the note to the wrong place. The rest of the training session had been a blur until he disappeared to the safe house they'd just left and raged in a drunken stupor until he had control of himself.

But now, he had a woman his father hoped to use as a bribe attached to his back. A distraction.

His *bride* clung to him and part of Hendrick reveled in it. But the rest of him twitched, irritated to allow some idea of his father's being right. To put a permanent halt to avenging Shane. His other option would be to let Kinley fend for herself. He could have let her run off, could have kicked her out of his truck all together and never laid a hand on her.

An inward sneer had him tightening his grip on the handles. He wouldn't have let her go on her own. His current situation wouldn't differ. Except he could have avoided kissing her. The smart way to keep distance would have been to state a monetary price. Transferring the funds back to her would be a snap of the fingers for Roen. Everyone comes out on the other end exactly where they intended to be.

But no. Hendrick licked his lips beneath his helmet, pulling in the last of her taste.

He pulled around to the back of *King Security*. Plenty of parking lined the street at the front of the building, but he didn't need his bike exposed. They'd figure out where they went. It wasn't about hiding. It was about keeping her safe while they entered the building. And keeping his bike intact.

The bike rumbled as he slowed to go underground. He punched in the code to open the gate. Hendrick slid his bike between Cole and Roen's trucks. The two of them parked like assholes, as if they'd been in a hurry. They'd left a large enough space between them.

He held out a hand to the side, waiting for Kinley to take it. He helped her off, then took off his helmet.

"Let's go see what our options are."

The woman crowded him, blocking him from getting off the bike. Small strands of hair frizzed on the top of her head from the helmet she now held under her arm, but the braids had stayed in place. Lowering her chin, she leaned toward him. "Giving me back isn't one of them. Even if what you say about Kit is true, and I wouldn't have to marry him. I'm not going back."

"You're not going back," he agreed softly. An easy thing for him to agree to, as he had many reasons not to allow her anywhere near her father.

"And what will they say to that?" She pointed her finger up toward the floors above them.

"They won't go against me."

Her shoulders dropped, and she stepped back to let him off the bike. "I suppose I should trust you."

Hendrick nodded, because to tell her she shouldn't trust a mercenary would be counterproductive. He pointed to the door on the other side of Cole's truck. With a hand on her lower back, he led her through and up the single flight of stairs, trying not to lean forward to take a bite out of her delicious looking ass ahead of him. He took her past the gym and past Roen's cave of computers. That level was eerily quiet. But when they came through the door to the lounge, a male voice echoed over a speaker.

"My man informed me you already have my daughter. Give her back." Kinley's father. Her spine stiffened under his fingertips and she didn't move further into the room. How much did she fear her father? Or was it a fear of being trapped again?

They still blocked the door, and five sets of eyes settled in their direction. Dak glared. It was easy to recognize the pissed off set to the man's stance, and likely pissed off at Hendrick for hanging up on him this morning without giving him all the information. King's features hardened, but a single brow rose as he moved his stare to Kinley. Cole, Roen, and the new guy, Archer, stared on with no emotion. It was a lot of weight for Kinley to handle, but she only focused her attention on the phone.

"I don't know what you're talking about, Curry. I don't have your daughter." King spoke, but his gaze didn't leave Hendrick and Kinley. He reached over and ended the call at the first sound of a tirade. "Explain."

"She doesn't want to go back." Hendrick shrugged. It was enough for him. Hopefully, it would be for the others.

"I've been trying to escape my father for years." Kinley pulled her shoulders back and stepped into the room. "I managed it last night out of desperation. He'll ensure I won't be successful again." She spoke her next words slower. "I'm not going back."

Archer and Cole shared a smirk while Roen nodded. But King and Dak didn't waver. They looked over her shoulder at him and he stared back. Hendrick secured a warning in his eyes to not go against him on this. He would wrap his arm around her middle and haul her back out of the building if they did.

"Understood." Dak conceded, but he didn't look any less pissed off. "How did you escape?"

Hendrick wanted this story too.

"I drugged the guards my father had waiting with me in the car. I waited until Cassius, the man my father just referred to, disappeared around a corner."

So many questions surged in his mind, and he read some of the same in the others' expressions.

"How many guards?" King leaned his hip against the table. That wasn't Hendrick's first question. Where the hell had she gotten the drugs?

"Two."

"How did you drug two of them at once?"

"Sorry, in house secret." One small shoulder lifted in a half shrug.

Hendrick snorted. He'd seen her fight against Cassius. While she couldn't best him, she didn't lack skills.

"I was out of the car before they slumped to the side. I ran for the thickest grouping of trees until I saw a lone truck."

"Where she stowed away." Hendrick filled in the rest.

"She was already with you when I called this morning." Dak's expression eased as he pieced things together. Being the last to know was what had pissed him off.

Hendrick answered with a single nod. "Cassius

found us. Which reminds me. I need clean up at one of my safe houses."

"How many?"

"Just one body." Clean up was something they sometimes did themselves, but they had people to hire for that job when time didn't allow them to take care of it.

"I'll arrange it." Cole pulled out his phone and started typing a message.

"All right, then. Let's see how this plays out." King pushed off from the table.

"She can stay upstairs," Dak added. He owned the building and the apartments that housed the upper floors. He lived on the top floor and kept the apartment next to his empty. For the most part.

An odd urge to wrap his hand around Kinley's arm rushed him. It felt as if she was slipping through Hendrick's fingers. When he hadn't wanted her there to begin with.

KINLEY WANTED TO feel relief. She tried hard to bring it forward. It should be there. Surrounded by mercenaries that agreed to help her. Except they hadn't. They'd only agreed not to hand her over to her father. But that was all she needed, and she should be grateful for it.

This escape was taking longer than she'd hoped. The one time her father moved uncommonly fast was to get her back when, in every other business decision, he dragged his heels until the bitter end. What was so important about her immediate return? The amount of men stationed in the map images she'd seen on

Hendrick's phone had been astonishing. Kinley wondered if her father had that many men. She still wasn't sure.

Hendrick swore Kit wouldn't want to marry, but would Kit have added his resources to find her? Or maybe it wasn't just Kit, but his family. His father. After all, if Hendrick was correct, Kit wouldn't have agreed to the arranged marriage any more than she, but an arrangement had been made all the same.

"I have to stay here?"

"For now." Hendrick answered from behind her, his hand running up her arm. The heat from his touch soaked into her skin. "As soon as we can get you out of town, we will. Unless you don't want to leave town."

Kinley frowned over her shoulder. Hendrick cocked his head to the side and his words from last night swam through her head. He'd offered to get her out, but he'd also offered to set her up right under her father's nose.

"Freedom from your father doesn't mean you have to leave town." Hendrick's hand squeezed gently.

"Or at least not permanently leave town." A man sprawled out on a chair had a narrowed expression.

"Or only pretend to leave town." A man with thick arms and dark, cropped hair mumbled from the back corner.

She supposed there wasn't anything to do at the moment, anyway. "Okay." She answered as if she had a say in what happened next.

They all tensed to move, but the phone ringing cut them off. The two that were in charge looked to Hendrick still standing behind her. He must have nodded because they answered the phone. He hadn't lied when he said they wouldn't go against him on this.

This band of mercenaries worked nothing like she'd imagined.

They didn't seem intimidating or terrifying. At this moment, anyway. She recognized the danger they each held leashed under their skin.

"King Security." The one she was sure was King himself answered with a chipper tone that didn't match his face.

"Cut the bullshit, King. This is bad for business. Hanging up on a client."

"I didn't realize you were a client. I don't remember striking a deal."

"What the..." Her father's voice lowered to one that Kinley recognized too well. To one that even she hid from while preparing to deal with the fallout. But a deeper, scarred voice cut him off.

"You made the request. I said I'd get back to you. We didn't even get as far as discussing payment."

"What do you think will happen to your reputation after this?" Her father's voice held a gleeful threat.

"Not a whole hell of a lot." King sounded bored.

"Where's my daughter?" Her father spoke with a calm that Kinley wasn't sure how to process.

Kinley pulled in a breath, ready to tell her father where to shove it, but a large hand clamped around her mouth.

"Not yet." Hendrick's whispered breath brushed over her ear.

"Couldn't say." King continued to control the conversation. "We'll let you know if we hear from the mercenary you requested and if he accepts the job."

"I don't care which one of you does the job." Her

father sounded strained, as if speaking through his teeth.

"We'll be in touch." The scarred-voiced man ended the call. "Where were you when you escaped?" He'd stared at the phone when speaking, but then he tilted his head to look at her.

She tried not to flinch, and she was pretty sure she'd failed. "At the Pierce family residence."

"And what were you doing there, Hendrick?"

Hendrick didn't answer right away, and Kinley wanted to kick herself for not asking him that same question before putting her trust in him.

Another long beat passed. "I'd parked my truck at the adjoining property. It's up for sale." Hendrick cut off any more questions by tugging on her arm. "I'll show you the apartment upstairs."

The others remained quiet, letting his non-answer slide as he pulled her away. But it suddenly became the most important thing for Kinley to know. She dug in her heels and whirled herself around.

"Why were you there?"

"Another job." Eyes that had been warm and fiery since she met him turned cold.

Kinley didn't imagine how the entire room tensed. The air stilled and thickened behind her and when she turned around, most of the others narrowed their eyes on Hendrick. Looking back at Hendrick, he matched their gazes. This wasn't any of her business. As long as it had nothing to do with her or her family.

Hendrick broke the stares of the others and reached for her again. She let him lead her away to an elevator. From the corner of her eye, she watched him visibly melt. The tension in his short answer vanished. The warmth returned to his eyes as he looked at her.

"We'll get you wherever you want to be."

"Must have been a hell of a kiss for you to accept only that for this much work."

He pushed off the wall of the elevator, peeling his body away like a wave. Heat rushed her.

It took extreme effort to only cock her brow, to hold back every other reaction her body begged for. She wanted to set her shoulders and brush her body against his. She wanted to wrap her hands around his neck and pull him down to her.

"It was one hell of a kiss. One I can't seem to stop thinking about. And that's rare." He tilted his head like he would kiss her again, but he didn't move closer. "I don't want kisses as payment."

Kinley stiffened. She hadn't wanted it as payment either. She wouldn't offer it again or offer anything more.

"I don't want any payment."

Now she frowned and leaned back to study his face.

"Not everything you've heard about *King's Mercenaries* is true. We don't always require payment when the job is something we want to do. To help."

"Oh." Relief and disappointment clashed, and she licked her lips and cleared her throat to drown out that miniature war. She didn't need him to detect either emotion. But the way his lips smirked said she hadn't been successful.

The elevator stopped and the door dinged as it opened. Hendrick backed off and let her out before the door closed.

He stalked to the door on the far left and punched in

a code on the electronic lock. Letting her go through first, he followed her and shut the door.

The apartment was sparse, but seemed to have all the basic furniture and kitchen appliances. The walls and shelves were bare except for the occasional colourful knick knack. Mis-matched cushions sat on the couches. It was as if previous tenants had left things behind and the landlord hadn't bothered to take them out.

"There should be a phone in here with all of our numbers programmed into it. The building has a lot of security. Call if you want to wander or need something. Wouldn't want you to get stuck somewhere. You wouldn't be the first." Hendrick hadn't moved away from the door.

"You're leaving?" She didn't need him or the company. She didn't need reassurance. Yet, the question escaped anyway.

"I don't have to." Hendrick left the door and walked toward her. A single hot finger traced along her jaw. "Is there something else you *want*?"

She didn't miss the emphasis. Her lips parted. But she forced herself to answer differently. "No."

His eyes dropped to her mouth as if he could see the whisper escape. "All right." Then he backed away from her and left.

The rest was up to her.

5

_____

HENDRICK HAD TO PAUSE INSIDE THE ELEVATOR
before going back down. Hadn't he just finished
scolding himself over his attraction to Kinley? Then
what did he do? He almost kissed her, pushed her to ask
him to kiss her. And the next kiss wouldn't be with his
hands behind his back.

With his head bowed and his eyes closed, Hendrick
breathed deep through his nose. He could be crazy, but
he wasn't impulsive. And standing close to Kinley made
him want to be. He gritted his teeth and reminded
himself who and what they intended her to be. A pawn
to bring him to heel. Used by his father. Although she
didn't realize it, Hendrick used that to keep his distance.

One more full breath and he started the elevator,
ready to face the scrutiny of the others.

No one had moved since he'd taken Kinley away.

"What job?" Dak's tone suggested Hendrick better not
lie. But to tell the truth would bring out an even bigger lie.

"A friend. I'm doing him a favour." The words

soured his tongue. His identity had been the only thing he'd kept from them, and even that was only a lie of omission. He always preferred to be called by his middle name, Hendrick.

By the looks on their faces, not a single one of them believed him. Or they didn't like the secrecy.

"What happened this morning?" King broke the silence and moved forward.

"They found my safe house. Based on the locations Roen sent me, I'm not surprised. They'd stationed themselves along that back road out of town, but they would have had to search the little side roads to find it. Three guys barged in, demanding me to hand over Kinley. She was hiding in the bedroom until she wasn't. The damn woman came out and stared down Cassius. She knows him well. Well enough that he's taught her to fight."

"So he's been with her father a long time."

"Seems so." And it grated at Hendrick the way he called her *kiddo* and patronized her. He taught her a lot, but not enough to defeat someone like him or any other potential threat she'd come across living in life.

He'd fix that.

Hendrick had to stop himself from reacting to his own thoughts. How would he fix that? When? The sooner they got her past their fathers' men and out of town, preferably out of the province and maybe even the country, the better. They knew where to find her. And while Dak and King had gone to great lengths to make sure a direct attack didn't happen at this building again, it wasn't impossible. Not if they kept her here for long and wore through their patience.

"Why does he want her back? Other than because she's his daughter."

"Family alliances. But other than that, I'd guess she knows too much. If she's been that close to Cassius and others growing up, she's learned a lot."

"We could ask her." Cole drawled from where he took a seat at the long table.

"We will." Dak caught Hendrick's gaze. He may have brought her here to get their help and keep her safe, but Hendrick wouldn't allow Dak to take over.

"I will." The air stilled with the veiled challenge. It was stupid. He didn't have any important connection to Kinley. In fact, he needed to get rid of her so he could go back to finding Shane's killer. But Hendrick found her, and Hendrick kissed her. She was his responsibility.

Cole and Roen smirked. The new guy looked confused. King's sigh filled the room and Dak's glare pierced.

Fuck them all. It didn't matter.

"What has Curry said?" Hendrick nodded at the silent phone on the table. The information from him would help in piecing together his father's plans as well.

"He's been vague. He isn't giving any details or reasons. Just that he wants her back. And before this morning, he'd requested you to do the job, but wouldn't say why except a friend recommended you." Roen rolled his neck as he spoke.

"Any idea who that might be?" Hendrick understood Dak's not-so-trusting mood, but it forced him to lie again.

"No." His father was an asshole. But he wouldn't have told Kinley's father who he was. He'd always kept his attempts to bring Hendrick back to the family private. That Hendrick left to become something other than the crime boss was shame on his father's head. And he stayed as far away from *King's Mercenaries* as possible. Shane did nothing to involve them out of respect for Hendrick, not fear or shame.

"Do you have a plan?"

"Wait just long enough for them to change their positions, their focus, then get her out of the province. At the least. They know she's here and now they know we won't give her back. We're playing a game of chicken."

"And how do you want to get her out?"

"Depends on where they put their focus. But the quickest and easiest would be a private flight."

Dak's eyebrows shot up. Although the quickest and easiest, it was also the most expensive. Not that money was a problem, but it wasn't the first option.

"She needs to be out of their reach as soon as possible." If she couldn't be used to marry him, what would they try to use her for next? Marry her off to someone even worse than Hendrick? He doubted they'd give her the opportunity to escape again.

"Okay. We'll have it ready and wait for them to move."

"Thank you." Hendrick said the words low. He appreciated their help, even if he intended to control it.

Dak nodded. "Roen, start digging into Kinley's father. And the Pierce family."

Hendrick's heart hammered. Whether he wanted them to find out the truth or not, they would. But not today. He'd had someone with Roen's computer skills hide any evidence of his connection to his family. There was still a record of Kit Pierce, but not Kit Hendrick

Pierce. The kid he'd hired had buried all images with his face and that name. Roen wouldn't find anything about Kit so soon. Hendrick still had time.

"I'm hitting the gym." Hendrick turned his back, turning away from the family he had now.

KINLEY HAD MADE herself lunch, cleaned the dishes, and searched the entire apartment by the time Hendrick came back. And she was pissed.

He let himself into the apartment and Kinley jumped from the couch and stormed across the room.

"Don't you dare stash me away again." She stabbed him in the chest with a single finger. "I've lived my life like this and now I'm free. If you leave here, I'm going with you."

"No. You can come with me wherever you want in this building, but you can't leave the building. You're safest here until we're ready to move you." Hendrick didn't flinch or cower. But his eyes lit up and his lips twitched.

She deflated. He'd taken all her anger and dispersed it with a few words. "That's all I ask." But it left her feeling empty. She'd been so angry about being stashed away with a warning not to wander for fear of getting stuck somewhere.

"Is the only reason your father wants you back so bad because he intends to use you for an alliance?"

"I assume so. He never seemed to care much for my well being. He doesn't realize how much I know about his business. I've tried to talk to him about it, tried to help and make myself an equal. He'd pat me on the head and call me cute. And when I pushed, I was told to shut up and locked in my room. He only wants me back for what it gains him."

"How is an alliance with the Pierce family worth the trouble he's exerting to get you back?"

That made her pause. Because she didn't know. She hadn't even known about the alliance until last night. There were other ways to make an alliance.

Hendrick frowned, and it seemed as if he wanted to see past her eyes, to see her thoughts. "I'll give you the code to the elevator so you can at least go downstairs. But I have to run an errand."

Kinley was certain this errand had just popped up. He hadn't walked in here with any intention. Something about their conversation gave him an idea that he kept to himself. "What errand?" She adopted the tone she used to use on the young new hires in her father's house. Before they realized she didn't hold as much power as she led them to believe. Of course, that didn't work on someone like Hendrick. Yet he answered her anyway, with a quirk of his brow.

"I'm going to see if I can find out why they want that alliance." Something in his voice cracked, but it was gone before Kinley grasped it.

Kinley gritted her teeth. She had to stay here, and that was the last thing she wanted. Free and still forced to hole up and out of sight.

"Something wrong?" He tilted his head, making his hair droop to one side.

Apparently, she still had more work to do to control her outward reactions. "I want to go with you. But," she continued before he turned her down, "I know I can't."

Hendrick pulled out his phone and started typing.

"I've asked Sophie if you can go over for dinner. Someone to keep you company. She lives next door with Dak. She'll show you around the building."

A quick patter of knocks hit the door behind Hendrick. He scoffed and opened the door. A small woman with light brown hair and bright blue eyes barged in.

"I love company." Not *she'd love to have company* or *she'd be happy to entertain someone*. The way she said it was with an odd emphasis that spoke of similar loneliness as Kinley often felt.

"Sophie, this is Kinley. She has to lie low here for a while."

"Understood." She nodded at Hendrick and stepped closer to Kinley. "Don't worry. We'll get you out of here soon." Sophie's back was to Hendrick, and she winked. Kinley wasn't sure if she meant she'd help her escape Hendrick or to trust in him to get her out of her father's reach.

Hendrick snorted. "I'll be back later." He met her gaze over Sophie's shoulder—hot, frustrated, and eager. What all that meant, Kinley wasn't sure. Except for the heat. That she deciphered as if it was a language of its own. One her body spoke fluently and had been trying to silence since he'd kissed her in the safe house.

"I won't ask your story." Sophie pulled her attention back to the present once the door shut behind Hendrick. "But whatever it is, it's terrible. You don't end up in the mercenaries' care unless it is. You're safe here, but if you want to get out before they deem otherwise, it won't be easy."

"I'm okay staying here. For now, anyway." That depended on how long it took to get past her father.

"For now." Sophie laughed under her breath. "Come on." She led her out of the apartment and down the hall. "Make yourself at home."

"Please, let me help with dinner. I don't want to stay still." Kinley followed Sophie toward the kitchen and stood beside the island, ready to be put to work. She refused to remain idle for fear of her curiosity over Hendrick's *errand*.

"I get that. How about a glass of wine? Unless you'd prefer something stronger." She paused with her hand in the cupboard. "Dak likes his whiskey."

"Wine would be great, thanks."

Sophie was being kind, her lips firmly stuck in a soft smile. But she moved around the kitchen with a practiced grace that made Kinley wonder what she did while living with the mercenary. She wasn't only living with him. Her touches were all over the grey and blue apartment in a way that blended the two people.

Kinley glanced at her left hand as Sophie passed her the glass. A slim band with alternating sapphires and diamonds sparkled in the light.

"Thanks." It wasn't her business to ask. Especially not after Sophie hadn't pried into how Kinley had ended up here.

"You're allowed to ask." Sophie started pulling stuff out of the fridge and cupboards.

Kinley shook her head. "I thought I was good at this."

"Good at what?"

"Not showing my emotions." Years she'd spent trying to hone herself as an equal to her father and the people who worked around him.

Sophie laughed. "You didn't. I remember when I first

got here, and I wanted to ask Ember all sorts of questions. Ember is King's wife."

"I'd heard rumours about a Queen of Mercenaries." How more dangerous King had become because of it always followed those rumours. After falling off the grid for two years, he returned with his queen and more deadly than ever. It made sense. If someone like the king of mercenaries had a weakness, then he better make sure the world fears him enough not to exploit it.

"So, you won't offend me by asking."

"I'll admit I'm curious. It isn't my place." Kinley set her glass down on the island with a soft clink.

"But?" Sophie waved her hand in a circle.

Kinley smiled. "What do you do? Do you have a job outside of here?"

"No. But I'm not stuck in here either, if that's what you wanted to know. I can't leave the building without someone with me, usually Dak, but I'm not stranded. I train. So does Ember."

After watching Sophie move around her kitchen, Kinley recognized the subtle flex of muscles beneath her clothes and her silent steps. "Do you work alongside the mercenaries?"

"Not yet. Even if Dak was ready to set me loose, I'm not ready. Ember does. For some jobs." Sophie kept looking over her shoulder as she talked while turning on burners on the stove and setting pots out.

"My dad's guards taught me to fight. But," Kinley recalled how easily Cassius had fought her. Thinking back on the spark in his eyes, she realized he'd only been playing with her, allowing her to think she'd had a chance against him.

"But not enough?"

"No. Not enough." Not enough to get past him, the one that would have always stood in her way. Until this morning, she might have considered them almost friends. He'd listened to her over the years. Listened to her ideas about how to make the business better. He took those ideas to her father, but of course never told him they came from her.

No. He kept everything between them controlled in a way that kept her in her cage without her even realizing it.

HENDRICK PREPARED HIMSELF to sneak into his father's house. But finding Hudson around the back made things easier.

The air didn't stir as he sidled up beside Hudson. They didn't look at each other, both hidden in the shadows from the other guards.

"I'm sorry." Remorse was heavy in Hudson's voice. "I wasn't with him."

"It's not your fault."

"It is. That was my job." He'd been Shane's most trusted employee. Like a second brother, growing up in this house. All three of them had played together as kids. And when Shane took over, he immediately raised Hudson in the ranks. Shane didn't go anywhere without Hudson.

"Do you know what happened?"

"Nothing." He spoke with the same rage Hendrick had boiling inside him since he found out. Rage and grief mixed to create a nauseous venom that ate at him daily. The twist of Hudson's face held the same. "I don't even know where he died. Your father said it was at the Raymond and Co. warehouse. He sent me to fetch the body. Shane had been moved. That wasn't where he'd died."

"Did he tell you of a meeting for that night?"

"That's the thing." Hudson broke his concentration on the night around them, and turned to face Hendrick —torture in his eyes. "He said he had nothing that night. He went home. I escorted him there myself."

"His apartment, or here?"

"His apartment."

Shane kept a separate home to use when he needed a break from their father. But it wasn't far away. If he'd distanced himself too much, he would have lost some of his control over his people.

"I wish I had something to give you. I would have reached out long before now if I had."

"And I've been avoiding coming to you."

"It hurts."

"Yeah." The pain lived in both of them. It changed Hendrick to the point the others were taking notice. But he didn't acknowledge it. He didn't want it there. Death happened all the time in his world, his life, his job, growing up, and it would always be part of his future. And not just death, but murder, assassinations. Hell, he was a fucking assassin.

But Shane was one of the good ones. He had a heart, unlike anyone in this business. Yeah, he still dealt drugs and weapons, but he was making changes to do his best to keep them away from kids. Away from innocents. Once a soul had been damned, he hadn't cared what they did to themselves, but he refused to be part of damning someone new. He'd treated his employees well. Better than their father ever had. He'd won their favor and their loyalty and increased their profits substantially.

"You've been digging?" Hendrick looked Hudson in the eye.

"I tried. Then the old man demoted me. I'm no more than a grunt. But I won't leave. I can't."

"Anyone else Shane trusted still working inside the house?"

"Not one. He's even handpicked additional guards just for you, awaiting your return."

Hendrick snorted, but sobered quickly. "I won't come back. I'm sorry."

"I wouldn't ask you to."

There was the smallest part of him that felt a responsibility to Shane's legacy. Someone needed to take over where he left off. His father would destroy it with his arrogance alone. But this wasn't the life for him. Hendrick didn't want to lead. He was never made for it the way Shane had been.

"Why is there an alliance with the Curry family?"

"That's why they were here?"

"Fuck," Hendrick cursed under his breath. His father was keeping things closer to his chest than he used to. "What's the urgency behind it? She escapes and her family has blocked every way out of town to find her. And I'm guessing my father has thrown some of his men into the mix. He gave Curry my name to hire to find her."

"To bring you back here."

"To introduce me to my bride."

Hudson's lips tightened as he held in his laugh.

"Careful. Don't strain yourself." Hendrick let his

own humour loose. He'd laughed his ass off when Kinley had told him, but standing beside someone who knew him, he relaxed, recognizing the ludicrous idea for what it was.

"I can only imagine the woman that would end up by your side. Your father is a fool to think he could bring you back with that."

"But that's just it. It might be something to lure me back, but they're going to extremes to find her. Even threatening King's reputation. They intend the marriage to be a true alliance, but why?"

Hudson sobered. "I'll see what I can find out."

"How much loyalty do you have around here?"

"Everyone who was loyal to Shane. A few switched to your father out of fear. But most of us learned he didn't have the power if we didn't bow to him. Some left. Most of us are waiting to see what comes of this."

"Good." Hendrick didn't want his father to hold the power he once did. "Keep in touch."

Hudson nodded, more sincerity in the gesture than any words could hold. They clasped hands and half hugged. They'd both lost someone important when Shane died. And they'd avoided each other since the funeral, avoided the pain.

Hendrick disappeared back into the shadows and took some time to scout out his father's property. He made notes of the guards, memorizing the faces that stood outside and inside the windows. If Hendrick hadn't still been healing from a deep stab wound in his thigh, he would have been here sooner, confronted his father sooner. Things weren't at a standstill anymore. His father was making moves. But towards what?

Hudson hadn't been the first person to say something about a future woman by his side—*I can only imagine the woman that would end up by your side.*

But Hendrick was imagining it now. *A woman would have to be as crazy as you are.*

Hendrick wouldn't call her crazy, but she was strong, forceful. He imagined a fearless, stowaway bride in the bed of a truck looking at him like he was an idiot.

6

IT HAD BEEN A LONG TIME SINCE SHE'D SAT DOWN AT A dinner and was encouraged to speak her mind. While her loyalty wasn't to her father, the business was different. She had a vested interest in that. So, when Dak tried to pry details from her, Kinley had been cautious of what she'd said, taking the time to consider each answer.

Did Dak need the exact security measures at individual restaurants? No. Would it help him help her to know the guards closest to her father and how she thought he would handle this? Yes.

Her father would rage, alternating between having control of his temper and losing it, and it would be Cassius he'd put in charge of finding and bringing her back. Kinley didn't trust herself to guess Cassius's moves. She made that clear to Dak. The extent they'd already put into retrieving her was a shock. Part of her hoped and wondered if her father might say good riddance.

Cassius had fucked with her, toyed with her eagerness to learn. Exhaustion pulled at Kinley when Dak finally declared Sophie needed rest. He walked her back to the apartment and the feeling of being escorted and guarded tightened her veins. Kinley whirled on Dak in the middle of the hall.

"I'm capable of walking the fifteen feet between doors alone. There is nowhere for me to go in this building without each of you knowing within seconds. Guarding me over my shoulder seems a little overkill."

"I'm not guarding. Because you're right, I don't need to." His jaw clenched and his brow twitched.

"Then you must have more questions." Kinley crossed her arms and cocked her hip.

"Several. You're good at evasion, by the way."

"Thank you." She loved the compliment. It was a skill she intended to hone further.

"You should take over your father's business."

She was shaking her head before he even finished. "There's nothing that would make him pass that business to me, especially after all of this."

"I didn't say he needed to give it to you. You should take it." Dak shrugged. "Or start from scratch and overpower him." He walked past her and opened the apartment door for her. "Just one mercenary's opinion."

"You said you have several more questions."

"I do, but not all of them are for you. Goodnight, Kinley."

Kinley slid past him into the apartment. Shutting her in, she was alone. She'd be lying if she said that some of her fantasies, when particularly pissed off, hadn't featured herself in a position of power and the rival of her father.

But that's all they'd been. Fantasies. Daydreams.

She'd learned today that everything she knew was only surface. Just enough to talk the talk, but not enough to walk the walk. She blamed Cassius for that. Sure, her father controlled everything, but Cassius had controlled her without her being aware of it.

Anger warred with her shame. Getting away last night had been a stroke of luck. But if Cassius had left her with any of the experienced guards, they would have stopped her hands holding the needles in the air.

She'd had those drugs stored in her room for a few years. Their potency may not have been enough to keep them out for long. But at least they still worked fast.

Any noise in her dash from the car would have alerted Cassius. He hadn't been far. She liked to think she'd had skill and had it all together, but her fight with Cassius at the safe house dissolved her inner confidence.

Could she take over her father's business? Or start one of her own? But how? She had no men loyal to her. Everyone who worked for her father trusted every word from his arrogant lips.

She had the money. And she supposed that was a start. Hell of a life to strive for—a crime boss rather than the ornamental crime boss's daughter.

Kinley kept the apartment in relative darkness, only turning on the kitchen light long enough to make herself a tea and turn on the fireplace.

Hendrick said he'd be back and she couldn't sleep until she knew what he'd found. Even if he came back with nothing. It would be something, one step closer to getting her freedom.

But her thoughts replayed every interaction with Cassius from over the years. He'd been around since she was only ten and had been the only one of her father's guards that hadn't ignored her. The more he spoke to her, the more others did, but not with the same friendliness. For a few years, she'd seen him as an older brother.

Not covering for her when she tried to sneak out with friends dissolved the big brother illusion. If that hadn't, then what he did to Brock would have.

She was staring at the flames like they danced the story of her life across their tips when the click of the door shutting pulled her from her thoughts. Hendrick stood at the other end of the room.

"You didn't find out anything, did you?"

"No." He was too relaxed to have learned anything exciting.

"Maybe it is as simple as it seems. My father hasn't always made the smartest decisions."

"Maybe." She heard the doubt in his tone.

"Want some tea?" She gripped the blanket as if to take it off her legs, but waited for his answer.

"No. Thanks." Hendrick sat on the chair across from her. His long, broad body blocked the sight of the small, cushioned seat as he leaned forward with his elbows on his knees.

"I was never good at waiting." She gave him a side smile, forcing the expression.

"Me either." Hendrick's eyes followed the mug up to her lips and stayed there even after she sipped her tea. She counted the breaths making his chest rise and fall before he spoke again. "Did you want to take over your father's business?"

Kinley started to speak, but stopped herself. Her eyes met his while she looked for her answer. "Dak suggested the same thing tonight. I've never allowed myself to wish for something he'd never grant. I'd hoped for something attainable. An equal. Not controlled. But I see now that would never have happened. But a competitor? That would be fun." If only to see the mottled rage on her father's face. "But those were only day dreams used to dim my anger."

"What about after he dies? Didn't you ever wonder about taking over then?"

"No. Too many of his men think the same way he does. And I was wrong about the friends and loyalty from some of them."

"You can fight. Physically, I mean. I watched how you fought against Cassius. You impressed me."

"I wonder about that, too." Her confidence thinned fast. Damn Cassius for doing this to her.

"Fuck that." Hendrick growled.

"Fuck what?"

"Don't sell yourself short, pretty girl." Standing, he towered over her. She craned her neck to continue to look him in the eyes.

Setting her cup down on the end table, she peeled the blanket off her legs and stood, forcing Hendrick to take a step back to give her room. "I'm not selling myself short." Her words clipped, and she jabbed him in the chest with her index finger. "I'm being realistic about my abilities. I'm allowed to relish in a pity party."

"Then what are you going to do about it?" He pushed back against her stabbing finger. The smirk playing on his lips taunted. And it worked, making her all the more frustrated.

She wasn't finished with her pity party to give her

future logical consideration. Narrowing her eyes, she fought the urge to stick her tongue out.

A sound like an internal chuckle escaped Hendrick. "I'm going to kiss you, Kinley." He slid his hand over her neck. She jumped at the contact. "And I'm not keeping my hands behind my back this time."

HENDRICK COULDN'T STAND the defeat in Kinley. He hadn't pushed her hard to get her to stand her ground. That little finger packed more punch than he expected.

He gripped the back of her neck and pulled her against him with his arm around her back. His lips were half an inch from hers. Those curves were pliant against him. Lips parted, she pulled in a breath, and he was ready to close the distance, eager to taste her again.

But that breath fed her voice. "Absolutely not." She shoved hard against his chest. His grip was too tight to put much distance between them, but he straightened.

"You're going to make me keep my hands behind my back again, aren't you?" To prove his dislike, he slid his thumb up the side of her neck to circle the sensitive spot behind her ear. He chuckled as she leaned into the touch.

"I could break your hands," she suggested with a faint growl of her own.

"But then you'd never know the things I can do to you."

"I don't want to know the things you can do to me." But those words hitched with hope.

"Liar." He pulled her tighter. For a bare moment,

Kinley relaxed. Hendrick realized too late that she'd forced her body to react that way on purpose. Her fist connected with his diaphragm. She packed enough strength to hurt, but she hadn't had the momentum to knock the wind from him.

Hendrick let her go and stepped back.

"Do it again."

She dropped her chin. "I'm done being played with, Hendrick."

"You are his equal. And you have the skills to fight." Hendrick relaxed his stance, but he stayed on guard, after Kinley had caught him by surprise more than once now.

"But I..." He cut her off by taking one large step toward her and grabbing her arm. He spun her until she landed with her back against his chest. She squeaked, struggling until he steadied her with an arm around her shoulders.

The moment she leaned into his hold, he used his other hand to grip her chin, tilting her head back and to the side. Bringing his lips close to her ear, he put all of his strength into his next words. "He only taught you what he wanted you to know. But I saw what you are capable of. And I'll teach you everything. The next time you have to fight Cassius, or anyone, you'll be the victor standing over him with a knife under his chin."

She gasped, her chest expanding under his forearm. He wanted to be the one to give her that power and watch her rise.

"You like that idea, pretty girl." Not a question. Hendrick recognized when a pulse pounded harder with excitement. He ran his nose over the space behind her ear.

"I like it," she whispered. "But I don't think I could follow through."

"You wouldn't have to. I'd be there to finish it for you." That promise shocked both of them. Hendrick pulled away fast enough to have Kinley swaying on her feet to catch her balance. She turned, the same surprise in her eyes as he felt in his gut.

The scene played out perfectly in his head. Kinley standing over the terrified face of Cassius, proving to him she wasn't someone to fuck with. But Hendrick was right there at her shoulder, ready to step in and do what she couldn't. And all of that had turned him on just as much as her body pressed to his.

He had no right to make that promise. No desire to be in that position. But he wouldn't take it back.

"You should go." The words lacked conviction, uttered in a hopeful whisper. Kinley may have pushed him away, but she was as drawn to him as he was to her.

"You should get some sleep." His voice was strained. Neither of them made a move in opposite directions. "I'm not leaving, pretty girl. And you aren't getting much sleep." He'd lost his chance to escape. His shock froze somewhere inside him. The image of this beautiful woman doing as he described kept him here. It didn't matter what happened next. He'd never take back those words.

"Awfully sure of yourself."

"Usually." He'd only put two steps between them when he tore away from her. Hendrick closed those in one move. Kinley didn't shy away. "You going to push me away again?"

A single, slender shoulder lifted. "Maybe."

"I wouldn't turn down the foreplay." He smirked,

surprising Kinley enough to widen her eyes and part her lips. A perfect invitation if he ever saw one.

He resumed his hold at the back of her neck and kissed her.

THE AIR FROZE in the back of her throat as Hendrick claimed her lips. There was nothing gentle about it.

Their last kiss had been devastating. It had brought out a side of her she'd forced dormant so as not to drive herself mad. She wasn't a virgin, technically, but that had been all about timing. Over the years, she'd learned to satisfy herself just enough to keep her wishes and daydreams away.

But when Hendrick had kissed her at the safe house, a beast inside her had let loose and she'd clung to him to give her more. Just as she clung to him now.

Kinley slid her hands up his chest and his muscles tightened under her palms. He growled low into her mouth and his hands moved.

At the back of her neck, he gripped, holding her in place. The arm he banded around her waist loosened and that hand explored, distracting her from the kiss. She let him invade her mouth while she focused on his touch.

Up her spine and back down. Over her hip and back to cup her ass. He pulled her against him and his cock pressed against her belly.

He'd only said a kiss, but could she tempt him further? Did she want to?

The answer reverberated as a loud *Fuck, yes!*

His hand slid under her shirt, pebbling her skin

from his light touch. She didn't want his touch to be light. Breaking the kiss, she looked up at him to tell him not to be gentle. But she froze as his hand wrapped around her side at her ribs. His thumb slid under the bottom of her bra.

"Something you wanted to say, pretty girl?" He moved his hand up, taking the cup of her bra with it.

"Not anymore." Kinley closed her eyes. He only held her by the back of her neck, making it impossible to move away from him. Hendrick captured her mouth again the same moment he rolled her nipple between his thumb and forefinger.

Damn, that thing was sensitive. And to think, she'd ignored them whenever she was alone in her room. She'd hadn't known what she'd been missing. Or maybe it wouldn't have mattered, because his hands were more than she'd ever experienced by herself.

She thrust one hand into his hair. His arm blocked her other one from raising above her shoulder. That simple roll of his fingers changed. He pinched, the tight pressure making her whimper.

"Make that sound again, Kinley. It's beautiful." His breath brushed against her lips, and he pinched again. This time, her whimper wasn't muffled. It was loud compared to their breathing.

Hendrick let off, thumbing the point. "Again." He waited a heartbeat before rolling it into a twist this time to create the sweet bite of pain.

Her whimper wasn't a whimper at all, but a moan that crawled down her body to settle in her core.

"There she is." He broke his hold and pulled her shirt over her head. "I didn't intend to go this far."

His honesty didn't douse the heat like it should

have. It was a second chance for both of them to pull back, to step away from each other and reconsider. But Kinley reached behind her to unclasp her bra.

"No." Hendrick lowered the hand at her neck and blocked her. She chilled. He'd just ripped her shirt off, but that was far enough for him. Talk about mixed signals.

"Okay. Right. Maybe a break is best." She looked away.

Fingers took hold of her chin and he brought her face back to his. He smiled. Not full and happy, but mischievous and cocky. "No. No break. I'm taking it off."

"Oh." Kinley dropped her arms and waited. He didn't reach for her bra. He claimed her mouth. And it was a claiming. His tongue thrust in and rolled over hers.

"Hold tight, pretty girl." His hands slid under her ass and he lifted her, settling her high on his waist so his face was almost level with her breasts. One was still exposed with the cup bunched on top. Hendrick nuzzled over the globe until he reached her nipple. He latched onto it with his teeth, and she cried out as he stalked to the bedroom, ducking through the door so she didn't hit the back of her head.

This was happening. And no one was going to come find her and take her home to lock her in her room. That had been so many years ago. A hopeful teenager looking for freedom and experience.

Hendrick let go of her breast and kicked the bedroom door shut behind him. "Are you going to answer my question now?"

His damn question and that fucking dress.

"Lies or truth, pretty girl. Which is it?" He held her

in the air. "I bet I could figure it out. But I promise it will be torture." He didn't make it sound like torture.

"It's both." She swallowed hard and lowered her lashes. Heat infused her cheeks. She hated the embarrassment. Although unnecessary with Hendrick, it filled her.

"Let's change one of those." A hand slid up her back and pinched the clasp on her bra. With his teeth, he pulled it forward. Kinley helped and took it off her arms. He grinned as it hung from his front teeth.

She laughed. He looked both insane and sexy. His grin widened, and he dropped her bra to the floor.

"What do you want me to do to you, pretty girl?"

"You're asking me?"

He chuckled. "It's a question only you can answer."

Her fantasies hadn't been that varied, but they had been specific. Being caught masturbating had been the most prominent. She suddenly wanted to know what Hendrick would do if he ever caught her. He had an unpredictable fire in his eyes that burned. But that wouldn't work right now.

Could she be brave enough to explicitly speak her fantasies aloud? Why shouldn't she be? Hendrick had told her not to lose herself. She was always bold with her words, except with her father.

Hendrick had encouraged her. And Hendrick was the one with her half naked in his arms, lazily circling her nipple with his tongue while she tried to think.

"I want to suck your cock while you force me to orgasm."

7

HEART PUMPING WILDLY, HENDRICK STARED UP AT Kinley, unable to keep his eyes from widening. An enticing mix of confidence and uncertainty deepened the colour of her eyes. She didn't back away from his gaze.

"Your wish is my command." No way in hell would he distinguish that courage by refusing her. If that's what she wanted, he'd gladly force climax after climax from her, ringing them from her body until she begged him to finish down her throat and put an end to it all. That was if he had the patience to last that long.

Her breath shook.

"Nervous?" His best guess was she was a virgin, or as close to one as possible. Being cooped up in her father's house and under constant guard wouldn't have given her the opportunity.

She shook her head.

"Don't lie." The warning was low. A reminder.

"A little."

"Have you ever sucked a cock before, pretty girl?"

"No." She leaned down and set her forehead against his.

"But..."

"I've fantasized about it."

That's what he'd wanted to hear. He wanted every delicious, dirty thing she craved. He'd expected her to whisper it. But she owned it despite the nerves he saw running through her. "I can't wait to hear more of those fantasies."

Hendrick tossed her on the bed and went to his knees between her legs. Reaching for the clasp of her jeans, he pulled them down her hips, lifting one leg to a time in front of him. Soft fabric covered her. He ran his finger over her, petting her while he planned how he'd make her fantasy come true.

"Hendrick?"

"Are you a virgin, Kinley?" It wouldn't change how he'd treat her. As he peeled her panties away from her cunt, Hendrick hoped he'd be the only one there.

"Not technically."

Hendrick paused and narrowed his eyes at her. "You're going to need to explain that."

Her cheeks changed colour. He had to fight not to grin.

Hendrick used his thumb to pull the hood up on her clit, exposing the bud. "Talk, pretty girl." Then he leaned forward and blew.

She gasped. "I was eighteen. I'd gotten away by sheer luck. We were in the back seat of his car. But Cassius found us." Each sentence was short and rushed. "He pulled Brock off me the second things... started."

"You mean as soon as he sank his dick into you." Not technically a virgin.

Kinley nodded.

"That night is the only experience you have, isn't it, pretty girl?"

"Yes. But I'm not..."

He finished for her. "You aren't naïve or inexperienced."

"I want this, Hendrick."

"As I said, your wish is my command." He closed the distance and sucked her clit into his mouth. Her legs tried to close on his head, but he gripped the insides of her thighs and forced them apart. He didn't have to treat her like a virgin, but when he entered her, he'd take his time.

When her legs relaxed under his hands, he moved one hand forward. He drew focused circles around her clit, never stopping. Using one finger, he followed the same pace as his tongue but at her entrance. Already wet, he slid the tip inside, stroking the sensitive nerves there.

"Hendrick!"

"Have you imagined a cock in your mouth when you come?"

"Yes! Please."

Hendrick pulled away from her and stood at the end of the bed, fully clothed. Looking at her laid out on the bed, he tried to remember how they'd gotten here. This hadn't been his plan at all. He hadn't wanted to get close to her. Fucking didn't mean getting close, but he knew deep down this wasn't just fucking. Not with Kinley. He'd known her for twenty-four hours.

Twenty-four fucking hours. He couldn't abandon her like this—they'd gone too far—but he could give her one hell of an orgasm while keeping all of his clothes on and then walk away. He could keep his promise and his distance.

But a small hand moved down her body, settling a finger over her clit.

"Don't you fucking dare touch it." The growl burst from him. Walk away? Hell would freeze over.

"Or what?" She drew a circle around the bud he'd just sucked into a swollen little mass. It poked out, begging for more.

"Or I'll tie your hands." He didn't know if Dak kept anything like that in this apartment. But Hendrick was creative.

Her finger paused, but didn't move away. He used the moment to pull his shirt off. She still hadn't moved by the time he tossed it to the ground.

"Should I count, pretty girl?"

"Maybe you need to." Kinley circled her clit and pulled her bottom lip between her teeth.

"Kinley." His warning fell flat as she closed her eyes and circled one more time. "One." An anticipation he hadn't expected burst inside him. His hands moved to the fly of his pants. If he ever played a game with a partner before, it had been at his instigation. But this was all Kinley.

She smirked, pulling her bottom lip free from her teeth.

"Two." His heart pounded, and dizziness swamped, pushing away all the reasons he shouldn't do this. Pushing away all the things he should focus on.

Kinley's eyes snapped open, and she lowered her chin to meet his gaze. Hendrick rid himself of the rest of his clothes, holding his belt behind his back, and stalked to the side of the bed.

"I wonder if you can take the punishment, pretty girl."

"Didn't sound like much of a punishment." She gasped as her finger didn't move in single circles anymore, but picked up a steady rhythm.

Hendrick laughed, a low chuckle that made her breath hiccup. That lilt of crazy always made people nervous. "That wasn't the punishment." He waited for her eyes to meet his. "Three."

Moving faster than her, he had her wrists in his hands and above her head with the belt wrapped around them.

"Now, what to do about that?" He let his gaze sweep down her body. She was slick and swollen—already aroused to the point of making her first climax easy.

But he thought a bit of edging was in order.

HE MOVED TOO fast for Kinley to have done anything to stop him, not that she'd wanted to. But knowing that tying her up hadn't been the true end to that little game had nerves coursing through her. Not bad nerves. The good, tingling kind of something new. In the back of her mind she hoped to always have those new-like tingles no matter how many times she experienced this.

His pupils dilated, making the hazel deepen. She'd seen them do that before, likening it to a fire in his eyes. There was something about Hendrick.

Kinley tried to pull each breath deeper, but Hendrick's touch on her lower belly made her jump. His chuckle that followed was sinful. He slid his fingers lower, and her eyes fluttered shut. It wasn't an exploratory touch. Every move was deliberate.

"If I say don't touch, you don't touch." His grin was loud through his warning, but it didn't make the warning any less harsh. Not that Kinley would ever listen. She doubted she wouldn't enjoy anything he'd do to her. Every delicious punishment would be worth it.

"I wouldn't dare."

Hendrick's gaze snapped up to hers and his grin spread. "We'll see, won't we?" He looked back down her body and slid a finger inside her. She closed her eyes and arched her back. It wasn't enough. But he worked slowly.

Digging her heels into the mattress, she tried to lift her hips for more.

"Try all you want. You won't get more until I want to give it."

She fell back to the bed with a whimper.

Hendrick set his thumb over her clit while he added a second finger. And then he orchestrated the nerves in her body like a choir. Each sensitive point sang at his command. Rising and rising.

He froze. The haze controlling Kinley's mind disappeared, but her body still hummed. He'd stopped right before her orgasm hit.

When she opened her eyes, he was looking down at her with narrowed slits, and a smirk settled on his lips.

She wanted to rage at him, but she wanted that orgasm more. Never had she brought herself to such a hazy state with her climax. Her mind was blissful and her entire body hummed, despite his touch only being in one place.

Hendrick chuckled low and curled his fingers.

Kinley pinched her lips together between her teeth to hold in any sound. She let her mind slip again and waited for her body to fall over the edge, waited for Hendrick to allow her over the edge.

But again, as the climax rose with a ferocity, he pulled away. The only sound she made was the high-pitched growl as she let go of her lips.

"If I say don't touch, what do you do?"

"Don't touch." It was a lie. She'd endure this again from him any day. "Please, Hendrick."

"Good girl." But the look in his eyes said he saw through her lie. He gripped her chin and tilted her head back. "You ready?"

She nodded, dropping her gaze to his cock. Damn, it was as big as the rest of him. He moved up the bed a little, so he was closer to her head, but could still reach between her legs. Lifting her head with a hand behind it, he propped her up on a pillow.

"Open up, pretty girl." He ran his thumb over her lower lip. She opened with his touch. He pinched her clit as he moved forward, sliding into her mouth.

Kinley worked over the tip and tried hard to pull him in further. He groaned, gripping the headboard, and held himself away from her.

"Slow down."

She shook her head as much as she had room to do. His taste exploded on her tongue, and she wanted more.

"Fuck," he cursed. He didn't work his fingers into her this time. He plunged them in and curled them upward. The shock was enough to make her pause. And he still hadn't moved closer. Kinley realized the battle they'd put themselves in.

She worked her tongue on the underside until his

eyes rolled back with his head. He growled and started pumping his fingers in and out, keeping them curled to hit the sweet spot over and over. She sucked him harder with every thrust until he caved and leaned over her.

"Fuck, Kinley." His hips twitched and she made a sound of encouragement around him. "Come, pretty girl."

With the tip of his cock touching the back of her throat, her body exploded. Her own hand could never hold a candle to Hendrick. Wave after wave of intense pleasure released through her blood. It had been the whole experience that made it so intense. Not just his fingers. His words, his control, and having a fantasy come true.

He was still hard in her mouth, but her jaw had gone slack with her orgasm. "Again." His hand had slowed, but he quickly restarted everything. This time, she was oversensitive. She cried out around his cock, and he started thrusting his hips again.

He worked her mercilessly until she broke, this one just as intense as the first. He pulled out of her mouth and body, lifting his hand to his lips. She tracked him with hooded eyes while he moved to the nightstand. He pulled out a condom and slid it on while still kneeling beside her.

Taking the pillow from behind her head, he slid it beneath her hips. "You're going to come again for me, pretty girl."

Her head fell from side to side on the mattress. He laughed.

"You don't have a choice."

She thought he'd slam into her, but he didn't. He made his way inside her with quick, shallow thrusts.

With her propped up on the pillow, he had the same angle he'd had with his fingers. The tip of his cock hit the spot that made her see stars.

She watched his muscles strain as he held himself back. They locked eyes and Kinley lost her breath.

"Now, Kinley." He set his thumb on her clit. Her body tightened and an orgasm she hadn't seen coming overtook her. Hendrick growled and broke his control, slamming into her with every contraction of her core.

He tore the pillow out from under her and covered her body with his. Claiming her lips in a brutal kiss, he continued to thrust until his cock throbbed. He nipped her bottom lip and held it between his teeth as he finished, his chest heaving.

Lifting his head, he looked as if he wanted to say something. It was the first time since she'd met him he looked lost for words. But she had the strangest feeling that he didn't want her to see that. Kinley closed her eyes with a sigh and arched her body into his like a contented cat.

Hendrick nuzzled her neck and pulled himself free, disappearing into the bathroom. Kinley's gaze trailed after him. That had probably been the best one-night stand she'd ever have in her life. She licked her lips. Maybe once she was safe from her father, she'd come back for seconds.

KINLEY WAS ASLEEP by the time Hendrick returned from the bathroom, a cloth in his hand. She tried to kick him when he cleaned her, and he caught her ankle in the air. She cracked one eye open to glare at him, then went back to feigning sleep.

Hendrick held in his smirk. But as he returned to the bathroom to toss the cloth in the hamper, he froze. What was he doing?

He didn't ask himself like his actions surprised him. No. He needed to know what he was going to do next. He'd more than fucked her, and had enjoyed it more than he ever had before. The entire scene came naturally to him. One minute he was ready to give her pleasure and walk away to keep distance, and the next he was edging her and driving them both crazy.

Each step back to the bedroom, he took carefully, unsure what emotion would slam into his chest when he saw her in the bed. Kinley's breaths were long and audible. His palms itched to run over her rounded hips and pull her against him. But he couldn't. He shouldn't.

A life with him would only make her a constant target for their fathers. And Hendrick had already waited long enough to go after Shane's killer. His father intended Kinley to be a distraction, even if it didn't work out the way he'd planned.

Hendrick pulled the blanket up over her. She stirred and looked up at him with a question in her hooded eyes.

"I have to go." He hadn't intended for the words to sound harsh. He settled the blankets on her shoulders, but Kinley sat up, pushing the blankets back to her waist and forcing him to stand straight.

"Is something wrong?" She held herself up with one hand braced behind her on the bed, the other relaxed on her lap. Kinley didn't hide her body. Her nipples hardened from the exposure, drawing his attention.

Fuck. She was stunning, and he needed to get away from her before he leaned down to latch onto one of those delicious buds.

"No." He had to clear his throat to release the growl. "Go back to sleep. We'll talk in the morning." He turned away, grabbing his clothes from the floor on his way out the door. The curses she muttered under her breath reached him as he shut the door.

Dressing in the living room, he listened for her to follow. Nothing. With a sigh, he left and made his way downstairs. He'd find somewhere to crash rather than going home. With only a few hours until he'd get up and make his way in, leaving was just a waste of time.

"You slipped up tonight." Roen's voice cut through the night. The door to the computer room was open a crack.

Hendrick pushed open the door with a finger and leaned against the frame. Crossing his arms, he raised a brow and waited for Roen to explain.

"You went to Pierce's."

Hendrick's throat tightened, but he made no outward reaction. Dak hired Roen for a reason. He was always one step ahead. Hendrick should have counted on Roen having eyes at his father's and on Kinley's father the moment he brought her in here. "Your point?"

"You were there when you found Kinley. And you went back tonight. You got through their security as easily as walking in here."

Roen still hadn't accused him of anything, so he stayed silent. He didn't owe Roen an answer for anything. That wasn't true. He owed them all the truth at some point. But not yet. Not now. And not before he told Dak and King.

"What were you doing there?" Roen stood from his creaky chair and took two steps toward Hendrick.

"A job for a friend." Hendrick hated the lie, but he wasn't ready to confide in anyone.

"And tonight?"

"Following my own leads."

"Care to share what you found?"

"I didn't find anything. My source didn't know about Kinley or the Curry family." Hudson would learn what he could, but being demoted didn't give him much access.

"You're hiding something, Hendrick. You haven't been yourself for months." The concern in Roen's voice had Hendrick grinding his teeth to keep himself from flinching. He'd thought he'd make it through life with no one ever knowing who he was. If Shane hadn't been killed, maybe he could have.

"I'm fine." Hendrick eyed the computers. He'd considered spending the rest of the night in here doing some of his own research, but that was too big a risk with Roen. He'd find every keystroke in the morning. Hendrick pushed off the wall, deciding to go to the gym. He'd either work out until he passed out or he'd crash somewhere on the mats.

"Kit Pierce." Roen threw the name out like a kick to Hendrick's spine. But Hendrick tilted his head up smoothly, no pause or hesitation as he regarded Roen.

"What about him?"

"Do you know him?" Roen's tone changed. The concern had vanished. And if they all didn't know each other so well, Hendrick might have missed the suspicion lancing the words.

"I know who he is."

Roen said nothing else. He didn't have to. They stared at each other in silence. The only response Hendrick could give him was a sigh as he walked away.

Roen knew. How he figured it out, Hendrick would never know. Maybe he hadn't known for certain and Hendrick had just given him confirmation. If any of them remembered the note sent to him as Kit months ago informing him of Shane's death, they might piece it together with the events of the past two days.

The truth had to come out.

8

THAT ROTTEN, FIRE-COATED, COWARDLY BASTARD.
Kinley had fallen asleep angry and woken the same.
Racing out of the room without even getting clothes on
demonstrated the height of cowardice. But the why
baffled her. One minute he'd been staring at her breasts
with enough hunger to make her core melt and the next
he'd been dashing out of the room. After the way he
took control, she'd never expect him to run from her.

With the curses still hot on her tongue, Kinley
crawled out of bed before the sun and showered. She
relived every minute of the previous night rather than
pay attention to her routine. He'd come back late and
had seen her down. She'd given up trying to hide
from him.

The things she'd realized about her life had brought
her to the lowest of lows for her. All her capabilities
seemed fake. Everyone around her had placated her if
they weren't shoving her away like her father. But not
Hendrick. He'd lifted her up and told her not to lose
herself.

Fine. If he wanted to be that way, she could move on and forget the night had happened, too. It was fun—a release. No need to hold on to a one-night stand.

Kinley dressed and dried her hair. She paused in the kitchen, debating breakfast, but that would take more time than she wanted. Breakfast wouldn't give her immediate answers.

She slipped from the apartment and punched in the code to call the elevator, and descended. The sun barely sent light through the windows of the main floor. Shadows still covered a mostly empty space. But she followed the low hiss of a coffeepot.

Dak stood at the counter, glaring at the black liquid. He looked up when she took a few steps into the room.

"Morning. Sleep well?" His voice sounded like it hurt.

"Um, no." She had no reason to pretend otherwise and no reason for her to have slept well—even without Hendrick's actions.

Dak pulled the pot out before it was full and poured two cups. The liquid hissed against the burner as he handed one to her. "I asked Hendrick what he'd been doing on the Pierce property. But I haven't asked you."

Straight down to business before the sun even woke. She shouldn't expect anything else from the mercenaries. "My father wanted an alliance." Kinley sipped the coffee and tried not to wince.

"Cream is in the fridge. Sugar is by the coffeepot."

"Thank you." She stepped around Dak, toward the fridge. He hadn't backed away to give her space, but Kinley didn't want to be under his scrutiny. After hearing their conversation with her father, she felt safe here. At least safe from getting handed back. Each of the mercenaries had a dangerous aura surrounding them. All a little different. But all deadly.

"And why did he take you to secure an alliance?" He spun, his gaze following her across the room.

"A bought and paid for bride." She shut the fridge door a little too hard.

"Good morning." Hendrick appeared in the doorway behind her. His voice crawled up her spine before she'd recognized his heat. She spun around without spilling her coffee. And it seemed like waves of steam rolled off his bare chest. Water dripped from the ends of his hair and he tossed a towel over his shoulders. His jeans sat low on his hips.

Kinley wanted to lick every crevice on his torso until she remembered how he'd abandoned her after fucking her. "Good morning." Oh, look at that. She pulled off an unaffected high-horse tone. The kind of thing she high-fived herself over. She'd practiced that tone over the years with her father and his guards. But the sight of Hendrick's bare chest was enough to crack it.

She turned away from him and stalked to the other side of the table in the middle of the room, looking into her coffee rather than closing her eyes for the mental break. Dak still stood on the other side of the room with a fixed gaze on her.

Others filtered into the room, looking either fresh or fully dressed and ready to conquer. She didn't want to imagine what.

Then Sophie came in. The only one of the bunch not looking ready to kick ass. She didn't make eye contact with anyone and shuffled her way to the coffeepot. Dak's attention shifted.

"Princess."

"Don't *Princess* me. If you want bright eyed and bushy tailed, then you and your cock stay on your side of the bed tonight."

Kinley chose the wrong moment to take a sip of her coffee. She coughed, holding her mug in front of her until the liquid made it down. A large hand patted her back. She hadn't noticed Hendrick move across the room.

Dak stalked toward Sophie and slid a hand around the back of her neck. It wasn't a gentle touch. He forced her to look up at him. Kinley turned away when he dipped his head to her ear. She didn't need to witness their private moment, even though the sight of it sent a shiver down her spine.

"Call coming in." Roen—Sophie had described him as the broody looking one—came in. All heads snapped in his direction. Roen's eyes landed on her for a brief moment before setting a phone down on the table and answering a call.

"Talk." Dak's attention zeroed in on the phone, but he'd adjusted Sophie so her back rested against his chest.

"Enough with the games. I want to talk to my daughter." There was something in her father's voice that she couldn't place.

Dak looked to Hendrick, as if this was his call. It was hers. She spoke before anyone ordered her silence.

"What do you want?" She stepped away from the body tensing behind her.

"I want to make a deal."

Kinley blinked. "A deal." She repeated the words with disgust. "I'm your daughter."

"What's your point, Kinley? You ran." Again, his tone was too calm.

"Go ahead, then. What's your deal?" She kept herself from scoffing.

"Take me off speaker."

"No. You have no leverage with this. Either say it or don't. It makes no difference to me."

"Money, Kinley. Enough money for you to keep yourself separate from your husband. But you will marry Kit Pierce. This alliance can't fail." Her father dropped the last four words with precision. Hendrick was right. There was something else he needed out of this alliance.

"Why? Why can't it fail?"

"That isn't for you to worry about. And beyond your understanding, anyway. Come back. Now."

"I have a secret for you." She waited, letting the hum over the phone grow louder. "I don't need your money."

"Stupid girl. I wouldn't be so sure if I were you." Her father's insult waned and something muffled fell over the line.

"Kinley." Cassius purred her name, and she outwardly cringed. She couldn't hide how much that sound hurt, not when he'd said her name that way a thousand times and she'd seen it as friendly, encouraging. "You're upsetting your father."

"It isn't the first time."

"No. It isn't." He paused. "We need you to do your part. You've always had an interest in your father's business. Now is your chance to be a key player."

"Bullshit."

Cassius sighed. "It wasn't supposed to be Kit. You would have liked the man he'd first lined up for you."

"What are you talking about?"

"You would have liked Shane."

The air whipped like an icy chill, and a hand wrapped around Kinley's throat. Anger rose in the heat of Hendrick's palm. The pressure wasn't enough to hurt her, but he could.

Cassius kept talking. "To be honest, I don't know much about Kit. Just that he exists somewhere."

"Keep him talking about Shane." Hendrick whispered in her ear. She didn't believe it was loud enough for any of the others in the room to hear, let alone Cassius.

"Why didn't the engagement with Shane go through?"

"It's a shame. At least for you. But I'm sure Kit is a fine substitute. Shane was a little softer around the edges, though."

"Spit it out, Cass. I don't understand."

"I know, kiddo. It's been cute watching you think you knew everything."

Kinley's throat closed off, and it wasn't from Hendrick's grip.

"Shane died. So now the deal needs to go through with his brother. But we need you back here to make it happen. Get yourself away from the mercenaries. Don't make me come get you."

The line went dead, and the only hum left in the room was the rage seeping off Hendrick like clouds of dry ice. Both hot and cold enveloped her back.

"What do you know about Shane?" He growled in her ear.

"I know of him. I didn't know he'd died."

"Murdered. He didn't just die." His fingers tightened

on her throat and she felt his pain. He still wasn't speaking loud enough for anyone but her to hear. Or that's what she thought, anyway.

Her breathing quickened. His hold was dangerous. "Let go, Hendrick." Kinley kept her voice soft. He wasn't trying to threaten her, but he wanted to threaten someone.

"Hendrick." Dak's gravely baritone shook the room. Hendrick still didn't loosen his hold. But in an instant, she was free.

A RED HAZE filled his head the moment Cassius uttered his brother's name. The only thing he focused on was that Kinley was a key to even a small piece of information. Shane had said nothing about an arranged marriage alliance with the Curry's. If their father had been involved, Shane may not have known.

Cassius, the fucker, knew something. Hendrick had the sickening feeling that, with Kinley in front of him, everything was coming full circle. Cassius didn't respect her like she'd thought, but he may keep talking for her. By squeezing her throat, by holding her, he felt in control of the conversation between them. But then the line went dead and panic seized his chest. He couldn't let go of Kinley. She was the closest thing to the truth he had.

"Let go, Hendrick." Her voice stroked him as soft as her hands.

Shane. *He was softer around the edges.* He wasn't a fucking monster like the rest of them, but he wasn't soft.

"Hendrick." The threat from Dak cracked against

him. He couldn't let go of her. Letting go of her was letting go of a clue.

But several hands grabbed his neck, wrists, and shoulders, pulling him away from Kinley. They held him back, so he didn't latch onto the sliver of hope she represented.

Sophie took his place and wrapped an arm around Kinley's shoulders. Kinley didn't fold in on herself though, didn't lean against Sophie for support. She pulled her shoulders back and narrowed her eyes at him.

She took a step toward him, but Dak stopped her. "Sophie, take her out of here." Dak, Cole, and Roen still held him tight, doubling their efforts as Kinley left the room ahead of Sophie.

No. No, no, no. Hendrick needed to know everything she knew. And then he was going after Cassius. Torture for information was something he thrived on.

They didn't release him until Gear and Archer blocked all the exits. Just in time for King and Ember to walk in.

Great. All eyes on him.

"What the fuck was that?" Dak was pissed and Hendrick couldn't blame him. He owed Kinley an apology. Hell, he owed her a lot more than that.

But the haze still lingered. An eruption was imminent. For months, he'd hidden the grief over Shane deep.

"I need to talk to you and King alone."

"No fucking way." Roen spoke. He moved to help block one exit with arms crossed over his wide chest.

"Why did you attack Kinley?" Dak sounded a lot closer to him now. King's eyebrows shot up, having not witnessed the reason behind the others holding Hendrick back.

"I didn't attack her. I needed Cassius to keep talking."

"You had to threaten her to make her do that?" Cole didn't hide his disgust. None of them were good guys, but they had morals, certain lines they wouldn't cross.

"Shane Pierce." Dak spoke the name like a test and Hendrick didn't quite keep himself from reacting.

"Kit Pierce." Roen added his own test. "Shane's older brother. He's been MIA for years, leaving Shane to take over for their father, who's been enjoying a cushy retirement. But he hasn't just been MIA. All digital evidence of him is almost impossible to find."

"He doesn't want to be found." Dak drew the correct conclusion. Or close to it. Hendrick didn't want to be associated with that family.

"Four months ago, a message arrived here for Kit." Cole revived the memory for each of them. And that's when Hendrick saw it. The realization of his identity flashed through each of them one by one.

"Everyone out." Dak was close enough for Hendrick to feel his breath.

"No." Gear spoke up this time, his eyes narrowing on Hendrick. "I want to hear this, too. He didn't just lie to you and King."

No, he hadn't. He'd have to come clean to each of them. Better to do it all at once.

"Agreed." King growled, then leaned down to say something to Ember. She sent him a look with a touch of sympathy. King nudged her lower back, and she left the room.

"Hendrick is my middle name. I haven't been Kit

since long before I became a mercenary. I hated my father and his business, never quite fitting in."

"Impulsive and crazy didn't sit right when dealing drugs and weapons?" Cole tried to joke, but the sneer flattened it.

"Shane had an ambition for it. But he'd been changing the way they did things. He was as good as one could get, being a crime boss. I never wanted that role. It was leave or get myself killed."

"Like Shane," said King.

"Not like Shane." He'd been running that place for nearly a decade. Hendrick's death would have looked like an accident or someone would have used some crazy action to justify killing him. "I don't know what happened to him. Or who."

"The job for a friend?" Dak gave him some space.

"Me."

"Does Kinley know who you are?" Roen hadn't relaxed at all.

"No." Hendrick met each set of eyes. He may regret lying to them about who he was, but he wouldn't apologize. He wasn't *Kit*. He'd never be *Kit* again.

"Your father has always known where to find you?" King didn't sit, but his shoulders lost some tension. No one was trying to hold him down or keep him from leaving. Still, Hendrick forced himself to stay and finish this.

"Shane always knew where to find me. He didn't tell him, but my father has his spies, I'm sure. He found out on his own that I work for you." It didn't matter to Hendrick if his family knew where he was. In fact, it made him feel damn good to be someone they feared. One of King's mercenaries.

"We all have pasts. None of them pretty." Cole shrugged and moved toward the almost empty coffee pot. He poured what looked like half of a cup and grimaced. He started making a new pot as if Hendrick hadn't just dropped his darkest secret.

"After that conversation, I'd take bets that Shane's death and this thing with Kinley are connected." Gear gave his opinion freely when he wanted to.

"I have everything lined up to get her out of here with a private flight if necessary." Roen sat down next to Cole.

As he looked around, Hendrick wished for the first time he'd pulled Shane out of the family. And into this one.

SOPHIE TOOK KINLEY up to the apartment she lived in with Dak. She wanted to go back to Hendrick, but reminded herself each time she turned toward the door that he'd fucked her and left her the night before. Those actions didn't deserve her consideration. But there was something in his touch, his hold, his voice. He was in pain. The threat inside him, waiting to be free, wasn't directed at her. Somehow she knew that. She sensed the difference in him compared to others she'd crossed in her life.

"I've never seen Hendrick act like that."

Kinley doubted he ever had. Because knowing the man for all of two days made her an expert on him. She rolled her eyes at herself. But that didn't stop her eyes from wandering toward the door.

"Are you sure you're okay?" Sophie had stood in

front of Kinley in the elevator, pinning her to the back wall without touching, asking with urgency if Hendrick had hurt her. But Kinley didn't think the way he'd handled her to be anything out of the norm for the mercenaries. She'd seen how Dak was with Sophie this morning and the night before at dinner. Each of them stood firm with a demanding presence. And it wasn't anywhere near what she'd grown up seeing.

None of that excused him, but Kinley wasn't damaged, physically or otherwise. "I'm fine. He's not."

Sophie tilted her head as she plopped herself down at the island while the coffee pot perked. Theirs had been interrupted. And what else would she serve this early in the morning—even if a shot of something stronger was what she needed to soothe her thoughts. "To tell you the truth. He hasn't been himself for months. Not since he was hurt because of..." Her lips pinched tight.

"Because of what?"

"Me. My ex-husband used me as payment to someone. They attacked, trying to collect. One of them stabbed Hendrick in the thigh. Pretty deep. It'd taken quite a while to recover. He hasn't been the same since."

"You feel guilty."

"I try not to. None of them would want me to."

"You shouldn't. By the way Dak looks at you, I doubt you had a choice but to stay here."

"You are not wrong." Sophie glanced at the coffee, then gave a nod as if coming to a decision. Reaching into a corner cupboard, she pulled out a brown bottle with a green label. Wagging it in the air, she gave Kinley a lopsided smile and poured a generous amount in the bottom of two mugs before topping them with the coffee. She set one mug in front of Kinley.

Kinley sniffed. The strong smell of the chocolate flavoured liquor was almost enough to make her eyes pop. After hiding the evidence, Sophie retook her seat.

"Why do they do that?" Kinley stared at the coffee while she asked, but then took a sip and let it sit on her tongue.

"Who's they and what's that?"

Kinley grinned. She liked Sophie. "Certain men, fathers, husbands. Why do they see women as pawns? We're used, manipulated…"

"Beaten," Sophie added.

"Sold." Another woman's voice followed the sound of the front door shutting.

Kinley looked over to see a shorter woman with long dark hair make her way toward them. A kindred spirit lingered in her eyes. Kinley closed her eyes and kept talking. "Beaten, sold. Why?"

"Two reasons. Insecurity or arrogance. And that's putting it simple. But I don't think you need us to answer that." The new woman eyed the coffees, then smiled at Kinley. "Ember." She squeezed Kinley's shoulder.

"I don't. Kinley."

"The mercenaries aren't like that." Sophie held her coffee between both hands.

"I know." Two days wasn't enough time to make that judgment, but circumstances made it possible. Hendrick could have kicked her out of his truck. Could have handed her over to Cassius. Could have tried to claim his own reward for returning her.

Ember opened the corner cupboard like this was a

natural routine for her—the two women drinking spiked coffee at ungodly hours of the morning. "So what did I miss downstairs?"

"Hendrick going a bit crazy." Sophie shrugged.

"He's always crazy." There was fondness in the words.

"Sorry. Crazier."

"That's not it." Kinley couldn't let them talk about him like that, despite the warmth she heard in their voices. Even she saw that crazy lilt to his eyes, the fire that burned under the surface. But that wasn't what happened downstairs. "He's in pain over something."

Ember, who'd walked in with bravado, now found her coffee to be the most interesting thing. "What brought you here?"

Kinley summed up the story she was already tired of telling. Runaway bride, crime family alliance, and so on. She took the time to relax as if this were a lifelong friendship where she got to vent her troubles. They'd all finished their coffee by the time she was done.

The muscles in Ember's face tightened, but she hadn't said a word the entire time Kinley spoke. "Let's go down to the gym. I'm sure the mercenaries are doing what they do best. We should have the place to ourselves for a bit."

"I've got some clothes you can borrow." Sophie gathered their empty cups and took Kinley to her bedroom.

The last time she had friends like this had been in high school. Not that the friendships had been strong enough to stand against her father's guards when they showed their faces.

Kinley didn't think her father's guards would frighten these two women.

9

HENDRICK GAVE ROEN EVERYTHING HE KNEW TO help him dig further into Shane and their father. And since Cassius knew something about Shane, Roen dug further into Kinley's family, too. Places that ran businesses like theirs, rarely kept clear evidence left for anyone to find. Transactions were all reported as something different. Without knowing their systems, it was difficult to decipher each transaction. And there were many done with cash. Most with cash.

After digging and talking in so many circles, Hendrick was dizzy. They concluded that the only people with answers were inside the two families.

"I don't suppose you're willing to let this go? The truth will make its way out." Dak stood with his arms crossed. Somehow, the truth always broke free. But that could take years. It had only been months, and the weight of Shane's murder was like a festering wound in Hendrick's gut.

"No."

"What about pulling Shane's guys out? Bring them

here. Maybe all the pieces from everyone will fall together." Cole's suggestion didn't have conviction. They were all grasping at straws, trying to avoid what needed to happen.

"Won't happen. Hudson said those that wanted to leave already have. Those that are staying won't leave. Not until they find out what happened to Shane."

They were all silent for too long. Even Hendrick didn't want to voice what he must do. To make it work, he needed Kinley. But he'd never force her. When she found out who he was, she may not agree to help him at all.

"How long do you think you'll be gone?" King let out a throaty sigh.

"At least a month. Maybe several. But I want to take someone in with me." He needed someone at his back. Someone he trusted absolutely. Hudson was one, but Hendrick had no guarantee he could manipulate the people in there, putting them where he wanted them. His father wouldn't trust him right away. A month was generous.

"I'll go." Gear spoke up from the other end of the table.

"I will, too." Cole volunteering wasn't a surprise to Hendrick, but he wouldn't take two guys with him away from Dak and King. Leaving them two short was bad enough. He wouldn't make it three.

"No. If I need more help, I'll let you know."

"Are you taking Kinley with you?" Roen looked over the top of the laptop while his fingers paused on the keys.

"That will be up to her." The looks he received as he left weren't encouraging. Roen had reported seeing the three women on the monitors going down to the gym about an hour ago. He didn't have to involve her. But it would make it easier, more believable, and would give him access to both families. Hendrick could ship her out of here and never have to see her again. How she felt about his true identity didn't matter.

Except it mattered to him.

He never should have treated her the way he did during the phone call with her father and Cassius. Despite how it appeared, he wouldn't have hurt her. And after last night, he'd wanted an excuse to get his hands on her again. Hendrick banned himself from touching her, from allowing her to distract him.

Now he needed her to play the distraction.

Hendrick silently approached the gym, getting close enough to overhear their conversation and their flushed faces from their sparring. Roen had let him glimpse his screen for a few minutes. Kinley kept up her own against the other two women. But Ember and Sophie ultimately won each round. Cassius taught Kinley routine strikes and defenses—enough to best a thug off the street, or even someone green, but he ensured she'd never win when it mattered.

Ember and Sophie did a good job of showing her that. Now, they discussed the type of training they endured being married to King and Dak.

"Part of protecting us is teaching us everything." At least they understood why King and Dak insisted on putting them through it all. Hendrick wanted the same for Kinley.

"They refuse to allow us to be less than them. And it's so fun putting King on his ass." Ember's smile infused her eyes. To watch the tiny woman best King was the best damn entertainment Hendrick had in a long time. And it was happening more and more. She'd worked hard since marrying King.

"We do everything that we just did for the past hour and more. My first time down here, all of the mercenaries circled me, attacking one by one for a solid hour." Sophie had learned more in that hour than any self-defense class she'd attended.

"Hendrick has been teaching us to throw knives. And he's usually the one who plays hide and seek. The others will join in too, but it seems to be a favourite of Hendrick's." Ember hated hide and seek. She'd improved, but it still wasn't her strongest ability. Sophie was excellent at hide and seek.

"Hide and seek?" Kinley asked.

"We seek. Hendrick hides. We have to find him without him spotting us. Sometimes he'll leave the lights on, but it has more of a thrill when it's in the dark." Sophie's answer held excitement for the game. Ember curled her nose.

And Hendrick wouldn't be him if let this opportunity pass. He slid into the gym and cut the lights. Their gasps fed his adrenaline.

"Come find me, ladies."

HER STOMACH DROPPED as darkness fell. The gym had no windows and Hendrick shut the door behind him. No light breached the room.

He had to have overheard their conversation. If she were him, she'd take advantage of the situation, too. But that didn't mean she appreciated being on this side of the game.

The moment his words lit her adrenaline, Kinley dashed behind the nearest piece of equipment. She didn't dare go far from where she stood. She didn't have the layout of the room memorized, and didn't want to run into something, giving away her position.

The only sounds were faint rustling, but so slight she may have thought she'd imagined it if she didn't know other people were in the room with her. But the direction of any noise eluded her.

Blinking rapidly, she tried to force her vision to focus. She didn't expect to see everything, but basic outlines would help.

Be smart, Kinley. Control your breathing. Slow and long, Kinley quieted her breath, listening for anyone approaching. They were all too good at this. She didn't hear a thing.

She stood, careful not to rub against the equipment. Her vision adjusted enough to make out the line of benches in front of her. With a careful peek toward the front of the gym, she stepped out and moved behind the pillar between the next two benches. The figure took shape only an instant before running into the other woman. But she couldn't tell who it was. Not until she flattened Kinley to her.

Ember turned Kinley back in the direction she'd come, holding her shoulder. A heartbeat later, Ember lifted her hand and nudged Kinley.

Kinley felt Ember's presence for two steps, then a whoosh of air replaced her. Panic rose. If Hendrick was close enough to reach Ember, he was close enough to reach her. She tried not to rush her steps.

Hendrick laughed, a cackle that echoed everywhere. The shivers didn't only race down her spine, but over her entire body. Her heart pumped wildly, increasing her breathing.

Fuck. She wouldn't win this. She wasn't even trying to find Hendrick. He hunted her.

Kinley weaved around the punching bags. A crack of light flashed from the front of the room. Someone left. Kinley spun back around, hoping to get a glimpse of Hendrick. It didn't surprise her when she didn't. Hendrick's presence was still a very real entity in the room.

She closed her eyes and tried to focus on that, as if to *sense* him.

Thunks and faint grunts came from the other side of her. Hendrick moved past her and Sophie attacked. Their shadowed forms became one. Had Hendrick not seen her, or was he saving her for last?

Kinley used their sparring as a distraction to move further from Hendrick. The idea of fighting against him terrified part of her. But sparring wasn't the purpose of this game. This was all about stealth.

Her other option was to move closer and help Sophie. The two of them together might best him. Sparring with the two women had been fun and eye-opening. Kinley could improve. Kinley would improve. But not in the next few minutes.

She hesitated, then took a step toward them. But Hendrick pinned Sophie against his chest. Damn. She lost. Hendrick's head lowered to her ear.

Kinley only had seconds before he turned his attention on her. She moved deeper into the shadows. A minute later, the door opened and someone left.

Don't panic. Breathe. Slow breaths were quieter. She closed her eyes and took control of her lungs, refusing to let the adrenaline get to her. She listened and heard nothing.

The purpose was to find him. Kinley couldn't stay out of his reach if she didn't locate him. Her eyes adjusted quicker this time when she opened them. The pillars in here created an advantage. Not all the equipment was shaped well enough to hide an entire body.

She peered around the side of hers and when she saw the still shadows; she moved around it, repeating the process to move to the next side and then another pillar.

Nothing ever moved. No sound echoed, except for any she made, but she hoped they weren't as loud as they seemed to her. He couldn't possibly hear her heart pounding.

The essence in the air was the only reason she knew she wasn't alone. Choosing to stay still for a moment, she looked, examining every shadow in the room. She scanned the entire room, then reversed her gaze, going over everything once more.

One of the weight machines appeared taller than the others. She blinked and gasped as his figure came into view. And the sound from her drew him forward. Damn it.

She lost control of her breathing and tried to put herself back into hiding. It took him seconds to cross most of the gym and wrap an arm around her waist, lifting her against.

The adrenaline did the work for her. She threw her head back to hit his chin and brought her knee up to give momentum for a backward kick to the knees.

Hendrick grunted and let her go, but his hand grazed her arm while she launched herself forward. Veering left, she dashed toward the back of the room, hoping to use the benches as a barrier between them.

"Running isn't the game, pretty girl."

Responding would only lead him to her. She intended to get lost in the shadows again, then attack as he got closer. Kinley tried to mimic the way he'd blended into the shadows of the equipment, unsure if she blended with the angles right.

He moved to the opposite side of the room, but didn't hide himself as much as he had. He'd already caught her—that part of the game was over. Kinley needed to time this just right.

She hoped that him tilting his head as if to listen meant he hadn't seen her. Hendrick passed the bench she stood behind. Kinley side stepped around it, then carefully put her foot up to launch herself into the air. The moment she pushed up, Hendrick froze and spun. Instead of landing on his back, she landed on his chest with her legs wrapped around his waist, and he'd caught her with one arm around her and a hand under her ass.

"You got me, pretty girl. What are you going to do now?"

Kinley's hands settled on his shoulders, but no plan came to mind. There must be some advantage from his position. With his face wide open, she should box his ears.

Bringing her hands up, she gently cupped them over his ears. Everything changed the moment he caught her. The adrenaline fueled the heat that had been between them last night. Kinley should still be mad about how he'd left. And she was, somewhere, although that anger was nowhere in sight.

"That's exactly what you should have done. But it's too late now." His hand crept up her spine until he gripped the back of her neck, applying enough pressure to show her the pain the hold could create.

She had more than enough time to take control of the situation. He saw her as a deer in headlights, trapped in shock. He wouldn't see it coming until too late.

But the rising desire had them both breathing hard. She was the trapped deer.

HE HAD TO admit, Kinley surprised him. But not until the end. He hadn't expected her to jump onto his back. The pressure her foot put on the bench had been his only warning.

Hendrick had her position pinned for most of the game, but he needed to be alone with her. He hadn't tracked her until he'd gotten rid of Ember and Sophie. Both women improved each time they played. Once he caught each of them, he'd whispered in their ears, asking them to leave so he could talk to Kinley. Ember knew his secret, so she'd left without question. Sophie had taken a little more convincing. After a threat to push her twice as hard the next time they sparred, she'd acquiesced, but with a glare.

As much as Hendrick wanted to move forward with the heat rising between them, he couldn't. Not until she knew the truth, and he asked for her help. His cock disagreed with him.

Her legs tightened around him and her fingers speared into his hair. She would have bent to kiss him herself if he didn't have the grip on her neck that he did. He needed her to recognize the threat behind that hold. Not the heat.

Fuck him.

"Kinley."

She blinked and leaned back into his hold. They were close enough he made out her features, not that he could read her expressions. Despite that, there was no mistaking what they both wanted right now. To lay her down on the mats and fuck her until neither could see straight. He needed to get it out now. Right now. No more waiting. Not even to make it across the room to turn on the light.

"I'm Kit Pierce." Hendrick felt the moment she'd registered what he'd said. Her shoulders straightened, fighting against his hold, and her ankles hooked tighter at the small of his back. Now that it was out, he breathed a little easier. The heat between them turned into tension he needed to deal with. He took steps across the gym to turn on the light, but he didn't make it.

As soon as they were past the benches and on the open mats, Kinley struck. Her palms slapped against his ears, creating a perfect seal and pop.

He growled—rough, low, and dangerous. Letting her go, he reached for his head. Kinley landed on her ass and rolled backwards over her shoulder and stood across from him.

"You thought to tell me this now? Not at your safe house? Not after Cassius attacked? Not once we got here?" Her voice had stayed level, but not with what came next. "Not before we fucked?" A feminine growl all men should fear spiked her question. She set one foot behind her and lowered her chin.

"Kinley."

"What? What do you have to say to me now, *fiancée*?"

But she didn't let him answer. She attacked, feigning right before passing him on the left to kick him behind the knee. Hendrick let himself drop to the floor and spun on his knee to face her, but the woman was ready for him. She swung up with a roundhouse kick in the direction he was turning. He barely ducked in time to miss it, but he also got a grip on the back of her ankle. Moving with her kick, he pulled her to the ground. He made a mental note to go over this move with her later. She could have continued to spin and gotten him with her other leg.

He set his hand between her shoulder blades and pinned her to the mat in seconds. Flattening out, he covered her body and put his lips next to her ears. She panted beneath him, but she didn't struggle.

"I haven't gone by the name Kit in a long time. It isn't who I am. I never fit into that mold." Hendrick held her attention. He kept going. "I was supposed to take over the family business. When I left, Shane took my place, easily. He was good at it, and making changes that mattered. I guess that's all about perspective." Being a dealer of drugs and weapons was bad no matter how you spun it. "Shane was the only one I kept in contact with. He was my brother. I loved him." Each of those words pierced a fresh hole in his chest. He'd never told his brother how important he was to him.

The tension in Kinley's body deflated the smallest of amounts.

"I want to find who killed him. And make them pay."

Kinley wiggled, twisting her shoulders. Hendrick backed off enough to give her room to roll over, but he was ready in case she tried to attack again. Her hand reached up to cup his cheek. The delicate fingers feathered over his skin. "I'm sorry for your loss, Hendrick."

He hadn't known that he'd needed those words. The other mercenaries said as much with sympathy in their eyes. Hudson expressed it, but he'd been dealing with the same thing. The words from Kinley gave him hope he could heal.

"I need your help."

She pushed on his chest and he stood, letting her up as well. Stalking to the front of the room, he paused near the lights.

"Shield your eyes, pretty girl." The endearment fell from his lips absently. She was gorgeous, and part of him wished she could be his. If she agreed to help him, she would be. Even though she had every right to refuse him.

He waited a beat before turning the lights on. Kinley had her forearm covering her eyes. Slowly, she peeled it away, her eyes squinting as she looked for him.

"I'll give you a choice. I can't force you to come with me, to help me. If you want out, I'll get you out of here today. Say the word and you'll be on the private flight we have ready and on your way to wherever you want to go."

"Come with you? Where are you going?"

"I have nothing. No leads to tell me what happened to Shane. All the answers lie within."

"You're going back to take Shane's place."

Hendrick nodded. "The place my father has been trying to put me since Shane died. He likes his retirement too much to let it go."

"Why do you need my help?"

"To be my wife."

10
––––––––––

"I'M SO TERRIBLY SORRY. MY EARS MALFUNCTIONED. Could you repeat that, please?" Kinley wanted to launch herself across the room and attack him again. How having her on his arm helped him, she didn't understand. But that was the exact life she was running from.

Except he didn't. He said he wouldn't force her. She could be gone today. Free and ready to take on her own world. Become a fearsome woman. Maybe she'd never be at the level of the mercenaries or the crime families, but she'd build her own life and stand tall doing it.

"It's more believable. I wouldn't go back for nothing. For anyone that knows me, they wouldn't fall for this either, but my father doesn't. He never has. He planned to introduce us that night and hoped the sight would help entice me home."

"This is ridiculous." She muttered it more to herself than for Hendrick's ears, but his heavy sigh reached her. "What exactly are you suggesting? I want every detail."

"I play on Shane's death as my reason for coming home, and for you. I'll let them think you've *enticed* me."

"You saying I haven't?" Kinley quirked her brow, then cursed her flirting. That was the last thing they needed. *You're mad at him, Kinley. You can't forget that.*

The look he pierced her with was the only answer she got.

"Then what?"

"We get married. They won't believe either of us is just falling into line. We'll have to make a deal, make it seem like we'll only come back if they meet our terms."

"Married? For real? Or fake it?"

"It can't be faked."

It was like a punch to the gut. Her air vanished, and she tried hard to remember how to breathe. He wanted to get married, standing in front of her without a care in his eyes, as if this wasn't a big deal. Maybe it wasn't a big deal to him.

"I've been searching for months. The only way for me to find out what happened to Shane is from inside."

"Right. And it's just a piece of paper. It doesn't have to be *real* real."

Hendrick crossed the room faster than her next breath. He had a fist holding her hair and a hand gripping her hip. His lips moved, but he didn't speak. Kinley waited for the denial practically seeping out of him.

"How long?" Her breathless question cut through his fierce hold. He stepped back.

"I'm not sure. A month. A year."

Panic tried to seize her throat. She didn't want to go back there for any amount of time. Definitely not for a year.

"Kinley." He must have seen her panic. It wasn't like she was trying to hide it from him.

"Why... uh... I need to think about it."

"Okay." Hendrick backed away from her and cleared the way to the door.

She made it to the door, but stopped with her hand outstretched. Turning her head over her shoulder, she had to ask one question. "Why did you leave last night?" She only let herself see him in her peripheral vision. Kinley couldn't take the full frontal rejection, but if she was going to give his plan real consideration, she had to know.

"I felt things I've never felt before. And that's a distraction."

A distraction from finding Shane's killer. She understood, but that didn't mean it didn't hurt. She hated him for only a second. The pain had been so apparent in him since she met him. Kinley wouldn't hold that against him.

Yanking on the door, she left. Sophie and Ember were standing at the end of the hall, leaning against the wall. When they looked past her shoulder, she knew Hendrick must have followed her to the door.

One look at the other women and Kinley kept walking. She passed rooms, some empty, some with the other mercenaries. In the break room space where she'd had the phone call, three of them stood around the table, clamping their mouths shut the moment she appeared. But Kinley didn't pay them any attention. She forced herself to the elevator.

Ember and Sophie squeezed their way in before the doors closed. No one said anything for the entire ride up. Kinley turned toward her apartment, but hands on her shoulders veered her toward the other.

"What did he say?" Sophie pulled her into the living

room and tried to get her to sit down. But Kinley spun away from the couch and started pacing.

"Did you guys know?"

"Know what?" Sophie sat and frowned, following her steps back and forth. But Ember stayed standing, her chin set high.

"You knew."

"I only found out today, before I came up here. Everyone found out today. I wanted to tell you, but it needed to come from him."

"It's okay. I understand." Hendrick had said he hadn't been Kit for a long time. Why would he have claimed to be him with the mercenaries? Other than his connections with the family, his name didn't matter.

Kinley continued her pacing.

"What's going on?" Sophie's voice hardened in a way that surprised Kinley. That woman had her strength well hidden.

"Hendrick is Kit Pierce. The man my father arranged for me to marry."

Sophie's shock helped ease some of her ire.

"And Hendrick didn't think that information was important to tell me. At any point. And certainly not before we fucked last night."

"You did what?" The two of them spoke simultaneously. Ember sat, and Sophie stood. Kinley wanted to laugh at how comical their shock was.

Oh, this helped. Someone to share her anger and frustration with. A friend. Two friends, as it seemed. Ones that had had similar experiences or lives.

Kinley sat and explained Hendrick's plan and the choice he gave her. "I don't want to go back." She was trying to have sympathy for Hendrick, but this plan came with its own dangers. If they found out the real reason they went back and that they intended to leave, they wouldn't make it out of there alive. At least Hendrick wouldn't. They would throw Kinley under lock and key for the rest of her life.

"Of course you don't." Ember's fierceness came through with every word. A hand landed on each of her knees.

Kinley had worked hard to make sure she could be free once she got away. The financial security she'd built was important. Not just because of the work she put in to build it, but she wouldn't get far without it. She'd always known she'd have to have her own security to keep her father from coming after. She didn't want to hide. She wanted to live.

"Do you have a computer I can use?"

"Sure." Sophie got up and walked down the hall. She came back a minute later with a small laptop. Setting it on Kinley's lap, Sophie sat down beside her.

"Thank you." Kinley opened the computer and waited for Sophie to put her thumb over the small square to unlock it. It only took her a few minutes to bring up the browser and type in the addresses of the banks where she kept her money. Money her father knew nothing about.

The loading circles taunted her for mere seconds, but she needed to plan. And to do that, she needed to check her finances. Having had to make her escape with a five-minute plan, she hadn't had time to secure her money. But there was no reason for her father to search for it.

The first page loaded, totaling the amount in her account to zero.

No. No, no, no. Kinley clicked to the next account. A zero stared back at her there. And the same on the third.

Her father's taunt flared in her mind. *I wouldn't be so sure of that if I were you.*

Years of creating her independence had vanished. Wasted.

———

HENDRICK FOUND GEAR in the weapons room. He'd wanted to follow Kinley, but he couldn't say what he'd do. She needed to make this decision without his influence. He'd find a way to do this without her.

"Are you sure you want to come with me?"

"Don't do that." Gear glared at him.

Hendrick sighed. "I had to ask. It isn't your scene."

"I'm there to watch your back and nothing else. Add it to the conditions to give your father. You get to bring your own man. Yours and yours alone. I won't take a single order from anyone else."

"I wouldn't expect you to."

"You trust Hudson." It wasn't a question, although it would have been a fair one. Hendrick was asking Gear to put his trust in Hudson, too.

"Yes." Anything he said wouldn't convince him. Gear would have to come to the conclusion himself. Maybe they'd even be there long enough for that to happen.

Darkness was covering his soul. He didn't want to go back there any more than Kinley. But for Shane, he would.

Shane had never once asked him to come home and help him manage the business. He'd understood explicitly Hendrick's need to get out. Just as Hendrick understood Shane's passion to put his stamp on that business.

"When do you want to get the ball rolling?" Gear was sorting through the weapons, cleaning and organizing. It's what he did when he needed to think.

"As soon as Kinley gives me her answer."

Gear paused and raised a brow. "How did that go?"

"She tried to kick my ass."

Gear grinned and nodded. "As she should have. You fucked her last night, didn't you?"

"I didn't intend to."

Gear shrugged. "Seems to be a theme." Neither King nor Dak had any intentions of keeping Ember or Sophie. And their relationships started out similarly.

If she agreed, Kinley would be his wife. The moment she claimed the marriage as just a piece of paper, he'd nearly lost it. His wife would be *his*. They couldn't fake it and have no one find out, but they couldn't fake it because Hendrick wouldn't.

"Aim that crazy in your eyes somewhere else."

Hendrick never hid his emotions, but they never appeared quite right. Part of what added to his crazy appeal, so he didn't change it. "Sorry." But he wasn't. "What weapons are we taking in? And what weapons can we give Kinley?"

Gear paused and turned to face him. "You should drag this out a little. Give yourself some time to work with Kinley before we move into the heart of the nest."

"I doubt I can. Once I make contact, we may only have a short time before they refuse the deal. But I can try to stretch the negotiations."

"Or don't make contact yet."

"They won't wait that long before they do something."

Gear nodded and sighed. "We'll give her a couple of knives and a small gun. All easy to hide. I'll help teach her."

"Thanks." Hendrick moved to the wall of knives. He had his own collection on his person and in his own home. He'd duplicated each of those and set them up here. No matter where he was, he'd always have his preferred knives. Hendrick looked each of them over, deciding which would fit Kinley's hands best. Which would be easiest for her to cause damage without having the weapon used against her. He needed to get her sheaths for them.

"There's a problem." Roen poked his head into the room long enough to meet Hendrick's gaze and left. Hendrick left first and Gear locked the door behind him. They found everyone in the computer room. Roen had returned to his usual seat and was clicking away.

Kinley stood behind him, her hands gripping the back of his chair. "It can't just be gone. There has to be an error on the bank's side of things."

"What's going on?" Hendrick stood beside Kinley. She tensed and stepped back from him.

"Someone has emptied her bank accounts.." Roen didn't look up from the screen.

"No. There's an error." Kinley said slowly, as if correcting the situation would change it.

Roen sighed. "No error. I'm sorry. I'm trying to find where they moved the money."

"And then what?"

"I'll hack the account and move it back." Roen shrugged as if it was that simple for anyone to do. Most of them had some hacking skills. But Roen was at a level Hendrick didn't think existed.

Kinley breathed heavily, her eyes following everything that happened on the screens. Her fists stayed at her side, clenching and relaxed in rhythm with her lungs.

"Fuck," Roen muttered.

"What? What is it?" Kinley was behind his chair again in a second, pulling it back with her grip and dislodging Roen's hand from the keyboard.

Hendrick took her wrists and pulled her back.

Roen righted himself at the keyboard again. "I found the money. They moved it to several of your father's accounts, but then they withdrew everything. You had a small fortune."

"I know." Kinley spoke through gritted teeth. Her eyes turned to slits and Hendrick saw her pulse pound in her neck.

A phone rang from the main break room. The timing was too perfect for it not to be Kinley's father or Cassius. They all followed the ring and when Hendrick and Kinley entered the room, King answered the phone, but said nothing.

"I've cut you off, Kinley. Come back, marry the boy, and do as you're told. You can have it all back if you do." A lie. The way he spoke, he didn't think her father realized *the boy* was one of King's mercenaries and standing next to his daughter. Hendrick's father always treated him like a dirty secret.

"You bastard."

"Careful, daughter."

Kinley's eyes widened, and she took a step toward the phone as if to attack it. Her lips parted, vitriol ready to fly. Hendrick slapped his hand over her mouth and pulled her back.

"Twenty-four hours, Kinley, or I'm sending someone after you."

Hendrick held Kinley until she calmed.

"If I were you, I'd do some research on the last man that attacked here." Dak's dark warning loomed as silence followed.

"Twenty-four hours." He hung up without clarifying his threat.

Kinley's feet shuffled as she moved away from Hendrick and sunk into a chair. Her cheeks paled and her breathing bordered on panic.

"Years. So many fucking years."

"For what?" Hendrick crouched in front of her and set a hand on her knee. She may not want the connection between them, but he needed it. He wanted it. He wanted her to say yes.

"That money. I've *earned* every dollar. It's mine." Fierceness poured from her, but her eyes were distant. She wouldn't look at him. She only saw her anger.

"You can earn it back." Hendrick squeezed her knee. Roen whistled behind him. "What?"

"You aren't wrong, but when I said a small fortune, I meant a small fortune."

"How did you earn that much money on your own without your father knowing? Or did he know?"

"He didn't know, and I don't know how they found it. I made it all online in a lot of different ways. Multiple side hustles, investing, small consistent jobs. No one way made me that safety net. And that's what it represented. All I had to do was get away from him, and I had the funds I needed to keep myself safe and live my life the way I wanted. I wouldn't have had to hide. Now?" Kinley looked at him. The spread of emotions moved over her face so fast he couldn't keep up. But the final one, sullen acceptance and determination. "I'm in."

Hendrick wanted to argue. But why would he turn her down? When having her made this easier, and her new situation only helped the tale he intended to weave.

HENDRICK TOOK HER hand and pulled her from the chair. No one else in the room said anything, and she knew they were all there. They'd all witnessed her fury and panic. But Kinley didn't dare meet any of their gazes.

He led her from the room and to the elevator.

"What are we..."

"Hush."

Hush? Did he just hush her? The elevator doors closed and still Hendrick held her hand. She tried to pull it away, but he squeezed tighter.

"Hendrick. Let..."

"Not now."

Kinley rolled her eyes and threw her free hand into the air. The elevator stopped at the top floor and let them out. Hendrick pulled her to the apartment. As soon as he closed the door, she tried to pull her hand back again.

"No."

She didn't bother trying to say anything else. He clearly had an issue he needed to rid himself of first.

"Why are you agreeing?"

"I thought that was obvious. To get my money back."

"You can earn your money again. Yes, it will take a long time. But I'll give you money to start you off with, to keep you protected from your father."

"Why would you do that?"

"Because I want to. So why agree?" He didn't ask her if she changed her mind. He was offering the same freedom, although it may require a bit more work than she'd intended, but she'd be safe.

"Because I'm fucking pissed. That's why."

Hendrick blinked. A small smirk played on his lips, but he shoved it away. She pulled on her hand again, and he released her.

"He tried to stomp on me one too many times. Stealing that money from me was the last straw. And it would take me years to earn that back. You aren't wrong. I could do it again. But that isn't the point. That money is mine. I earned it right under his nose while he thought I was a clueless chit. And then there's Cassius." Her voice dropped to a tone she'd never heard come out of herself before. Low and ugly, and it felt good. The anger rising pulsed in a way she wanted to embrace it to soak in its energy. "That manipulating bastard needs to be taken down a notch."

Hendrick tilted his head back, regarding her with a heated scrutiny. Kinley breathed through her anger. Now wasn't the time. Although, she still had a mixed anger toward Hendrick. She was about to marry the man in front of her. The demanding, crazy, utterly sexy man in front of her. Who'd lied to her.

Damn it. Kinley turned away from him, closing her eyes. Would that lie matter at all if they hadn't slept together? She had to push that aside. But fucking him again should stay out of the equation.

"Okay. We'll contact them in twenty-four hours. We're doing this on our terms. They'd be suspicious of anything else. So, pretty girl. What are your terms?"

"I get a say?"

"As much as I can give you. The alliance was meant to make me the heir to your father's business, was it not?"

"Yes. I'll insist that still stands. But he may not honor the agreement if he thinks I treat you any differently than he does."

Kinley sneered.

"I hate it, too."

After a deep breath and a long sigh, Kinley lifted her chin to meet his eyes. "What kind of wedding will it be?"

"Whatever we want."

"What do you want?"

"We aren't talking about me, Kinley."

"Please?"

"I want to get married before we go back. Elope. I don't want a single one of those assholes to witness this."

"I'd wanted a big wedding, but it wasn't with my family. I would have been on my own, had built my life, friends, and a family of sorts of my own. A church wedding ending with a starlit dance." A small laugh escaped her, and she cleared her throat. "We get married before we go back. No wedding with them, that's my condition."

"Okay, pretty girl."

"And my money returned to me."

"As soon as it is, we'll get Roen to secure it. They won't steal it again."

"I don't know what else I want. I just want us to get out of there as soon as we can. Can you promise me that?" There was a small fear that he'd learn to like it there and choose to stay. "Even if you don't want to leave when you find out what happened to Shane, will you still let me go?"

"You have my word, Kinley. I won't want to stay, but no matter what happens. I'll let you go when the time comes."

"I won't live under my father's roof."

"We won't be. He doesn't have the answers I need."

"Cassius mentioned your brother. Do you think he knows something? Why would he?"

Hendrick shook his head.

"I was supposed to marry him."

"Shane wouldn't have forced you if you didn't want to marry." Hendrick chuckled. "He would have called me to come get you out."

"So I'm right where I would have ended up, anyway."

"Yeah, pretty girl." His voice softened, and he took two steps toward her, but she took a step back. Her bottom lip stung, and she realized she'd bitten it.

"So, what do we do today?" She'd decided, and she was going to charge ahead. She'd get her own revenge from the inside, just like Hendrick.

"We pack. Plan the wedding. And we set you up with some weapons."

"One of these things is not like the others," she mumbled.

"How many weapons do I have on me right now,

Kinley?" Hendrick didn't hesitate this time when he stalked toward her. He closed the distance even as she backed away. Only a few steps and she hit the wall.

She opened her mouth to answer, but he cut her off. "You didn't look."

She'd kept her eyes on his. Swallowing, she forced herself to look up and down his body. There was a gun in a holster at his ribs. And she'd seen the sheath for a knife at the small of his back before. Kinley assumed that never left him. "Two."

"Wrong. Seven."

She couldn't stop her eyes from popping open. "How many will I have?"

"Three to start, but we'll hide weapons around the house as well when we get settled. You'll know where to find them if you ever need them."

"I can fight. I've never used any weapon. Cassius refused to teach me how to shoot."

"Because that worked for his benefit. We'll teach you everything."

Her hands shook. She made fists at her sides.

"Kinley." Hendrick raised his hand to run his fingers down the side of her neck. "I'll keep you safe. And I'll get you out of there."

Kinley nodded. She might be mad at him, but she trusted him.

11

HENDRICK HAD LEFT Kinley hours ago. He'd sent Sophie and Ember up to help her plan the wedding with instructions to leave the location, ceremony, and reception to him. They needed to help her with her dress, flowers, and a cake, sending the information for the flowers and cake to him.

He couldn't give her the exact dream, but he was damn well going to give the closest thing.

Married. Fucking married. Hendrick had zero regrets about his bride, but he'd never considered getting married, or even finding someone permanent. He was a little too crazy for most people's tastes.

Kinley's father was forcing her into this. She had no reason to agree just for him. In fact, when he'd asked why, he hadn't been any of her reasons. She didn't care about helping him. That wouldn't change his promise to get her out.

He considered calling his father and striking the deal with him now, but that left time for him and Curry to talk. Curry didn't know Hendrick was Kit. At least he didn't think he did. And he'd like to keep it that way until they walked in the door as newlyweds.

He needed to pack.

Dak and King stopped him in the parking garage. "Hendrick," Dak called out to him as he reached his bike.

"I have to."

"We're the best at what we do. Hell, you're one of us. We can get the information another way."

The thought of kidnapping his father and torturing the information from him had crossed his mind every few days over the past several months. The old man knew something, or didn't care. But that put Hendrick too close to him, in a way that was worse than going back. Torture carried a touch of intimacy.

The other two men nodded, somehow under-standing that Hendrick needed this. He'd felt himself slipping away since losing Shane. He didn't know how much further he'd fall or what he'd emerge as on the other side. That crazy part of him always stayed under his control, but it could slip. Someday.

"You call."

Hendrick understood. They meant for him to check in, and they meant for him to ask for help. He would, only if he had no other choice. This wasn't a job. This was revenge.

He nodded and slid his helmet on before swinging a leg over his bike.

His apartment seemed cold after not being there for several days. Not that he had many possessions. He had his comforts and his knives.

What would Kinley need in a home? He'd have to give the appearance of controlling her to an extent, but he'd give her everything within those confines. She wouldn't be trapped the same way she'd been growing up.

Hendrick made calls for the wedding while packing his things. Maybe they had a day before they needed to leave, maybe a week. But he didn't need anything here in the meantime. His skin itched, prickles crawling over him. If he wasn't ready to move, he might not do it.

But he wouldn't back out of the wedding. There was a small church in the heart of the city. A tiny temple that had stood the test of time surrounded by buildings three times its size. The one beside it was a hotel owned by Archer. They'd hold the reception there.

The priest made his displeasure with the short notice and rush of the wedding known, but he'd agreed with one condition—if Hendrick delivered a sizable donation to the church in person. Hendrick didn't see that as a hardship.

It didn't take long for Sophie to message him with the flower and cake details. He pushed Shane from his mind to do what he needed for Kinley. Going back was for revenge. But this wedding wasn't. It wasn't fair to her.

Hendrick left his bags by the door of his apartment and set out to make their wedding the best day of his bride's life.

KINLEY WAS BUZZED when she answered the door and a man with both sides of his head shaved, and tattoos covering the bare skin, stood on the other side. Sophie and Ember had insisted that planning a wedding required wine. At least they'd waited until after lunch to pour it. By that point, they'd had the flowers and cake done. Only her dress remained undecided.

She should be excited. The haze of the alcohol should be pleasant. But her fake smile had been slipping. Until she saw the look on the man's face when he saw her cross one foot behind the other to stop herself from swaying. If she'd been sober, the fierce glare would have terrified her, but her inebriated brain made it clear none of the mercenaries would harm her.

Kinley snorted.

"Have you come to join the party, Gear?" Sophie asked sweetly. The two women came up behind her.

"I came for Kinley. But she's in no state to shoot a gun." He crossed his arms over his chest and stepped into the apartment.

"I didn't invite you in." This was supposed to be her temporary home.

Gear raised a single brow.

"Well, I didn't. But come on in." She swept her arm back, smacking Sophie behind her, then let the door swing hard behind Gear.

"To the kitchen!" Ember darted off and opened the cupboards. When she pulled out a bottle that wasn't wine, Gear made it to her in three strides and pulled it from her hands.

"No." Oh, that growl was sexy. Kinley wondered if Hendrick growled like that. She imagined all the mercenaries did. But that growl wasn't enough for her. Unruly hair, flaming eyes, and a tendency for knives did the trick. Kinley wasn't so far gone to not hold back the groan at the thoughts of Hendrick.

Kinley finally made her feet move to follow them all

to the kitchen and saw Gear put a bottle of amaretto high enough that none of them could reach. But Ember didn't look deterred.

"If you're going to crash a bachelorette party, then you have too many clothes on." Sophie grumbled and then slapped a hand over her mouth and another over her eyes.

"I think it's safer for both of us if Dak doesn't find out you said that."

Sophie nodded while still keeping her hands covering her face. Kinley appreciated the other women more than she knew how to say. They'd wrapped her up like one of their own after only being here for a day. They made planning a wedding she didn't want special.

Kinley had tried to make the simplest choice to get it over with, but both women refused to let her. They'd pushed her to get the details of her dream wedding, and they helped her find the best match.

She sighed and finished her glass of wine. Moving around the island, she reached for the open bottle. A large hand wrapped around her wrist.

They froze in a clash of wills. "Let go."

"You need to sober up."

"Not right now, I don't." Kinley ripped her hand from his grasp and took the bottle, finishing its contents into her glass.

"That a girl." Ember knocked her shoulder with her, then hopped onto the counter with a single motion and grabbed the bottle of amaretto. "Have a shot with us, Gear."

"Fuck." He shook his head and grabbed the bottle again, but Sophie was right behind him. She grabbed the bottom and pulled down so the neck slipped out of his hand.

Ember had the shot glasses down by the time Sophie ran around the counter. Gear took a step toward them and Kinley blocked his way.

"Please. You can teach me to shoot in the morning. I have no interest in getting shit-faced. But… Please." Kinley needed what these two women could give her. Friendship with strangers. They'd forced her to see this sham of a wedding as something special. They at least made it possible for her to pretend.

He took a step back as if it was a sign of good faith.

"Let's choose that dress." Sophie pushed a shot glass into Kinley's free hand. The three women stood in a half circle. They clinked the shot glasses, tapped them on the counter, then tipped them back.

Gear stayed in the kitchen like a damn guard as they returned to the couch and the laptops they had opened to pictures in white.

They'd passed her dream dress over several times. Kinley didn't know how they were going to get any gown on this short notice. Especially since leaving the building wasn't possible. Ember and Sophie kept waving her off.

It was Gear that noticed she hadn't closed the picture. The wine was making her cling to something she knew she'd never have. That's where some of the sadness came from.

"Kinley." His voice appeared behind her. "That's the one you want, isn't it?"

She looked over her shoulder. "It doesn't matter."

"Tell the truth, girl."

"Why didn't you say something, Kinley?" Ember

moved in beside her to inspect the pure white, full skirt dress. "It's gorgeous."

"And not possible to get on short notice." She assumed they'd elope as soon as possible, so there was no way for their fathers to intervene. Even waiting a day may be too late once they hit her father's twenty-four-hour deadline.

A rough sigh rumbled behind her. "I'll be back." He had his phone to his ear as he left, but not before they heard the words he'd snapped into the line. "Keep an eye on your women."

He sounded so frustrated that Kinley had to laugh.

"We'll find you the perfect dress, but let's narrow down to that style." Sophie tapped away on the laptop in front of her while Ember poured a second shot and refilled their glasses.

She started some music on her way back to the kitchen. "I think Sophie had the right idea. The next man to crash this party better lose their clothes along the way and shake that ass."

"What was that, little girl?" The squeak that escaped Ember had both Kinley and Sophie falling over in a fit of laughter. King stalked across the room with Dak behind him. Sophie's laugh dried up fast.

Kinley turned her attention back to searching for a dress. But wondered if Hendrick would have the same possessiveness over her. They wouldn't be in a true marriage after all.

HENDRICK HAD IGNORED the messages from Gear, King, and Dak for as long as he could. The wedding was set. After significant tips to each establishment, they'd all promised to have everything ready. Kinley would have a wedding day to remember.

Hendrick let himself grieve again for his brother. He let the loss wash over him, and oddly, it gave him strength. The strength to succeed and find who killed him. And the strength to be there for Kinley, to keep her safe.

Outside *King Security*, Hendrick gave the messages his full attention.

Gear: Your woman is getting herself into trouble.

Hendrick's lips quirked.

Gear: Dress is looked after.

Dak: They've been drinking. I'm taking Sophie home soon.

King: Kinley shouldn't be alone.

Hendrick: On my way up. Hendrick sent the message before calling for the elevator. When the doors opened, King and Ember stood inside. King held Ember with her back against his chest while he leaned against the wall.

Hendrick stepped inside and put his hand against the door to keep it open for them.

"Don't get her hurt, Hendrick. I like her." Ember's eyes held a glassy sheen, but she wasn't drunk. If the others had been with the women, they wouldn't have let them drink too much. Not with a den of carnivorous crime families waiting for an opportunity to strike. She walked in front of King with her own strength and straight steps. Mostly straight steps. Hendrick wondered how much concentration she put into her feet.

He shared a look with King as he passed—one he had no hope of deciphering. Not with his head full of

Kinley, Shane, and his own vengeance. Hendrick let the elevator close and made his way to the top floor.

The door to Dak's apartment shut the same moment the elevator opened. Kinley was alone.

Slipping into the apartment, Hendrick settled in the entry. Kinley carried empty glasses to the sink. She set them on the counter and then braced her hands on the edge, leaning forward. Her shoulders dropped with a sigh.

"I was never really free." The defeat pushing her down was practically visible.

Hendrick made his way further into the house. Kinley stiffened and the small gasp from her lips was louder than his steps. He reached for her and slid his hands around her hips, pulling her back against him.

"You're free right now, Kinley. You can change your mind. I'll get you out of here and set you up to be on your own and safe."

Kinley let her shoulders settle back against him.

"I know. And thank you. But I can't accept it. Not like that."

"That offer doesn't expire, even after we're in."

She turned in his arms, her hands settling on his chest.

"I heard you were getting yourself into trouble." Hendrick let the heaviness drift away, changing the subject.

"Gear doesn't look like a fink." She tilted her head to the side. Her eyes were clearer than he'd expected after seeing Ember in the elevator.

"What makes you think Gear said something?"

She frowned. "Never mind. He might not look like a

fink, but he was acting like one." Clear eyes, but not a clear mind.

"How much have you had to drink, pretty girl?" Hendrick forced his hands to stay gentle rather than pull her closer to him. She held them apart with her hands.

"Enough," Kinley said, tilting her head to the other side. "It was a bachelorette party. Or so I was told." Her lids dropped for a moment before she looked back up at him.

Hendrick leaned forward and placed a kiss on her forehead.

"I want to be mad at you. I should be. But then you go say the things you say and do the things you do." She shook her head, then lifted her chin. Narrowing her eyes. He saw the buzz glimmer now. "I am choosing to be mad at you," she declared loud enough to echo in the empty apartment. But her hands moved. They slid until the tips reached his shoulders and she brought them back down.

"And how is that working out for you?"

"Not very well." The scrunching of her nose followed her whisper.

Hendrick pushed past her strength until he crushed his body to hers. He pressed her against the counter and reached past her. Pulling a tall glass from the upper cupboard, he filled it with water behind her. She didn't move her gaze from his. Hendrick felt her eyes soak in everything from him. He wasn't trying to hide much. He may not have wanted the distraction, but he didn't like the idea of a marriage in name only. Hendrick wanted her. Before, during, and after. Especially after.

Bringing the glass between them, he wrapped her hand around it. "Drink."

"Bossy." But she took the water and sipped. Hendrick waited with patience he didn't have while she took her time. He watched her lips around the glass and watched her throat work as she swallowed.

Their breathing changed. Heavy, audible huffs from each of them ratcheted up the heat between them. Hendrick had the urge to push her to her knees, trapping her between him and the counter while he fucked her mouth. As if she saw the images play out in his mind, her knees quaked.

Hendrick wrapped an arm around her waist to stop her from sinking down.

"Finish the water, Kinley." He needed to get her to bed before he lost all control of himself.

She tipped the glass back, chugging the last quarter of the glass. Hendrick took it from her and refilled it. Slowly, he let go of her waist and took her hand. He led her to the bathroom and found the painkillers in the medicine cabinet. Shaking out two, he passed them to her and passed her the water.

"Take those."

One at a time, she tossed them back, but seemed to struggle to get them down. She set the glass down by the sink and then hoisted herself onto the bathroom counter. "I'll tell you a secret."

"What's your secret, pretty girl?"

"I stopped drinking two hours ago. The shots are still buzzing my system, but not in the same league as Ember or Sophie."

"And why are you telling me this?"

"Because we both wanted something in the kitchen."

Hendrick crossed his arms over his chest and waited. When he didn't answer, she hopped off the counter, her shoulders rolling inward.

"Or I go back to being mad at you." She stepped away from the counter. In one swift move, he had his hand splayed on her stomach to stop her.

"Neither of us is in the right state for what I was imagining in the kitchen."

"What were you imagining?"

"You aren't in the right state to hear it, either."

"Then I guess we should talk about what happens next. Set some rules."

"Rules?" Hendrick crowded behind her, herding her to the bedroom.

"Yes, rules. For after we're married."

"What did you have in mind?" Hendrick slipped her shirt off her while he spoke. Her breath caught.

"What image do we need to portray? Did you force me into this? Are we together happily?"

Hendrick took his shirt off as well, enjoying how her words trailed off and her eyes dropped. "We are what we are and nothing else. I won't put on a show."

"And when there's no one around?"

"Still no show. But I have one rule." With his shirt hanging from his fingers, he pulled her against him. His cock hardened further the moment their skin made contact.

"What rule?"

"This marriage isn't fake. It isn't just a piece of paper." He kissed her. He had to. Crushing his lips to hers, he slid his tongue in and devoured her, drinking in her air. She tasted like wine. The dry fruit tickled his tongue, but there was something that was sweet. He assumed it was the shots they'd had. Stroking over her tongue some more, he tried to figure out what it was. Amaretto. Fuck. Some day, he'd lick stuff off her entire body.

He slid his hand up her back and pinched the clasp of her bra. Pulling it away, he dropped it to the floor. Before his cock told him what to do, Hendrick lifted his head and slid his t-shirt over hers.

She opened her mouth to speak, but nothing came out.

Hendrick reached under the front of the shirt for the fly of her jeans. As he pulled them down her legs, he couldn't resist leaning forward and placing a kiss to her centre through his shirt.

Her fingers speared into his hair, but he kept the contact brief.

"Hendrick. Please." Her eyes were closed as she tried to pull his head back to her.

"You need to sleep."

He stood, lifting her with him. Laying her on the bed, he kissed her, but not enough to stoke the flames.

"Goodnight, pretty girl." He tucked her in and slid into the shadows of the room while her eyes were still closed. He wouldn't leave her. Not a single night would pass from this point on where he'd be away from her.

12

KINLEY WOKE TO A COMMOTION ECHOING FROM THE living room. With a sigh, she settled herself deeper into the mattress.

Throwing the covers back, she sat up and looked down her body. *Hendrick*. She remembered every touch, kiss, and look from him last night. He'd put her in his shirt and tucked her into bed. She couldn't go out there wearing only his shirt.

She made her way to the closet, but paused. Knowing she still had to shower, she didn't bother with clean clothes. She slid on the jeans and shirt from the night before and strode out of the bedroom.

Hendrick, King and Ember, and Dak and Sophie waited for her.

"Hey, beautiful." Sophie came forward and hugged her. Ember joined her. But the content vanished, never quite taking hold.

"It's time." Hendrick locked his eyes on hers. It was time to make the call that would seal the deal.

Kinley nodded. She couldn't voice this reality anymore than she had to.

Dak pulled out a phone, scrolling before pressing the call button. He put it on speaker and set it down on the kitchen island. Stepping back, he gestured her forward.

Okay. They were jumping into this fast. But as she glanced at the clock blinking on the stove, the twenty-four hours her father had given her were up in five minutes.

"Yes?" Her father's smug answer churned her stomach. She had to close her eyes and breathe through her nose to make the nausea pass. She couldn't believe she was about to cave.

A knuckle pushed under her chin, lifting her head up. She looked up into Hendrick's eyes. They flared with anger, but he didn't direct it at her. He didn't want to do this any more than her. She saw that.

"Your choice," he whispered so that his voice didn't carry to her father.

"Fine." Kinley snapped loud, the single word carrying everything she felt toward her father and what he was doing to her.

"Kinley?" He stretched her name, searching for more from her.

"If you give me *my* money back."

"You'll get it back once you're safe at home."

"Is the alliance still in place?"

"That's not for you to worry about."

"But it's for you to worry about." She stepped around Hendrick to close in on the phone. "You want me back, then you are going to tell me everything right now."

"I'm sure this conversation has an audience."

"Too bad."

"What makes you think you have the upper hand? You don't come close to the level you think you do."

Hendrick squeezed her shoulders, offering support she wasn't sure she wanted. But at the moment, it helped.

"I don't need to come back as much as you need me to come back. Is there still a deal with the Pierce family?"

"Yes. Your mother hasn't stopped planning your wedding."

"What are the terms of the alliance?"

He scoffed. "Don't be foolish. I'm sending Cassius to collect you now."

"No." King interrupted their conversation. "She leaves on her own in her own time. No one will force her out of here."

"Your services are no longer needed." Her father spoke through gritted teeth.

"Too bad I'm not working for you. Although that still wouldn't work."

"Then the deal's off, Kinley. Either Cassius comes to get you now and you get your money back, or you don't get it back at all, regardless if you come on your own time."

"This choice is out of her hands. If Cassius sets foot in this building, he's dead. If he or any of your other men lay a hand on Kinley before she has said she is ready to leave on her own. They're dead."

"I'll give you another twenty-four..."

Hendrick whispered in her ear, drowning out her father's voice. "Try to scream." He wrapped his hand around her mouth but not tight enough to cut off all sound. After encouraging nods from King and Dak, she did as he asked and let out every ounce of her frustrations from her lungs. Hendrick clamped tight. But she didn't stop, making it a genuine struggle to contain her fury. Any other time, and the vibrations from his insane laugh would terrify her. But this was a show for her father.

"Don't think to control this. Your daughter made her deal with you, against our advice. But I wouldn't want you to forget for a second who has her. Don't fuck with me, Curry. It won't end well for you. My words aren't a threat." King ended the call.

Hendrick released her, but didn't take his arm away. He moved it to her waist, grasping lightly.

"He won't give me my money back, no matter what I do, will he?"

"That was never the point. We'll take your money back from him."

Kinley tilted her head back, focusing on her future husband. "From the inside."

"From the inside," he repeated.

"COME ON. YOU can borrow some more of my clothes." Sophie pulled Kinley away from Hendrick.

"I can make do with what's here."

"Not for what we're doing."

The apartment had a few essentials, likely left by Ember and then Sophie, but it was all a mismatched array of things.

"What are we doing?"

"You have a shooting lesson to make up today and you're training. I made you a promise last night." And the vision wouldn't leave Hendrick's mind. He was obsessed with making her as powerful as the rest of them.

"I have some yoga pants and sports bras that you can use for the next few days until we can get you your own." Sophie restarted her trek to the door. Kinley looked at him, but he wouldn't stop this. This had been his choice. He'd asked Sophie and Ember to help get her started this morning. Until he came down and pushed her limits.

Ember followed them out, and he was alone with King and Dak once again.

"You're going to go in there and blow everything up, aren't you? Figuratively, of course." King tilted his head back and crossed his arms.

"That's what I'm good at." But it didn't hold the excitement it usually did. This would be the one time he'd have to fight to control his crazy. In the centre of that environment, surrounded by his father, that crazy could snap. "I don't expect to get far with Curry. I don't give a shit about his business. He just needs to think I do."

"Your father won't hand everything over to you the day you arrive." Dak stated the obvious.

"I don't expect that either. I'm not sure if his desire to return to his retired life outweighs his mistrust for me."

"If he doesn't trust you, then why does he want you back?" Dak eyed the kitchen, pausing on the pot of coffee on the counter.

"He thinks he can mold me, control me. He's been trying to get me back ever since I left. Quietly. He doesn't draw attention to the son that didn't belong and that abandoned the family." The old man was going to experience a rude family reunion.

"He sounds like an idiot." King scoffed.

"He's arrogant." That arrogance would get him killed one of these days. "Are you both joining training today?" Hendrick didn't want to talk about his father anymore. Didn't want to imagine living under that roof. He intended to walk in there and let his father see the mistake he made inviting him in.

"Yes. We're letting them get warmed up on their own first." Dak leaned against the counter, nursing a large cup of coffee. The man could drink an entire pot on his own when in the right mood. And right now, he seemed on edge.

"See you down there." Hendrick left before more questions flew about his plans that he didn't have the answers to. The apartment door closed, syncing with the sound of his phone. One of his phones. He pulled it out of his pocket and cursed. The devil's ears must have been burning.

"Getting into an elevator, old man. Better talk quick." Hendrick punched the button for the elevator as he answered. The doors didn't immediately slide open, meaning the women must already be on their way down to the gym.

"What are you doing with the Curry girl?"

"You'll have to be more specific in your question. I'm not doing anything *with* her." Hell of a lot *to* her. Though his father didn't need to know that.

"Curry hired you to bring her back. Why the hell wouldn't you?"

"How King handles clients is his business." The

elevator rose and the doors dinged. It was unlikely he'd lose service, but Hendrick could hope.

"I want to talk to you. An official meeting, if that makes you feel better."

"No."

"Kit." His father snapped, using a voice that used to make Hendrick cower until he caught up to his father's height at twelve. He soon realized he'd outweigh his father one day and there would be nothing to fear.

Hendrick could lay it out now, tell him he was coming back with his own conditions. But if he let the plan loose, he had no way of controlling what his father told Curry or if his father had something to force Hendrick's hand and make them return now. No, he'd wait until the last minute.

"I have a proposition for you."

"No." Hendrick cursed the clear signal he still had as the elevator descended. "Oh, what a shame. I'm losing signal and can't hear anymore of the bullshit coming from your mouth."

His father growled over the line as Hendrick ended the call.

Days. They only had a matter of days to put this off. They'd force them both back and then Hendrick wouldn't have the upper hand.

KINLEY FOLLOWED ALONG with Sophie and Ember as they warmed up. Their routine made her realize she wasn't in the best shape she could be. She wasn't struggling and heaving, but her stamina didn't match theirs with the weights.

"The guys should be down here by now." Ember hadn't stopped glaring at the door.

"We should get some sparring of our own in before they show up." Sophie tipped back a bright blue and pink water bottle.

They took turns sparring, starting light. It was Ember that kicked things up, throwing in more forceful kicks. But the three of them laughed as Ember put both Kinley and Sophie to the ground.

Kinley had enjoyed sparring with them. They were kind in their corrections and made the exercise fun. It had been fun learning from Cassius growing up. He'd led her to trust him with those playful lessons.

The door opened, making them all whirl toward the entrance. Hendrick stalked into the room. His eyes were clouded and his shoulders seemed thicker. Kinley swallowed. Nothing about training with Hendrick would be fun. The other two women insisted he was the one that added a spark to training. But looking at Hendrick now, there was no spark. He looked as dark as the night they'd met.

"We're starting with what you tried to do the other day." He was bare chested and his pants hung low on his hips.

"Which part?" Their fight had become a blur as she'd processed the information and then dealing with her father stealing from her.

"You're off on your back of the knee kicks."

She'd perfected her aim. To the exact spot Cassius had taught her. Her eyes closed as embarrassment emblazoned over her skin. The heat in her cheeks scorched.

"I knocked you down." She held onto hope that

maybe she'd done something right. Maybe she'd kicked him hard enough to force him down, even if it hadn't been in the right spot.

"I went down because it gave me an advantage." Hendrick circled her on the mats, and she mirrored his motion. Sophie and Ember moved to the other side of the room and continued their own sparring, leaving Kinley to fend for herself.

Hendrick stopped his circling and moved toward her. He dropped to the floor, his hand running down her back, over her ass and down the backs of her legs.

"Right here." His hands pressed on a tendon and her knee buckled. She gripped his shoulders to keep from falling into him. Although he was already close enough to have a hold on her. "Use the strongest part of your foot. The ball or the heel. And don't pull back your kick."

He stood and stepped back, his lips tilting up to the right.

"But you have to make it past me first." His position looked relaxed, but she recognized the same taunt he'd used on Cassius. Each muscle twitched, ready to strike.

Kinley didn't mimic him. She wasn't at the level to pretend or taunt. Setting her stance, she tried to remember how she got past him last time. But would he expect her to do the same thing, or would he expect something different? Trying to figure out how his mind worked in this state would drive her as crazy as others claimed him to be.

He didn't show any weakness and Kinley didn't expect one. She'd caught him off guard last time. Right now, his full attention was on her. Her only choice was to go with her gut.

She lunged to his left, tilting the other way as if to feign, but continued full force on his left.

He grinned and blocked her. He reached for her arm, but she evaded his hold, retreating to her original position.

"That's the only time I'll let you retreat, pretty girl."

Fuck it. Instead of trying to get past him, she attacked. She stuck to what she knew, even if it was flawed. There must be some strength in her, or Hendrick wouldn't insist on doing this.

He blocked her first kick and had an arm ready to grab her second, but she pulled back and used her other leg, landing a roundhouse on the outside of his thigh. Still, she didn't pass him. She struck again, aiming for his other leg. When she landed against that one, he sucked in air through his teeth.

She'd hurt him. But if she stopped and showed concern, he'd have the upper hand. And what would a mercenary like Hendrick do with that?

Kinley lunged to his right again, making it past him far enough to kick back, focusing on the position of her foot and setting the exact spot he'd shown in her sights.

He went to the ground, a rumble vibrating through, but it didn't slow him down. He swept back to kick her feet out from under her. Kinley repeated the kick she'd done the other day, and he managed the same hold.

"Here. Push your weight into this foot." He squeezed the one in his hand. "Use it as a pivot point. Spin. Put your hands on the floor and kick up with your other foot. Always use momentum. Whether it's yours or your opponent's."

It was difficult to put the right amount of force behind the move, scared of falling to the ground. She'd always focused on kicks, punches, and blocks. This relied on the strength in her shoulders and her core.

Hendrick helped lift her other leg, pulling it straight and directing it at his head. He feigned the blow, so Kinley came full circle with the move.

"Again." He let her go and pushed himself up. Kinley caught the tightening around his lips.

"I hurt you." The second kick to his thigh. She'd wanted to stop, but known he would have attacked her instead.

"That was the point, pretty girl. Now, do it again."

"Hendrick."

"Do. It. Again. Kinley." He stood as straight as he'd started. There was no sign of pain. But a mercenary like him knew better than to allow for a weakness. How she'd seen it, she wasn't sure. She must have hit directly on an old injury. But how old?

She avoided kicking him this time, but it took longer to get past him. Hendrick didn't fall to the ground this time.

"Fuck," she cursed. She must not have hit the right spot. Scrambling away from him, Kinley made it out of her reach by the time he turned.

"Again."

Attack. Pass. Kick. And he was still standing.

"Again."

Attack. Pass. Kick. Hendrick fell. Kinley was quicker to kick him and quicker to get her hands on the floor. He caught her other foot once she kicked it up and directed the move.

"Good. Again."

13

HENDRICK PUSHED HER UNTIL THE IMAGINATIVE
curses spilling between her heaving breaths stung even
his ears. They'd worked on her kick to the back of the
knee and the following kick for a solid hour before he
sent her off with Gear for a shooting lesson. But the
moment they'd finished, Hendrick brought her back to
the gym to spar.

"Fuck off, Hendrick. I'm done." Kinley pushed up
onto all fours on the mat and sneered at him. With a
sigh, she dropped her weight. Her forehead slapped
against the mat.

His thigh burned. While he tried not to favour the
four-month-old injury, he'd completely let down his
mental guard he'd placed around it when facing off
with Kinley. He'd learned by now not to underestimate
her. Her speed was her advantage.

Sweat dripped over her body. Despite the pain in his
leg screaming at him to stop, Hendrick wanted to do
more. He wanted her to win at least one match. The
others had finished ages ago. Dak and King had sparred

with Sophie and Ember, letting them break part way through before coming back. But Hendrick had an obsession.

"Okay."

"I wasn't asking." She groaned and pushed herself to stand in front of him. Kinley shuffled toward the door.

"Look at me." He needed her to see she wasn't broken or beaten.

Her only response was a finger over her shoulder.

He took one step forward to grab her, and she stopped, dropping her chin over her shoulder.

"Don't you dare lay another hand on me. I said I'm done, and I meant it."

It was her tone that kept him from grabbing her. She could hate him now, but in the end, it would be for the better. "Be back down here tomorrow morning."

"I'll be lucky if I can move." She resumed her stroll toward the door.

"I wasn't asking." He mimicked her response, but dropped his own brand of threat into the words. He could hear her teeth grinding as she held back a response.

Gear slipped into the gym as she slipped out, not sparing him even a glance.

"You never push that hard."

"Sophie and Ember aren't mine to push."

"Is Kinley?"

"Is Kinley, what?" He blinked and moved his eyes from the closed door to Gear.

"Yours to push?"

"Yes." The answer was simple to him. Her freedom from him and this life were hers the moment she asked for it. But for now, she'd agreed to marry him. She was his.

"Why don't you let someone else train with her tomorrow?"

Hendrick narrowed his eyes. "You volunteering?"

Gear didn't answer. It was a jealous question, but Hendrick didn't feel that way. Possession and control rode him hard.

"Just my two cents." Gear shrugged. "She did well shooting today."

Hendrick nodded, trying to push away his tension. But the further that receded, the more the burn in his thigh made itself known.

"You should start with knives tomorrow." Hendrick didn't miss the smirk on Gear's face. He likely thought he was a fucking genius, suggesting Hendrick give the pissed off woman a blade and teach her how to maim.

Of course, Hendrick's blood pumped with a heavy beat at the idea.

———

———

"I'VE DUTIFULLY SHOWN up three days in a row, and at the end of each day, I've told him to fuck off. I even thought I was creative with it last night." Kinley sat in a comfortable chair in the front lobby of King Security. It was the only place she hadn't used to hide from Hendrick, and the only place he hadn't looked for her.

"What did you do?"

"Front kick, uppercut, cock, knee. I spelled it out for him with each strike to make sure he understood."

Kinley had chanted like a cheerleader and Hendrick had cupped his groin while falling to his knees. Then she'd stormed out of there with a finger over her shoulder.

Sophie threw her head back with a laugh. "I'd never get away with that with Dak." She tipped back the small glass she held between her fingers. The two women had brought down a bottle of Dak's whiskey and sprawled themselves in cushions, sipping away until someone discovered them. A closed sign gleamed outside the front door, and had been there since her father threatened to send someone after her. They weren't letting any clients inside.

Kinley drained the last of her first drink and held it out for Sophie to pour more. "He isn't this harsh when he works with you and Ember, is he?"

"No." Sophie's softness appeared when she whispered. She topped off her drink as well. "But Dak isn't always easy on me and King isn't always easy on Ember." Her tone was still soft. It wasn't the same as what Hendrick had been putting her through.

Some hours, he'd been silent, forcing her to spar with attack after attack. Others he'd try to taunt her, but when his taunts didn't work, he'd stopped. But he'd learned her hatred for Cassius was her motivation, and he used it. He dangled the image of her holding a knife to his throat like the proverbial carrot.

"You two are about to go into a dangerous den." Sophie's lips twisted as if that was a good excuse. Except it was. Kinley knew his reasons. But...

"His touch burns." She let the alcohol run down her throat to mimic the effect.

Understanding dawned in Sophie's flared eyes. "What kind of touch?"

"Every single one." It was almost enough to distract her, but when he tried to use it to distract her, running his hands over her middle or down her arm, she had to force herself not to falter. The hardest one was when his hand circled her neck. They'd been nose to nose so many times in the past days, trading desires with only a look.

Infuriating.

Calming.

Heating.

"Have you two...?" Sophie let her hands finish the question for her, waving them back and forth as if that meant something.

"Not since the night before the bachelorette party." But with every figurative foot of distance their sparring put between them, the tension thickened just as much. Kinley wanted him, and there was nothing she could do to stop herself. It didn't matter that she intended to stay mad at him for leaving like a coward after the fact, or that she needed to hate how hard he'd pushed her. She wanted him.

Sophie whistled and took another sip. Kinley sighed and leaned her head against the back of the chair. The lobby looked similar to an accounting office without the filing cabinets. It was oddly bare except for the necessary furniture. Plain desk, a computer, and chairs. They made the entire front wall of several large windows. Sophie had explained to her that no one could see inside, even though they could see outside. It had been a relief for Sophie while escaping her husband.

Early sunlight gleamed off the few cars out this time

of morning. The shops, restaurants, and other businesses opened one by one. But a particular shine caught her attention. A glare off of familiar shaped sunglasses. Kinley lifted her head, her throat closing over.

"What is it?" Sophie followed her gaze.

"Cassius." He stood across the street, arms crossed and wearing a leather jacket. Kinley stood and walked to the centre of the room. He stared directly at her, a confident smirk playing on his lips. She knew he couldn't see her, but it felt like it. A piercing burned in her chest from his gaze.

He'd called daily, needling her to step outside, to return home. Her father had been a bit more erratic with his calls. Sometimes calling in a rage and others where he tried to coax her.

"Princess." Dak's deep baritone filled the space behind them, but Kinley didn't turn around to see the look on his face. She imagined he aimed it at the bottle of whiskey hanging from Sophie's fingers.

But Dak wasn't the only new presence in the room.

"Hiding from me, pretty girl?" Hendrick closed in on her back.

"Wouldn't dream of it." But her challenge didn't hold any power, not while still staring at Cassius across the street.

"He's back." Dak sidled up next to Sophie and took the bottle from her hand.

"Back?" Kinley swung around. "He's been here before?"

"Every day." Hendrick answered.

"And you haven't bothered to tell me?"

"He's never stepped off that sidewalk." Dak didn't let Hendrick answer her. "And it's only him. We haven't been able to find anyone else watching the place. But that doesn't mean they aren't there."

"He comes and goes several times a day." Hendrick set his hands on her shoulders and pulled her back in front of him.

"It's like he can see us." Sophie leaned toward Dak. Kinley understood the feeling now that she understood what Cassius thought of her.

"He can't. He stands exactly like that, whether or not someone is here. Thinks he's intimidating." Hendrick scoffed, but Kinley heard the danger. He didn't find Cassius's stance amusing.

"Time's up, Hendrick." Kinley shivered at Dak's low announcement. "He hasn't crossed the line yet, but he will soon."

"I agree. Time's up."

Kinley spun and tilted her head back. Hendrick didn't look at her, though. He glared at Cassius through the window, his struggle clear. He would have loved a reason to kill Cassius for crossing the line.

HENDRICK HAD TO cut the training short this time. It wasn't him pushing limits, but Kinley. Seeing Cassius put her into a blind rage that had been building since she discovered the weaknesses in her he'd created.

Everything he'd pushed to teach her over the past few days had stuck. Kinley landed blow after blow and had creativity of her own. She was as prepared as he could make her.

"That's enough, Kinley."

She stopped short from lifting her back foot for a

front kick. "Really? You've pushed me to my breaking point every single day, but only an hour down here today is enough?"

Hendrick closed the distance. "Today is enough."

"Well, I'm not finished." She set her foot back.

"Kinley." He set his hands on her shoulders. "We're having the wedding tomorrow."

She froze, tilting her chin up to look at him. "Tomorrow." It wasn't a question. Something seemed to snap. Hendrick saw a recognizable flash in her eyes. Slow steps took her out of his hold and out of his reach. She backed up to the door, her hands behind her to find the handle.

"You can still change..."

"Don't." She cut him off. "I'm not changing my mind and we both know it."

"Okay." He let her go, giving her the moments she needed. Before now, the wedding didn't have a set day or time. There was always the slim chance that something might absolve them from going through with it. The finality of the situation had slapped him in the face as hard as it had Kinley. But he'd had years of experience to control himself.

Hendrick didn't leave the gym. Not until he knew Kinley was settled in her apartment. Only then did he move to shower, talk to Gear about weapons, and talk to King and Dak one last time about his plans that didn't exist. After phone calls to the priest, the hotel, and the florist to set everything in motion for tomorrow, he made his way upstairs to find Kinley.

He couldn't let this distance that had grown between them to stand before tomorrow.

The elevator doors opened to take him up and

Kinley stood inside, freshly showered and dressed in jeans and a tank top.

The look she gave him said more than he could decipher. Hatred, sadness, anger, and desire. They may be at odds, but the attraction between them burned brighter than ever.

Kinley moved to step past him, but he blocked her with an arm around her waist and pushed her back inside the elevator. He punched in the security code and slammed his finger against the buttons to close the doors, but not to send them up. She struggled between his arms and the wall.

"What are you doing?" She pushed on his arm, but he didn't budge.

"What I've wanted to do for days." He waited until the elevator was halfway to the top floor and pressed the button to stop it. Ever so slowly, he lowered his head to kiss her, stretching out the tension living and breathing between them.

"Hendrick." His name on her lips had a whine that was both desperate and frustrated. He felt the same.

Their lips touched. Hendrick wanted to grab her with a fistful of hair and chase the storm brewing inside them, but he kept it gentle.

"I'm proud of you, pretty girl," he whispered against her lips.

"You're what?" Kinley set her head back against the wall.

"You've done amazing every day."

"But you've..."

He'd been an ass. "We didn't have time for me to do it any other way."

"Bullshit." She tried to move away from him, but he wouldn't let her. "Why did you push me so hard?"

"Because I won't let you fail."

Kinley gasped. "You lied. You fled. And you've declared there won't be anything fake between us. I don't understand what you want."

"I want you, pretty girl. I lied to everyone. I fled because you're a distraction. A distraction I have no hope of dissolving and I've decided I don't want to." Any more declarations than that, and they'd be treading into territory neither of them was ready for. So he kissed her, this time allowing himself to devour her flavour.

"I'm still mad at you," Kinley said when Hendrick moved his lips along her jaw, but there was no conviction to her statement.

He chuckled. "Whatever you need to tell yourself. As long as you don't make me stop."

"I can't make you stop. I don't want you to stop." Her hands pulled at the bottom of his shirt.

Hendrick ripped his shirt out of her hands and over her head. He pulled at her clothes, shoving hard on her jeans over her hips. Kinley worked to free his cock.

Once she released him, he dropped to his knees to get her jeans and panties off her ankles. The scent of her arousal floated toward him. Leaning in, he ran his nose over her clit and breathed in.

"Hendrick," she cried.

She smelled too good not to taste. He lifted one of her legs over his shoulder, putting her on the tiptoes of her other foot. Her clit poked out from under its hood, begging and throbbing. He didn't tease her. Hendrick flattened his tongue over the bud and worked her into an instant frenzy. Her fingers speared into his hair, pulling until pinpricks pierced his skull.

He needed her to come. Plunging two fingers inside her, he curled them and forced her climax. Her legs shook.

She hadn't yet finished, her walls still clamping around his fingers, when he pulled from her and stood. He took her with him to line his cock up with her heat. Slamming her against the wall, he rocked into her.

"Hendrick?"

"Shh." He only wanted to focus on the feeling of her body.

This had been building for days. Every touch between them had burned a fresh brand of her on his hands.

He palmed her ass and set a hard pace, forcing them both to the brink. They set their foreheads together as their bodies took over, feeding on the heat between them.

Kinley gripped his shoulders, moving herself on him.

"Come," he growled.

She cried out as her body obeyed. Hendrick pulled out just when her core tried to force his climax with hers. The hot spurts of his seed coated her stomach and his.

Their breaths filled the small space. Still holding her against the wall, Hendrick hit the button to start the elevator.

He carried them into her apartment, leaving their clothes behind. Kinley laid her head on his shoulder, holding tight making it impossible to put her down, even as he started the shower and stepped inside.

"You can't let Cassius get to you." He spoke while the water rinsed away the light sweat and arousal.

"I can't help it. Seeing him…" She sighed. "I was angry, but seeing him raised it to a whole other level. I feel so naïve and used. Please tell me I don't have to be meek and mild when we go back."

Hendrick slid one hand up her body and gripped her chin. "Never. They're going to see the real you. The woman they unknowingly created."

14

HENDRICK HAD FORCED ALL UNCERTAINTY AND anger from her the moment he'd kissed her in the elevator. He'd taken her again after the shower. Every slow, harsh thrust a mirror to the beating of the blood through her veins. And with a promise that she wouldn't regret putting her trust in him, he'd left. His goodbye had been a kiss that only looked chaste, but had been nothing close to that. Even now, waking in the cool sheets, her lips and body still burned.

Closing her eyes, she forced herself to focus on what they had to do. This was it. Pulling herself from the bed, she paused as she looked across the room. A blush lounge set hung on the back of the door. Pants, a tank top, and a cardigan to wear over it all. Something a bride would wear while doing all the things of the day to get ready.

"It won't be that kind of wedding." Kinley spoke to no one but herself. But she couldn't resist covering herself with the soft fabric.

A quick, two-tap knock preceded Sophie's voice. "We're here!"

Kinley emerged from the bedroom and saw Sophie and Ember settling themselves in the kitchen with expensive looking coffees and a box of pastries. "You guys didn't have to do this."

They both paused and stared at her. "Yes, we did." Soft smiles helped warm her melancholy state. No matter what kind of wedding this was, it was hers. She should grasp any memory she could. And instant friends like Sophie and Ember were all she'd need to turn this day into a special memory.

Only minutes later, someone else knocked on the door, but this time, they didn't let themselves in. And from that point on, there'd been a steady stream.

The first had been three masseuses, all carrying their own tables and bags. They had spoiled Kinley and the others with a massage and facial. Ember and Sophie relaxed into the fun, helping Kinley to do the same. The next to arrive had been an esthetician team for pedicures and manicures. At that point, it didn't surprise her when a stylist and makeup artist walked through the door. Each team had been ushered up by one mercenary or another.

And Hendrick had arranged each of them. He gave her the entire experience of a desired wedding.

Damn it. She was supposed to be mad at him, although that hadn't stopped her yesterday. But that was becoming impossible with everything he did for her.

The last was a slim, older woman wearing a wrap dress with a bold sash that tied it around her waist escorted by Gear. She held a garment bag over her arm. Her wedding dress. Everything about this day had been perfect. And while the dress she'd settled on was magnificent, it wasn't the dream she'd imagined for so many years.

Pulling in a deep breath, Kinley reminded herself that the dress wasn't what was important. And Hendrick had already done so much for her.

Kinley smiled at the older woman who greeted her with the same. She leaned her head back. "You are a beautiful bride, my dear." She held one hand out, shaping it around Kinley's face without touching. "I have your dress. I have everything with me in case we need to make any quick alterations. As I understand it, we have a bit of time to allow for that. Although, it's not as if they can have the wedding without the bride. They'll wait." Her wise eyes sparkled.

The seamstress held the dress up high with one arm and unzipped the bag.

Kinley gasped, unable to reach out toward the white fabric. "This isn't the dress I ordered."

"What do you..." She turned her gaze on Gear. "You went over a bride's head and chose a different dress? I knew you were evil, but I didn't think you were that evil."

"Mrs. Wilson." Gear tried to cut through her anger, but his voice didn't hold the same firm tone he'd used on them the night before.

"I don't care about the circumstances of the wedding. I refuse..." She hugged her arms around the garment bag and turned her tiny might on Gear. "What did you just call me? Don't you *Mrs* me."

"Nana Marie." Gear's tone changed into something softer, almost loving. Kinley saw the wide-eyed looks Ember and Sophie were directing at the man. "This was the dress she wanted, but wouldn't let herself have."

Nana Marie shook her head, pursing her lips. "You have no idea the risks involved with surprises at weddings," she muttered, more to herself than the others in the room.

Kinley slowly took the garment bag from Nana Marie. Tears flooded her vision.

"Well, maybe not so evil." Nana Marie's words were soft.

"It's... it's stunning." Her perfect dress.

"Well, it isn't yet, but it will be as soon as you put it on. Hurry it up, child." Nana Marie started shooing them all toward the bedroom. She swung her head over her shoulder. "What are you still doing here?"

"That's my cue." Gear grumbled, but he had a smile for Nana Marie.

"It was your cue the moment you dropped me off in the room, devil boy."

Gear placed a kiss on Nana Marie's cheek and left.

"Wait!" Kinley set the dress down over the couch and rushed toward Gear. He frowned down at her. "Thank you." She put as much emotion as she could without letting her tears loose and ruining her make-up."

"You're welcome, Kinley."

Kinley placed her hand on his arm and used the leverage to reach up and place a kiss on his cheek. He met her halfway, still holding his frown over his eyes. She let him go and he left with a soft click of the door.

"Devil boy?" Ember asked.

"I've known that boy since he was knee high. Hell on

chubby legs. Legs might not be so chubby anymore, but he's still trouble."

The three women chuckled through their shock, helping Kinley push away the tears at seeing the dress.

In the bedroom, they all dressed. The only alterations needed were small tucks to make the bodice fit tighter. The V between the breasts dipped lower than she'd imagined, but she loved it that much more.

Kinley stared at herself in the mirror. She just might have the wedding of her dreams. But she wasn't yet sure about the marriage.

Ember and Sophie appeared behind her in red, satin dresses with empire waists. Nana Marie stood beside her, patting at the dress as if there was something left to fix.

"Now, it's stunning."

HENDRICK STOOD AT the front of the church dressed in his black tux with the waistcoat and pocket square matching Kinley's flower colours. Gear and Cole stood with him. He'd tried to make everything perfect for Kinley. The only thing he couldn't do was fill the pews. Dak, King, Archer, and even Thane, the doctor they often called, spread themselves out over both sides. Roen was with the women as a guard and would come in last. Ember and Sophie would stand with Kinley at the front of the church. Kinley hadn't asked them, but Hendrick had. Gear had escorted a woman he'd called Nana Marie to the front pew as well.

The priest smiled beside him, pleased with the donation this wedding was giving to the church.

Flowers decorated the ends of the pews. The exact colour roses, but Hendrick took it a step further and found a florist with smaller roses that would keep the leaves and thorns on the stems. Sophie had messaged Hendrick everything little detail Kinley let slip, before she'd settle on the easiest option.

Now he waited for his bride. The bride he never imagined.

Music trilled over the speakers. The doors opened. Ember and Sophie swung them wide and kicked the stoppers down. Ember walked down the aisle first, her sharp gaze only for King. Sophie followed, her eyes softer.

The music faded and a new song rose. Hendrick felt the change in the room. Everyone stood.

Hendrick locked his eyes on the open door. His breath seized as they remained empty. He'd promised her she could change her mind at any time. But he'd never considered that he'd be abandoned at the altar.

But then white flowed forward on the floor and with each step Kinley came into view. A full skirt and a slim bodice that exposed the entire centre of her torso between her breasts. His gaze lingered there for only a second. He'd have time to explore that later. If she'd let him.

She paused after her first few steps. Jaw slack, her eyes took in the entire church. The flowers, the runner covered in petals. The tulle decorating the front of the church. And then Hendrick. She blinked away the shine in her eyes.

He met her stare as she took the steps down the aisle with a slow rhythm. *Fuck.* She was magnificent.

Hendrick held out his hand to help her up the two

steps to join him. Running a finger over her cheek, he slid it down her jaw, her neck, and her chest. She shivered under his touch.

"You're gorgeous, Kinley."

She blushed, running a finger of her own over the edge of his waistcoat. "Thank you. For everything about this day."

The priest cleared his throat. Neither of them looked toward him, but Hendrick guided them into place. He listened with half an ear, repeating when he was supposed to. And he soaked in every word Kinley repeated as well.

The photographer he'd hired had slipped from the side long ago, catching everything from the moment the doors opened. He didn't think Kinley had noticed him. Hendrick insisted he be discreet so as not to take away from the atmosphere of the day. The man would get a significant tip if the photos turned out as well as Hendrick expected.

Gear passed him the rings as the priest prompted. It had been hard to pick out a ring for a woman he barely knew. He knew her strength. And he'd used that and everything Sophie and Kinley had messaged him about her wedding dreams to pick out a round cut diamond engagement ring that sat in a wedding band with a nest of deep rubies.

Kinley passed her bouquet to Sophie. Hendrick slid the band of rubies on first and topped it with the diamond. Her intake of breath had told him he'd chosen right. Warmth filled him. He never wanted to give her a reason to regret her decision.

Her soft fingers ran over his hand as she slid the plain gold ring on his finger.

The words Hendrick had been waiting for rang from the priest. "You may kiss the bride."

Hendrick slid his hand over the side of her neck, stroking her jawline with his thumb. He bent his head and pressed his lips to hers. Gentle and soft for the camera. But then Hendrick let the lick of heat push them into the kiss they both wanted.

Chuckles rumbled through the room. Whistles pierced the air from Cole behind him. Even Roen and Archer joined him as the kiss kept going.

And Hendrick refused to break from that kiss until he was ready. Sliding an arm around her waist, he pulled her against him. He slowed the kiss, topping it with soft embraces as the cheers and whistles faded.

He turned them to face the small audience. The photographer stepped forward, making his presence known to ask to take more pictures.

"I've got all the candid shots I could ever imagine, but there are some poses I always love to do."

"You've got thirty minutes."

The mercenaries not in the wedding party spread out to stand guard. The photographer posed them in several positions, together and alone. He set up wedding party shots and even got one of Nana Marie next to the bride.

"Nana Marie?" Hendrick leaned toward Gear while they sat in the front pew, waiting for their next turn.

"Seamstress. She asked to attend." Gear wouldn't look his way and there was something in his eyes as he looked at the older woman.

Hendrick didn't need to pry into the other man's past.

Kinley let out a full sigh. She was tiring, swaying

from foot to foot. "That's a wrap," Hendrick called out to the photographer, who'd straightened and let his camera hang from his neck.

Gear took Nana Marie's arm and led her from the church. Dak and King each took their women and did the same.

"Let's go, pretty girl." Hendrick held out his arm and followed the other. The last of the mercenaries and Thane brought up the rear with the photographer as they all switched locations to the building next door.

Strings of lights decorated the rooftop. A handful of tables had centrepieces made with Kinley's flower choice.

"Hendrick." His name was a breath from her lips. "You did everything, didn't you?"

"Yeah. I did."

"This is amazing. It's better than any dream I had. I don't know how to thank you."

"You don't. What we're about to do tomorrow won't be easy. The least I could do is give you this."

Kinley turned her body toward his and tilted her head back. "I supposed I don't need to stay mad at you today."

Hendrick laughed low and bent his head. "I don't think you do. Be mad at me tomorrow, but not today. And definitely not tonight."

Her breath hitched, and Hendrick took advantage, kissing his wife.

KINLEY'S EMOTIONS WERE raw. These people she barely knew did so much for her today. Just to make this forced marriage special. There's no way the wedding her mother was planning held a candle to this.

And Hendrick. Yes, he'd lied to her. But he lied to her through pain. She hadn't missed the single longing look he'd cast at the space of the best man. She doubted he'd have had his family at his wedding, but he would have had his brother.

Kinley wondered if she would have been attracted to him all the same in an alternate universe. The universe where she ended up engaged to Shane, who'd passed her off to Hendrick to get her free.

Inwardly, she shook her head. Those thoughts were a waste of time. This was her life. Even if it was short. Her life was next to Hendrick.

He led her around the tables and to the small dance floor set up under a circle of lights. Instrumental music flowed from unseen speakers. Pulling her against his body, he swayed.

"This dress has no lies."

Kinley laughed. She couldn't help it. She felt happy. It was chipping away at the melancholy that had squeezed her since she decided to marry him. "What do you think this dress is saying?"

"A woman with sassy confidence who knows what she wants. Who isn't a coward. But she's feminine. And a perfect fit for me."

"When you say it, that's the woman I feel like."

"Good." He kissed her, devouring her mouth. Kinley soaked in his taste and touch. One more night to be free. One night to stand tall with sassy confidence and not a cowardly bone in her body. A woman ready to claim her husband.

He'd said no fake marriage, and this was her wedding night.

The song ended, and they pulled apart. He sat them at a table for two, ahead of all the others. Servers wheeled in carts of food. Hendrick had done everything to have every moment played out perfectly. The timing was impeccable. No lulling moments of wondering what to do next.

They ate, laughed, danced, and drank—minimally —until even the city below them had quieted.

Gear had taken Nana Marie home a few hours ago, and had returned, putting himself in the position of guard. Terrifying and large, he stood watch. Slowly, the others without a woman on their arms joined him.

Hendrick tensed beside her and she narrowed her gaze at King and Dak, seeing the same tension.

"Is something wrong?"

"No. It's just getting late. None of us are comfortable being this exposed for so long."

"Seems like a good time to call it a night, anyway."

"Let's go, pretty girl." Hendrick nodded to the others and everyone moved with practiced choreography, filing out the door and to the elevator. They broke apart in groups so that Gear and Archer took the lead and Cole and Roen had the rear. They held the same pattern with the vehicles to drive them back to *King's Security*, except for King and Ember, who kept driving to their own home.

Kinley didn't know where the other mercenaries went for the night after they'd all made it to the building. But that wasn't what she focused on. The change in all of them was visible once they were inside. They were safe here. Kinley soaked that in and let herself relax.

They rode the elevator up with Dak and Sophie, but no one said anything. The other couple were in their own little world in the corner. Dak held Sophie's chin, lifting her face toward him. He spoke low. Kinley heard the hum of his voice, but couldn't make out the words.

Hendrick held Kinley with her back against his chest. He slid a hand up the front of her torso, letting his fingers dip and play in the opening of her bodice.

"I can't decide if I want to keep the dress on you or not." Hendrick nipped the shell of her ear.

Kinley tilted her face toward his when he released her. "Why not both?"

His breath brushed her neck as he was about to say something else, but the elevator door opening cut him off. Hendrick nodded to Dak and Kinley waved to Sophie. The other woman looked as flushed as Kinley felt.

The door shutting sounded loud in the quiet and dim apartment. It was the only moment Hendrick let any distance between them. But it didn't last.

His hand skated down her arm and gripped her wrist. Pulling, he spun her toward him.

"What are you wearing under the dress, pretty girl?"

"That's for me to know and you to find out." Kinley was letting go for tonight. Just for tonight. And that meant saying and doing whatever the hell she wanted with this man.

"Hell of an invitation. I wouldn't dare turn it down." He backed her toward the kitchen. He moved one of the island stools away and set her in its place beside its mate. "Hands behind you on the island."

Kinley lost her breath at the demand in his voice. It was such a contrast to the playful side of him. But she obeyed without question. Why wouldn't she? Not when obeying him got her what she wanted.

"Foot on the bottom rung of that stool." He pointed to the stool next to her, then dropped to his knees. "Eyes on me."

He trapped her gaze. His eyes held so much emotion and power. Kinley saw why people called him crazy. The colour of his eyes was so vibrant, they didn't settle on one emotion at any one time. He took her breath away.

Hendrick grinned sideways. "Keep your eyes on me, pretty girl." His grin widened. "For as long as you can see me."

He gathered the layers of her dress in front of him and lifted. With a wink, he ducked beneath her skirts and let them fall down his back.

"Fuck, Kinley. You dirty girl." He spoke with heated desire, sending a shiver over her spine. That shiver spiked as he thumbed her exposed clit. Kinley had worn nothing beneath her dress. Not for the lack of lingerie choices. Something about being this bold woman had grabbed onto her attention. As soon as she'd seen her dream dress, she'd tossed the plans for the lacy briefs. The dress screamed confident femininity, and Kinley hadn't wanted to waste the power of that feeling.

She closed her eyes and threw her head back, stiffening her arms to keep herself in place. Hendrick blew over her folds in between small licks with his tongue.

"You're going to come so many times tonight." His lips moved against her thigh, then he nipped.

She yelped, but pushed her hips forward. He didn't have enough urgency for her liking.

He chuckled and bit her again, this time holding the

bite a little longer.

"Hendrick!" She cried out and squirmed, pulling away or pushing toward him, she wasn't sure.

He soothed her thigh with his tongue, then kept it going up her thigh to her clit.

"Yes. Please." Kinley couldn't keep herself quiet. The bodice of her dress felt too tight and her breasts were craving his touch.

Hendrick gripped her hips and went to work. Every lick had a distinct purpose. Some of her fantasies had centred around this, but she hadn't been sure if she'd enjoy it. She had her answer now. She never wanted him to stop.

Uncontrollably, her hips bucked with each lap at her entrance. His grip changed, and he threw her leg over his shoulder, then thrust his tongue inside her. His other hand worked her clit, putting enough pressure on the button to make her explode in seconds.

A garbled scream escaped her.

He stayed under there until her breathing slowed and he'd lapped at all of her cream. But it only made her ready for more.

He came out from under her dress, wiping at his mouth with his thumb.

"Pick a number between one and ten, pretty girl." He ran his fingers over the straps of her dress and down her back to undo the clasps.

Her mind raced. "Six." Seemed like an evil number to her.

Hendrick pulled the straps down her shoulders and helped her pull her arms free. He palmed her breasts. "One orgasm down. Five to go."

Oh dear God, what had she done?

15

———

HENDRICK WANTED TO DO SO MANY DEPRAVED things to this woman. Half of them involved this dress, but he took a moment to think. Throughout the evening, he'd heard what Gear had done, getting her dream dress when she refused to consider it herself.

He couldn't risk damaging it. But there was at least one fantasy playing in his mind that wouldn't harm the delicate fabric.

Bending, he laved her nipples. She gasped with each lick, her body sensitive to every touch. The bodice hung loosely below her ribs.

"You ready to take me?"

"So soon?" She shook in his hold. Her gaze held a greedy look.

Hendrick chuckled. "It's only the beginning."

"But…" She trailed off, her tongue licking her lips as she dropped her head.

"Fuck," he cursed to himself. He had too much he wanted to do to let her take the time to suck him off first. "You'll have to clean me off instead, pretty girl."

Her hands fisted the waist of his pants. Hendrick pried them off him, feeling her pulse race in her wrists.

"Turn around. Hands on the island. Then step back until you're bent over. I'm going to fuck you in this dress."

Kinley rushed to do as he said, and he stepped back with her. Crouching down, he gathered her dress the way he had before. Running it up her legs, he threw it over her back, but stopped it below her shoulders so he wouldn't lose sight of her face.

"The sight of my sweetest dreams." Hendrick glided his hand over her ass, thighs, and back up again. When he moved down, he used his finger and trailed it between the smooth globes of her ass. Her intake of breath was sharp.

"Hendrick?"

"Yeah, pretty girl. Some day."

She shook her head, but Hendrick ignored her. He tapped the inside of her thighs. Kinley widened her legs without him saying a word.

He wasted no more time. She wouldn't be able to stand like that forever and Hendrick needed to get her naked as much as he needed to fuck her in the dress. Releasing his cock, he set one hand on her hip and lined himself up. He dipped the tip into her heat before grabbing hold of her other hip.

Squeezing, he controlled his initial thrust, sitting himself all the way in and holding there. They both needed to catch their breath.

"Fuck, Kinley. You feel so good." He'd taken her bare. And he found he didn't give a fuck. She was his. With his next breath, he tried imagining her with child. His cock twitched. Well, that was news for him.

Shaking off his revelation, he pulled back to start a rhythm sure to get her to the peak. He wasn't ready for a child. Despite the heat that hit him, he may never be. He wouldn't come inside her. There were other places.

"Hendrick. I can't hold on."

That made two of them. "Come. Now, pretty girl." Hendrick clenched his jaw as her walls squeezed him, her body trying with all its might to force him to come with her. He wouldn't.

Her arms gave way and Hendrick grabbed her around the waist. He flipped her back and lifted her into his arms. Once in the bedroom, he stopped.

"I need you to stand so I can take the dress off you. Think you have the strength for that?"

Kinley lifted her head from his shoulder, nodding. She held onto his arms to steady herself as he set her feet on the floor.

He cupped the side of her neck, using his thumb to lift her chin. He kissed her while working on the lower clasps around her waist. Sliding his fingers along her hips, the dress moved to fall to the floor. Hendrick lowered himself to help her step from the fabric and to pick it up from the floor.

"I can't do it again, Hendrick."

"Do what again?" He put her dress on the hanger waiting on the closet door, then started stripping his tux. His cock still hung from his open slacks.

"Come. I can't."

Hendrick grinned. "You can. And you will. You asked for six."

She gave a shocked laugh that sounded more like a series of scoffs. "I didn't *ask* for that many."

"Sure you did. I said pick a number."

"I didn't know what that number was for."

He'd hung his jacket and vest, and was peeling his shirt away from his body when he decided he was done joking. "One night, Kinley." He closed the distance. "We have one night to be this free. And safe. You're taking everything I want to give you. Everything."

"What about you?" She ran her hands over his abs.

"What about me?"

"Do you have to take everything I want to give you?" She raised a single brow, and Hendrick's heart skipped a beat. What would she want to do to him? He wrapped a hand around her neck, rubbing his thumb up and down the side column.

"If you still have the energy when I'm finished, you can do whatever the fuck you want to me."

HER BODY WILTED, submitting to him. He was right. Only tonight was certain. She didn't know what to expect tomorrow or from their marriage. This heat between them wouldn't last under the pressure of revenge. They both had their own missions to complete with the end promise of setting her free.

Kinley let him have the power over her for tonight, knowing she had the same over him. His wild eyes seemed just as undone as she felt.

Hendrick used the hold on her neck to push her toward the bed. "On your knees." He didn't let go of her neck, but he used his other hand to take hers and help her up. She knelt upright on the edge while he stepped away. Rigid muscles covered his body. The odd tattoo. Kinley couldn't stop her eyes from roaming.

And why would she want to stop herself from looking at the magnificent size of him jutting from his open fly?

"Like what you see, pretty girl?"

"Very much." She licked her lips.

Reaching under the bed, Hendrick pulled out a small paper bag. Kinley didn't bother questioning where it came from or how he'd gotten it in here. He wouldn't be a very good mercenary if he couldn't get past her.

With a hooked finger, he pulled out a thin chain. One end split into a Y and all three tips had jeweled tweezer clamps.

"Looks like you know what this is." He moved in front of her.

She nodded, but her thighs dampened from the rush of desire. His laugh told her he didn't miss it.

"Just the reaction I was hoping for." He bent his head and sucked one nipple into her mouth while holding her steady at her waist. Pulling hard, he let her go with a pop, and replaced his mouth with his thumb and finger.

The chain clinked as he let it all drop from the one clamp he held.

"Eyes on me." His lips smirked and his gaze flamed. Kinley wanted to look down, to watch him tighten the clamp. When she caved and dropped her chin, Hendrick squeezed, giving it a slight twist to shock her. "Try it again, pretty girl." His dare wasn't much of a warning, but she lifted her chin and met his eyes. "Good girl."

The rubber covered tips slide over her skin. She knew when he tightened it, because his lips twitched and his eyes narrowed. The pressure increased past the point she lost her breath.

"There it is." He focused on her face and held her gaze as he bent to run his tongue over the clamped nipple. Breaking the visual contact, he took her other nipple into his mouth.

He repeated the entire torture, forcing her to look at him instead of what he was doing to her body. But it was the third clamp that worried her.

It was harder to keep her eyes open and on his. He used only his fingers, stroking up and down the sides of her clit. It throbbed and her core clenched. She whimpered, and he rewarded her with a light kiss before he lowered to the floor, putting his face in line with her core.

This time, he didn't order her to look at his eyes. He let her watch him pull the hood back and slide the clamp over the swollen bundle. He licked her gently while he tightened the tweezer.

When he finished, he stood, lifting her with hands under her ass. "Fucking gorgeous. I might decorate you for every special occasion."

He crawled onto the bed and sat on his heels. Kinley clutched at his shoulders, wrapping her legs around his waist.

"Red and green bells for Christmas. Amber jewels for Thanksgiving. Flowers in May, and icicles in January." Hendrick reached between them, taking himself in hand. He lowered her onto him.

With every movement, the chain pulled at the clamps. Her core wept for him, and his words only heightened her desire. The thought of being precious enough for him to decorate constricted her chest.

He slid into her with no effort.

"Still think you can't come again, pretty girl?"

She made a keening sound that wasn't an answer.

"Do it. Make yourself come." Hendrick let go of her hips and leaned back to grip her ankles, holding her feet flat on the bed.

Kinley blinked. He wasn't moving. Fully seated inside her, he throbbed as much as her, but he stayed utterly still.

"Now, Kinley."

His demand snapped her into action. Before she processed his words, she undulated on him, using her grip on his shoulder and her planted feet for leverage.

"Good girl." But his praise came out strained. Her eyes roamed over his chest. He was tight, holding himself tense. And that drove her higher. This was all on her to take her own pleasure. Hendrick was forcing her to take it after saying she couldn't. He controlled her. That should scare her. That wasn't what she wanted. But her body didn't want to listen.

The pull of the clamps blended with the rest of the buildup. Her entire body hummed, making it hard for her to breathe.

"Look at you. Chasing your own pleasure without a care in the world. Take me harder, Kinley."

Her head fell back, the ends of her hair tickling the top of her ass. The chain pulled tighter. Hendrick's knuckles grazed against her stomach. And that was all she'd needed.

A slight pull up on the portion attached to her clit shoved her over the edge. Her orgasm was sharp and electric, racing through her body.

"Fuck, Kinley. That isn't enough." Hendrick pulled

hard, and the clamps popped off her. Hot sensations flashed into her nipples and clit. She screamed as the pain pushed her into another climax before the other had finished.

Arms wrapped around her, flipping her back to the bed. He pressed his groin to hers, easing the throb in her clit. He covered her breasts with one hand and his chest.

"Did that count as one or two?"

She almost cried. "Two. It was fucking two."

Hendrick laughed, nuzzling her neck. He didn't fuck her hard. Slow and soft, he moved inside her until her body calmed. He pulled out and settled his cock along her stomach. "That was torture."

She burst into an exhausted laughter. "Poor big bad mercenary." Kinley wasn't sure if she spoke loud enough for him to hear. She couldn't hear herself.

He joined in her laughter, but despite the tension in him, he sounded much clearer than her. "Careful what you wish for, pretty girl. We aren't finished yet."

———

SO MUCH FOR no distraction. His focus was going to be on his now wife, and not where it needed to be to find out what happened to Shane. But Hendrick couldn't summon any regret for that. She was his match in every way.

Kinley had one heel off the floor, ready to kick him away from her once they were inside. Hendrick had seen the moment she gave in to the magic of the day, but it hadn't reached every part of her. She held something back from him. He couldn't let her go now. But in the end, it would be up to her.

Hendrick liked to play dirty, and he'd already told her their marriage would be real in every way. Tonight wasn't their only time together.

Her eyes drifted closed, but Hendrick's cock still throbbed between them. And he wouldn't allow her to say he didn't live up to his word.

Stroking up and down her sides, he woke her slowly. She arched into his touch, pushing her breasts against his chest. Hissing, her eyes opened. The sensitive peaks were a dark pink now and still straining. He moved his hand up to trace his fingers over them.

"Hendrick." His name was more of a plea on her lips. He intended to take her every night from now on, but the danger under his father's roof was unknown. Tonight, and for tonight only, they had all the freedom they may ever have. Hendrick wouldn't waste it.

Lifting his hips, he lined himself up and thrust in. She whimpered beneath him, but lifted her hips to meet his.

"Don't make me do it again."

Any other night, he might give her mercy. "This body is mine, pretty girl. If I want you to come again, you will." Hendrick wasn't a complete monster. He moved in and out, building her up to an enjoyable release rather than one that might have been painful after all he'd put her through.

Several minutes passed when her breathing changed. He hadn't thought it was possible for her to get any wetter, but he felt a fresh surge. It was becoming painful for him to continue to hold back his climax, but it would be worth it.

He ran his hand down her leg and lifted it over his hip. She gasped at the change of the angle. A growl vibrated through his chest. Her walls squeezed unbearably tight while he hit the most sensitive spot inside her.

A sting of pain appeared on his chest. He hadn't realized he'd closed his eyes until he looked down and saw her biting him. Kinley was his. He just hoped she never asked him to let her go.

Hendrick slid his fingers into her hair and pulled her off him. Holding her head to the bed, he touched his forehead to hers and ground his pelvis against hers. These last two had to be on the heels of each other again. He wouldn't last.

"Fuck, Kinley. Now."

She came with a strangled scream. Hendrick gritted his teeth and groaned as her body milked him, but he held back long enough for her to crest the peak and reach the right moment for him to force her into a second one.

He ripped himself from her and slid down the bed. Her cunt dripped, and he watched the muscles there quiver. He covered her clit with his mouth and sucked. Shoving two fingers inside her, he curled them.

Kinley cried out and shoved both hands into his hair to pull him off. His scalp stung, but he didn't relent. Her body obeyed him beautifully. The orgasm hadn't faded completely. He felt her body tighten and rise again. She came with a whimper. Her entire body shivered.

He changed his touch to soft pets until her body stopped squeezing his fingers. Gripping himself in hand, he moved back up the bed and knelt beside her.

"Open your eyes, pretty girl."

"No." Her mutinous whine made him smirk, but

that's all he could do. His cock was ready to explode and he wouldn't have her not looking at him when he came on her body.

Gripping her chin, he turned her face. "Eyes open, now." This time, when he spoke, his voice sounded rough. A thread of danger echoed through it.

Her lips parted, and she opened her eyes. When she realized what he was doing, her lazy gaze dropped to his cock. The purple head stuck out as he pulled at himself with harsh strokes.

Her tongue licked at her upper lip. "Please?" She was half asleep below him, begging for him.

"You don't have the energy." He shook his head, yet still scooted closer.

"I want it, Hendrick."

"Then come and get it."

She struggled to get herself up on her elbows. Angling herself, she set her tongue out flat as an invitation.

"This won't take long."

"I know. It's just a taste."

Hendrick supported the back of her neck and thrust forward. Kinley relaxed her jaw and throat. The sounds she made wrapped around his cock. Seconds. That's all it took for his orgasm to explode from his spine and down her throat. He roared, then choked on it as a small hand cupped his balls.

He let her play. But then she pulled back until just the head of his cock was in her mouth. She swirled her tongue and lightly scraped her teeth over the most sensitive part of him. Painful pleasure shot down his cock. The woman wanted to torture him like he'd tortured her.

Fucking made for him.

He let her, enjoying that side of her for as long as he could stand it.

"Fucking minx." He pulled her off him. She fell back to the bed, eyes closed, and with a satisfied smile on her lips. She looked happy with her taste of revenge.

He left her to run them a bath. The time was counting down, becoming impossible to ignore. But he had to, for a little longer. With the bath running, and bubble foaming, Hendrick returned to the bedroom and lifted Kinley from the bed.

"If you force another from me, I swear the next time your cock is in my mouth, I'm going to bite hard."

"That isn't much of a threat." Hendrick ran his nose up her neck before biting down hard enough to make her arch in his arms.

"Of course you'd find that enticing." She whimpered and her eyes cracked. "What are we doing?"

"A bath."

"That's not fair."

Hendrick chuckled. "You'll have to explain that one to me, pretty girl."

"You can't make a girl choose between a bath and sleep."

"I'm not making you choose."

She hummed and kissed his chest. "I'm supposed to go back to being mad at you."

"Sure you are. But that can wait a little longer." She'd try to put distance between them, but her anger had already vanished.

"You don't fight fair."

"Did you expect me to?"

"No."

Hendrick set her down in the water. "You'll have to wake up long enough for me to get in behind you."

That had her popping one eye open, reminding him of the night he found her in the bed of his truck. Turning the water off, he motioned her forward and crawled in behind her.

Dak didn't build small apartments in this building. Each one had a luxurious bathroom. The bathtub was more than big enough for the two of them to fit.

They settled under the bubbles. Hendrick held Kinley against him, placing a light kiss to her temple.

"You didn't have to do everything you did for me today." Her voice was still soft with sleep. "It meant more than you know. Thank you, Hendrick."

"You're welcome." And he'd do it all again, and more.

Something nagged at his gut, but he couldn't decipher it. Instead, he wrapped his arms tighter around his wife, and nibbled her ear until she roused enough for them to wash and get some sleep before their world turned upside down in a few hours.

16

COFFEE AND PASTRIES STIRRED HER SENSES. THE
aroma grew stronger, pulling harder at Kinley to
wake up.

"Time to wake up, pretty girl." *Hendrick*. His voice
stirred pleasure that still pulsed in her body, but with a
throbbing soreness that made her clench her thighs.
The crazy man had tortured her before soaking her in
the most relaxing bath and tucking her into bed. And
Kinley knew she had no hope of stopping him from
doing it again. Next time he asked her to pick a number,
she'd pick one. Or two. Maybe three. But no more.

Turning her head over on the pillow, she cracked
her eyes open, fearful of any morning light. Hendrick
stood beside her in only a pair of sweatpants and
holding a tray.

A stupid tear crowded the corner of her eye. Why
was he doing this? Why was he treating her like
someone special? Or was this just the aftermath of their
wedding night? In a matter of hours, it would all be over.

Kinley pulled her to sit up, holding the blankets over her chest. Hendrick settled the tray over her lap.

"Good morning. Wife." He kissed her before settling himself back in bed beside her. His hair was tousled in the sexiest way. Leaning back against the headboard, he regarded her with lazy eyes with one arm behind his head.

"Good morning." It was like a shield surrounded them, creating an alternate reality they might have had. Kinley let the warmth of that fill her, turning her attention to the breakfast for two in front of her. "This looks wonderful."

He filled two plates with three different pastries each. Extra large cups of coffee sat in either corner. The buttery crust made her stomach rumble. Kinley started with a sip of her coffee.

Hendrick devoured a pastry within minutes. When she still hadn't touched one, he held one up to her lips. Not wanting to disturb the atmosphere, she opened her mouth. Somehow, he made this breakfast as special and remote as the entire wedding and all of last night. He licked at the crumbs and the glaze left on her lips after every bite. Her body hummed, but exhaustion still weighed on her.

"You wore me out last night."

His only reply was an evil grin that made her knees weaken. Thankfully, they were still in bed.

"I suppose it's almost time…"

He leaned in and nipped her bottom lip, cutting her off. "Not yet. Don't go there yet."

Those words held the same pain when he talked about Shane. Kinley studied his eyes. Going through with this plan was costing him. She shouldn't rush these moments.

Nodding, she kissed him. Soft and chaste, because her body was not up to the challenge of taking him again so soon.

He devoured another pastry and fed her another until she had to push him away. Hendrick set the tray on the floor. They sipped at their coffee together, him with his arm around her shoulders.

It didn't take long for his lips to find her neck. He nuzzled, kissed, nipped, and she tilted her head to give him access. This time together was all theirs. Neither of them wanted it to end. It didn't mean reality wasn't pushing against whatever barrier their desire for each other built.

After setting his coffee on the nightstand, he used his hand to peel away the blankets from her breasts. Her nipples peaked from the air.

"You're beautiful, Kinley," he whispered as he drew lines over her bare chest. She turned toward him, tilting her head back to let him do as he wished.

Hendrick's cell phone vibrated on the nightstand. He tensed, but ignored the call and buried his face in her chest. Kinley felt the pressure from the outside world before the phone started buzzing again.

He looked up and locked his eyes on hers. This was the moment she would become trapped again. He kissed her, tasting her as he licked at her lips. He reached for his phone before he released her.

"Yeah." He answered, but kept his arm around her shoulders, pulling her down to the bed with him. She heard the voice on the other end, but couldn't make out what they said or who it was. He squeezed her shoulders before hanging up the phone and letting her go.

"Time's up, isn't it?"

"Yeah. Your father sent two men to retrieve you." Hendrick's face changed. Dangerous insanity flashed in his eyes.

"Where are they now?"

"Waiting for me."

Kinley frowned, not understanding, until Hendrick got up from bed and changed into a pair of jeans. From the top of the dresser, he collected his knives. She lost her breath at the sound of the steel and the glint from the light.

She peeled herself from the bed and stalked across the room to him. Leaning up on her toes, she set her hand on the back of his neck and pulled him down to kiss him.

The mercenary took over the devastating husband she'd had for the past hours. And Kinley had no desire to stand in his way.

———

THEY HAD HIDDEN dungeon-like rooms in the basement. And that's where Dak and the others stashed the two men. Curry crossed the line, but he hadn't used Cassius. According to Dak, Cassius had returned to his station across the street an hour after these two set foot inside the building. And all this transpired before Hendrick had even made Kinley breakfast.

Hendrick hadn't been able to pull them from that apartment to face what came next. He'd held onto those moments for as long as possible. Going back was the only way to find out what happened and to find closure for himself.

His priorities and desires were shifting quickly enough to leave him confused. An eagerness to fuck these guys up more than usual pulsed inside him. They threatened Kinley. His crazy swirled in all sorts of shades as he opened the heavy steel door.

A knife hung from each hand and he nestled the others in their sheaths on his body. He hadn't bothered with a shirt that would need burning. King had delivered the threat to Curry. Any of his men stepped on their property, they'd die. Hendrick was just the one to follow through. Happily.

"Did your boss tell you he sent you both to your death?" The two men looked young. There was a smoothness to their skin that belied any constant beard growth. Instead of showing fear or begging for their lives, they snarled.

Hendrick spun one knife around his wrist, catching it with a flourish honed by years of practice. Their snarls froze and their eyes widened. One of them sniffed as if unphased by the threat in front of him. The other seemed to possess some smarts. His defiance faded from his features.

"You won't get anything out of us."

"I didn't intend to. You two have nothing we want. Curry knew whoever he sent here would die. King made it clear. Curry wouldn't send anyone who wasn't disposable."

The one on the right paled. He understood his fate. Hendrick might show him a bit of mercy and end him quicker.

Sometimes, a part of him worried about himself.

These two were young. They had a chance to turn themselves around. But the likely scenario was they'd continue on the same path and get themselves killed by someone else. Or Curry would get them killed. They weren't so young they didn't understand the bed they'd made. Holding onto pride and acting cocky didn't get you far. A lesson learned by time.

"King can't do his own dirty work?"

Hendrick laughed, the sound starting low in the concrete room. "King's hands are dirtier than I could ever hope mine to be." He held his palms up to stare at them. That statement only held truth because the man was almost a decade older.

"Then just get it over with, asshole."

Hendrick dropped his hands and tilted his head at the one who took charge. The other shook in his seat, No silently forming on his lips. "I don't torture just for information. I torture for fun."

The shaking kid pissed his pants and the brave idiot pulled at the chains. But finally, fear flared bright. While these two wouldn't have any information about Kinley or Shane, they might have some insight into how Curry ran things.

"I think we need some one-on-one time." Hendrick typed out a message to Cole. Minutes passed before he walked in. "Help me move bold-and-brassy boy here to another room."

"You going to drag this out?" Cole questioned.

Hendrick let Cole see the true emotion in his eyes that ruled his plans. Sure, he had the logical plans of getting what he could out of them. But they represented the threat to Kinley that was her father. It wasn't just another torture job.

Cole sucked in a breath. He saw it. Kneeling down, he unlocked the chain from the floor behind the chair while Hendrick did the one in the front. With one on either side of the chair, they lifted and carried him from the room. He'd tried to struggle, to topple their balance, but with a quick tip backward, they upended him. He stopped struggling.

They locked him back down in another room.

Cole leaned in close to speak so the idiot didn't hear. "You want help with this?"

Hendrick shot Cole a look. He controlled his crazy. Always.

Putting up his hands in surrender, Cole left.

"Now, for some foreplay." Hendrick threw a knife so that it sliced the outside of his arm before clanging against the wall behind him.

He screeched, yanking himself to the side as if the knife was still there. Hendrick threw another to do the same to his other arm.

"How does it feel being a useless lackey sent to your death so one of his higher ups didn't have to?"

He bit his lip hard enough to make it bleed.

"You two thought you were good enough to walk into the home of the king of mercenaries and succeed in whatever Curry wanted you to do? Or are you too young to know what King is capable of?"

"He's just a man. Like you. Like me. Like Curry."

"Interesting comparison." Hendrick pretended to consider his words while he slung small blades to land in his torso. Not long enough to do anything more than sink into the muscle. They'd hurt like a son of a bitch, but wouldn't cause any damage. It was all a warm up. But at the last, he whimpered. "You're no man. I haven't met Curry, but I doubt his quality. I even have my doubts about myself." He laughed at his own joke while closing the distance. "But King? Yeah, he's just a man. But not one like you've ever imagined. He didn't give himself that name. He earned it."

The idiot didn't see the knife Hendrick pulled from his back. He still stared at Hendrick's face as he sliced at the tendon in his elbow.

He screamed.

"I imagine you felt pretty damn important getting sent to retrieve the boss's daughter."

"He said it would be an easy in and out. And that the girl wouldn't give us any trouble."

"Easy to get caught. Easy to get killed. In and out. He had that right. But the girl? She would have kicked your ass. You wouldn't have gotten her to the front door."

The reality of his situation settled hard. He lost his fight and obstinate attitude.

"Ah. Now you understand."

HENDRICK WALKED BACK into the first room. He'd wrapped all of his knives and blades in a cloth. Dropping them on the floor, he sat against the wall and started cleaning them. The idiot's fear didn't satisfy him as long as it would have.

This kid's fear served more of a purpose. He hadn't tried to act bigger than he was. Hendrick wouldn't send him back to Curry, but he may not have to kill him. That depended on a few things.

"He wouldn't tell me how old he was."

"He was twenty-two."

Hendrick had to hold in his chuckle at how quickly this kid spat out the words. "And you?"

"Nineteen."

That's what he'd thought. "You're going to tell me a story."

"Wh... what story?"

"A little about you. How did you come to be in Curry's employ? What the job has been like. Oh, and make it entertaining." Hendrick rolled one of his small blades between his fingers and back. "You wouldn't want me to get bored."

The kid started with foster care, listing off the years like a grocery list. Hendrick feigned a yawn, and the kid changed his tone to make it sound like an epic tale. The kid might live after all.

Focusing on putting emphasis and excitement into his life that led him to here, he gave Hendrick information that he didn't realize was important. Like how Curry gained certain employees. How he turned the employees in his restaurants and clubs, getting them involved without them knowing. Then they have no other direction than to follow along or keep quiet to save their life. Bus boys became either runners or cleaners. This kid chose runner knowing he got nauseous at the sight of blood.

"You've missed some characters, kid. Who do you answer to?"

"Eric is his name. His dark hair always puts a shadow over face. We know he's near because of the smell of cigars. A specific brand that makes three flavours, but Eric only smokes one of them."

Hendrick struggled to keep his laugh inside. He'd cleaned every blade he had twice while the kid told his story and he hadn't noticed. The kid kept talking, embellishing every so often. He hadn't needed many prompts. Once on the topic of who he answered to, he continued to list off the other jobs and the people in charge of them.

Business managers dealt with Cassius. "If you aren't a manager and you've caught the attention of Cassius, you need to hide. But there's no use." He dropped his tone for dramatic effect.

"Who else has the same power as Cassius?"

"No one. Other than Curry himself. It's a full pyramid power structure."

"All right, kid." Hendrick slid the last knife back in its sheath and stood. The kid squeezed his eyes shut, flinching away. "I liked your story. I won't kill you."

Hopeful eyes looked up at him.

"Today." Hendrick couldn't allow the kid to lose his fear. But, fuck. He couldn't see himself killing the kid.

Hendrick left, locking the heavy door behind him. Blood had dried to his chest, arms, and jeans. He tossed his jeans into a bin to be burned later, and showered in the utilitarian bathroom they had down here.

The others were waiting for him somewhere, certain they'd been watching and listening. At least Roen would have. But Hendrick took the elevator straight back to Kinley. He didn't have any spare clothes up there, but they had a few phone calls to make.

Kinley was pacing back and forth in the entryway when he opened the door. Her hands tightened into fists at her sides. Whipping her head toward him, her hair flew across her back.

"What happened?" She rushed him, but paused

when her eyes landed on his wet hair. "You've showered."

"Yes." He set his hands on her waist, waiting for her to either come to him or step away. She didn't move.

"They were disposable to him. He knew what he'd sent them into."

"*Were*?"

"You heard King." Hendrick could tell her one still lived, but he needed to know she could handle him. Because few lived at his hands. And part of him enjoyed it.

Her breathing quickened. Hendrick recognized the flash in her eyes. She was angry.

"He's such a heartless monster."

Hendrick blinked. *He*? She was angry at her father. But she didn't come closer to him to take comfort. Stepping away, she squared her shoulders. His wanton bride from the night before was gone. And he didn't have time to reel her back.

"It's time to make some calls, isn't it?"

"Yes." Hendrick was going home. Out of everything he'd done and seen, that was what made him sick to his stomach.

———

KINLEY WAITED BESIDE Hendrick. She knew what he was, what he did, and she wanted to go to him. To hold his hand and wrap her arms around him. But she'd stopped herself. That wasn't where their focus needed to be.

Hendrick had led her to the elevator and downstairs

to meet with the other mercenaries. He'd grabbed a clean set of clothes from the gym.

"I need a favour." Hendrick started by setting his phone on the table, but before calling anyone, he looked at the others. "I need the body from downstairs packed up. I'm taking it with me back to Curry." His eyes darted sideways to look at her, but it didn't last.

"And the other?" Roen asked.

"Keep him here. You guys can decide what to do with him. He tells a good story." Hendrick smirked.

"You didn't kill both?" Shock smacked the words from Kinley before she could think through everything he'd said.

"No. I didn't need to."

There was more to these mercenaries than the world realized. It was evident in Ember and Sophie. And everything they'd done for her with the wedding. Seeing the torturous assassin rise from her bed had made her forget for a moment. She wouldn't make that mistake again. They were two parts of the same man that worked together.

Hendrick sighed before swiping his finger over his phone screen and leaning both hands on the table, facing off with the voice that answered.

"You win." Hendrick spoke through his teeth.

"Kit?" The older male voice had a touch of smugness.

Hendrick winced. "Is the alliance with Curry guaranteed?"

"I won't ask how you found out about your bride-to-be. She's caught your eye. That's good."

"The alliance." Hendrick growled.

"Already signed. It takes effect the moment you two

marry. We'll host the wedding in a month, after you've got your feet under you here." His father sounded proud, and a little excited. He really wanted Hendrick back.

"No. The wedding will be my way. No exceptions."

"What are you playing at, son? I'm happy to have you come back, but I'm sure you have an alternative motive. Maybe something to do with who you work for?" His voice lowered, but sounded louder, as if he'd put his mouth closer to the speaker.

"You know better. The mercenaries want nothing to do with your business. Won't touch it with a ten-foot pole. I'm doing this for Shane."

"Whatever brings you home."

"Happy to hear you say that. I have stipulations."

His father laughed. "What is it you want, son?"

"You'll find out when I get there. I suggest you plan dinner with the new allies tonight."

"So, you returned the girl. Interesting."

Hendrick cut the call, breathing heavily enough Kinley felt the tension from the others. Although none had moved, it felt like they'd taken a step back. But Kinley moved closer. She laid a hand on his bare shoulder. He jumped, turning his head to see who dared to touch him. The colour of his eyes was bold, snapping all of her focus. Lighting a match in this room would be lethal for all of them.

"Is there anything at your father's house you want? Things you would have taken with you when you ran?"

My fucking financial information. "No. Nothing sentimental. But I'd like to have more than one change of clothes and other essentials."

"Make a list. We'll get all of that soon."

"When you're done making the list, you're having another shooting lesson." Gear's voice rumbled from the corner of the room.

Kinley nodded.

"I'll help with a list." Sophie pulled out paper and a pen from a drawer and moved to stand beside Kinley.

Hendrick straightened. The energy flowing off him was dangerous. It heated her face through his touch where he'd cupped her jaw. He pushed her face up with his thumb.

"We leave in four hours." He kissed her, but it wasn't the same as it had the night before or that morning. It felt forced.

Time for Kinley to be the smart woman she was. She was the wife of a mercenary this morning. And now she was the wife of a crime boss.

17

HENDRICK WENT OVER HIS PLANS WITH GEAR ONE last time before gathering his packed bags from his apartment. He felt like setting fire to the place. He felt like setting fire to everything in his wake. Until Kinley set her hand on him. He'd never had that kind of grounding person in his life. The heat still burned, simmering and ready to lash out.

He feared what walking into his father's house would do to him.

Gear waited with his own bags at his townhouse. They'd left the weapons at King Security. "I still think we should have two vehicles."

"We will. Cole and Archer are following us with the body. They'll leave a vehicle behind."

"Yeah."

All this driving around was Hendrick's way of wasting time. Procrastination wasn't something he did. But there was no way to prepare himself to do this. Kinley waited in the parking garage with two large suitcases. Seemed Ember took her job seriously. Good.

Hendrick didn't know how these first few days were going to go and he couldn't let down his guard for a moment. Not to shop for something she might need.

Gear moved past everyone to gather the weapons they'd packed from the weapons room.

Kinley stood with her shoulders back and her chin high, ready to go to war in a red dress. Hell of a statement from the one he'd found her in. But the dress served more purpose than words to her father. The skirt flared down to her knees.

She shouldn't have to do this. Hendrick let go for this moment of safety. Closing the distance, he bent his head and kissed her. He tried to pour everything from the night before into that single touch.

She hummed into his mouth, but resignation filled the sigh that came from her as she pulled away.

"I'm sorry, pretty girl." Hendrick murmured the apology for her ears only. "You can still back out."

"No, I can't."

Bags thumped on the concrete floor as Gear came back. He pulled out the knives and gun they had chosen for Kinley. "You wearing the holster and sheaths I gave you?"

"Yes."

Gear passed her the weapons one by one and they all watched her lift the hem of her dress to slide them into place on her thighs.

Both Sophie and Ember embraced Kinley. "Be safe." Sophie let her go and Ember grabbed her shoulders as if to impart wisdom, but all she did was nod. The silent communication unknown to any of the men in the room.

"You remember what we told you." Dak growled as he wrapped an arm around Sophie's shoulders.

"I will."

"I have a parting gift for you." Roen stepped up with another duffle bag similar to the ones holding weapons. "Surveillance. Set it up wherever you can, whenever you can. I'll be here to listen and watch."

"My father has scanners at every house and business." Kinley shook her head at the bag.

"So does mine. But I'll take it, anyway." There had to be somewhere they didn't have covered.

Everyone waited awkwardly. Gear shook his head and started gathering bags. He was right; they needed to go.

Hendrick took Kinley's suitcases and led her to the vehicle behind Gear, where he hid the weapons and surveillance in a floor compartment. The moment they stepped into the SUV, his focus changed. The melancholy of leaving became something different. It turned into a desperation to survive. A desperation to protect.

They weren't on the road for more than ten minutes when Gear got a text. "Cole and Archer have left."

"What do I do when we get there?" Kinley leaned forward between the two front seats.

"You don't leave my side without looking at me first."

Kinley pursed her lips and sat back against the seat.

He glanced at her in the rearview mirror and, sure enough, she was glaring at him. "It's setting boundaries from the start. You're mine now. Not your father's."

Her face softened, and she nodded.

"You're not kept like you were, but everything is for protection."

"Anyone, including both of your fathers, won't hesitate to use you against Hendrick." Gear turned in his seat to help explain. "It doesn't matter what is between you two or how you feel about each other. You're his wife and to these men, that has something to do with their pride. They'll assume Hendrick's reaction toward you is for the same reason."

Hendrick held her gaze in the mirror for a heart-beat. They hadn't had time to analyze their time together. With doom looming overhead, that time had been precious to Hendrick. And if the time with her had been precious, then so was she. He'd torch anyone who hurt her with a fucking flame thrower.

Pulling in a painful breath, Hendrick pushed his focus back to the evil den they were about to walk into.

Driving into the circular driveway of his father's house made him cringe.

No. Not his father's. If he was going to get anywhere, he had to walk in there like he owned the place. Like he owned every person in the room. Thanks to the alliance that was sealed when he and Kinley married, he did.

Two other large SUVs sat in front of them. "Those belong to your father?"

"Yes."

"Then let's not keep them waiting." Words that would have an exciting lilt to them any other day sounded ominous coming from him now. He needed to shake off this dread.

Getting out of the vehicle, he stretched and looked around. He knew where most of his father stationed most of his men. Spotted most of them. He even knew where he'd station extras with the Curry family here, and especially when expecting Hendrick.

"Stay here. Keep her in the car until I get back."

Hendrick spoke to Gear, but his attention was everywhere else. He strolled around the driveway, drifting away and toward the grounds. He felt the eyes on him. The more he walked around aimlessly, the more they struggled to keep up with him.

Hendrick ducked into the shadows and from there stayed out of sight. He made his way to the back of the house. It took him a few minutes, but he found Hudson in the same position as he had last time.

"Report to the house in one hour."

Hudson flinched.

"Need to stay more aware, bud."

"I knew you were close, but didn't realize you were at my shoulder." Hudson tilted his head. "Why am I reporting to the house?"

"I'm back."

Hudson abandoned his attentive pose and turned toward Hendrick.

"Just until I found out what happened to Shane. Until then, I'm taking over. Which means you're getting a promotion." Hendrick squeezed his friend's shoulder and sank back into the shadows, leaving him stunned.

When he got back to Gear, Hendrick opened the back door for Kinley.

"Cole and Archer are two minutes out."

"Tell them to pull over and give us ten minutes."

"Where did you go?" Kinley looked off into the darkness.

"To talk to my brother's right-hand man." Hendrick set his hand on the small of her back and kept her beside him. Gear brought up the rear.

Two men stood guard at the door. They each set one foot to the side to block the door.

"Weapons." The tallest of the two held out his hand.

"No thanks. We have our own." Hendrick kept walking past them, stepping over their feet and holding his hand out behind him to help Kinley. Chains clinked as Gear pulled his out from wherever he kept them. Hendrick caught sight of him throwing it over the back of his neck and holding onto each end on his chest.

They entered the house in the middle of an argument.

"Where is your daughter?" Hendrick's father had his arms crossed. The two families stood on opposite sides of the dining room.

"You promised the mercenaries would bring her back."

"They did."

"Well," Hendrick interrupted what Kinley's father was about to say. Heads snapped around and guards took protective stances. "Sort of." Not a soul in this room had been aware of the threat that had approached. Fuck, he hoped it hadn't been like this for Shane. Hendrick might sneak up on Hudson, but he was the exception. Hendrick had insisted on teaching Shane and his closest men a few things. More than a few.

Curry took one step forward, but stopped when Cassius set his hand on his arm. Leaning in, he said something no one else could hear. But Hendrick let his grin widen, knowing the information being passed.

Curry sneered at Hendrick's father. "You didn't say your son worked for the mercenaries."

"It worked, didn't it? They're both here." He stuck out his chest, boasting of a perfect plan.

Curry sighed and reached back for his wife that

stood behind him. "Kinley." He smiled. "Come here." He set his wife in front of him, who spread her arms.

"Oh, I'm so happy you're safe, Kinley."

Kinley reached for Hendrick's arm and squeezed. She looked up at him with wide eyes. It wasn't her face that he saw. This was the practiced compliance she'd had to live with. He wondered if she even realized she did it.

Hendrick held her gaze until he saw the compliance crack. There weren't so many in the room that he or Gear couldn't get her away from her father and his men if he tried anything. The guards were all set outside the house.

He nodded and dropped his hand that had moved to the back of her neck without him realizing. His breath seized as she walked away from him and toward her parents.

KINLEY WALKED TOWARD her parents. She made each step blindly, unable to track her progress or figure out how she left Hendrick's side. She'd been upset on the drive when he'd demanded she ask permission, but it turned out she'd needed that permission.

Her mother folded her arms around her and her father added one of his. She tried to find comfort in her mother, but she couldn't. Her mother had followed along with the plan to use her. Had she even fought with her father about it? Had she even tried to save her daughter from this life?

The moment her mother let her go, her father's hold

changed. His hand gripped her arm, and he tried to pull Kinley behind him. Cassius hovered close by.

"I've almost finished the wedding plans." Her mother started chatting, oblivious to the struggle between Kinley and her father. "We'll go dress shopping first thing tomorrow."

Her father's grip tightened and Cassius stepped closer. Kinley pulled back, setting her foot behind her to add strength.

"Let my wife go, Curry." A wisp of steel echoed Hendrick's words. Her father didn't release her, but his shock loosened his grip enough for her to free her arm. But Cassius wasn't frozen. He lunged forward.

Kinley rushed her steps, but she didn't need to. The whip of a chain through the air didn't sound like she would have expected it to. The end of Gear's chain lashed Cassius's wrist. He snatched it back, holding it to his chest.

"Don't try that again," Gear warned, swinging his chain back over his shoulders.

Hendrick stepped up to her back rather than pulling her back toward him. They now stood between the two families. "Let's all play nice. As boring as that is."

"Wife?" Her father moved his gaze from Hendrick to her.

"What does he mean, wife?" Her mother looked only at Kinley.

"You can cancel the wedding plans, ma'am." Hendrick reached around her and lifted her left hand so that it rested flat on her chest. "It's already done."

"You fucking bastard." The moments her father's temper took root were the moments he made a mistake. Making that kind of mistake against a man like

Hendrick would cost him his life. "You stole my daughter."

Hendrick chuckled. "Not even close."

Kinley's own grin threatened. She'd been a stow away bride. His stow away bride. Kinley ended up in the fate she'd wanted to escape. Fucking irony.

She turned her head so her cheek touched his chest. The movement was unconscious, but when he tilted his head to look down at her, she felt comfort. No matter what, her situation wasn't the same.

"Hendrick." Gear never moved from his position.

Hendrick nodded and turned an icy gaze on her father. Kinley pulled in a breath to ready herself for what came next.

"I brought you a gift, Curry. But I'm sure you were expecting it." The door opened. Kinley kept her gaze forward. She hadn't seen the body back at King Security and she didn't think she wanted to see it now.

But Cole and Archer strolled all the way in front of her father, dropping the cloth wrapped body at his feet.

"You're smart enough to know a couple of kids wouldn't have made it past King's mercenaries and grabbed Kinley. I assume you wanted to test King? See if he was bluffing?"

"Where's the other one?"

Hendrick sucked in air between his teeth. "Too many pieces."

Even knowing the other was still alive didn't change her reaction to the image Hendrick created. She pinched her eyes tight.

"I believe we're all here for dinner. My mother has always made an excellent meal and by the smell of things, that hasn't changed. Please, everyone, have a seat."

If Kinley hadn't seen the effect coming here had on Hendrick, she'd never guess he hadn't wanted this role. He settled into the centre of it all with a stronger authority and presence than she'd ever seen. Her father was pissed, but Hendrick's was just coming out of shock and only now watching him with suspicion.

Slowly, they all moved toward the table. His father pulled out the chair at the head of the table. Hendrick cleared his throat loud enough to catch everyone's attention.

She looked over her shoulder to see him shaking his head at his father. Hendrick moved them to the head of the table. He shooed her father down to the next seat. Kinley stared as her father moved down. Hendrick held out the chair for her.

He looked at his father. "As soon as we're finished eating, I want to see the contract for the alliance. And any other current contracts." Hendrick sat and waited for his father to take the seat at the other end of the table.

The food filled the centre of the long table, all in covered dishes. Hendrick lifted the covers of the ones closest to him and dished up her plate first and then his own. He passed the food to her father, forcing him to take it and for the food to flow.

Her father sat next to her with her mother on his other side. Cassius sat across from him and next to Gear, who sat next to Hendrick. Men she didn't recognize filled the last three spaces separating Cassius and her mother from Hendrick's parents.

Cole and Archer hadn't left, but everyone seemed so

focused on Hendrick that they hadn't noticed. Cole leaned against the door between the kitchen and dining room, not bothering to hide, but Archer settled himself against the back wall.

"There won't be any need for you to see the contract. You'll be getting an annulment."

"No." Kinley spoke while air still resided in her lungs. The room silenced, dishes stopped moving down the table and silverware hung in the air.

"What did you say, Kinley?" Her father asked.

She looked up at Hendrick. He settled his hand over hers.

"She said no. Too late for that anyway."

"A divorce then."

"No." Hendrick stared down her father.

Kinley was caught in his eyes. They flamed with that dangerous insanity. She heard the sharp breaths from others at the table. They feared him. She didn't.

"Your daughter is mine, Curry."

———

HE HADN'T INTENDED for Cole and Archer to stay, but Hendrick had to admit that their presence made him feel better.

The women had been the only ones to fill the silence throughout dinner. They'd tried to pull Kinley into their conversations, but she wouldn't say more than single-word answers. Most of what they'd discussed had been the wedding and how they were upset to have missed it.

"Come, Kinley. You can tell us more while the men discuss business."

His skin bristled. He didn't want Kinley out of his reach. But he doubted their fathers would discuss the contract with Kinley present.

He looked over her shoulder to find Cole had moved to the opposite wall as Archer, rather than staying in the open in the kitchen. Cole nodded, knowing exactly what he wanted.

Hendrick lifted Kinley's hand and kissed her palm, holding her hand to his lips longer than necessary. "Go ahead."

Cole appeared behind her and pulled out her chair. He held out his arm to escort her from the table. The man was flourishing his charm, but only for Kinley.

"Excuse me, sir." One of the front door guards walked toward his father. "Hudson Patel is trying to get into the main house. He said the boss called for him."

"Send him..."

"I did." Hendrick spoke over his father. "Let him in."

"Kit?"

He ignored the name. The guard hesitated, but he took in Hendrick, Gear, and then Archer, still standing at the wall. He left and held the door open for Hudson.

"The office is still in the same place, is it not?" Hendrick stood and motioned for the men left at the table to go ahead of him. The office was on the other side of the house, past the kitchen and at the end of the dining room.

The two crime bosses stepped through with their own individual guards on their tales. Cassius hadn't stopped glaring at Hendrick most of the night. The man would get what he deserved soon enough.

Stepping into the office took his breath away. It still looked like his father belonged here, but it smelled like his brother. The cologne and the cigars Hendrick had thought he'd only smoked with him. He'd topped it with leather and old books. The books had been an addition of Shane's. He'd always been the kid in the corner reading. It was why he'd surprised everyone by stepping up with an interest to run the business.

Pushing the emotion down deep, he added it to the fuel.

Hendrick cleared his throat for the second time that night when his father sat behind the massive desk. "I believe that's my seat." Hendrick rolled a small blade between his fingers to a rhythm that only played in his head.

"*I believe* you're getting ahead of yourself, Kit."

Hendrick flipped the knife in the air and caught it the moment he snapped his gaze to his father's. He'd known he'd always been right not to have a knife on him when coming face to face with his father. The smallest flick of his wrist, and Hendrick could sink the blade into his father's chest.

"Sit down over there and we'll try to resolve this issue you've created. You're not out to the best start."

Hendrick stalked toward his father. Gear cut off the guard that tried to stop him. "That isn't how this is going to work. You want me back here so you can continue to enjoy your cushy vacation homes. I have my own reasons. But I can leave. We do this my way, or not at all. Now, move."

"Watch yourself, Kit. You lost your breeding for this position." His father stalked around the desk and sat, sprawling himself to seem as large as possible. He snapped his fingers at the guard. Stepping away from Gear, he moved to the side and poured drinks. He set one in each of the waiting hands of the older men, and ignored Hendrick.

Hendrick held back his laugh at Gear's snort. The slight wasn't subtle.

"The contract?" Hendrick sat and tried not to imagine Shane sitting here. Gear took up position near the door and Hudson stood at Hendrick's shoulder as if taking his rightful place. And maybe it was.

"The top left drawer." His father tipped back his glass.

Hendrick leaned back and opened the drawer. The contract and a pen were the only things in it. He bet if he opened every other drawer and door in this room, he'd find it empty.

Pulling out the papers, he read them, taking his time to absorb every word. He wanted to know how much control he had over both businesses.

He had full control of his father's, taking the position of his brother. But control of the Curry corporation wouldn't happen for five years. In those five years, he'd apprentice under Cassius. At the end of the five years, he would co-own the business alongside Curry until he retired.

"If you don't find the terms acceptable, you can always divorce my daughter and return her as I hired you to do."

"It doesn't matter what happens with this contract. I won't divorce your daughter. But I have one problem with the contract. Only one," he added excitedly, as if they should all find that exciting, too. "I'm not apprenticing under him. I'll agree with the timeline. It makes sense since I wouldn't know anything about how you run your business. But Cassius there, can go fuck a dead horse for all I care."

Cassius tensed. Hendrick lifted his lips, taunting the man. Any excuse or chance to take out the other man would make his day.

"I'm not handing my company over to you at all. The contract is null and void since you walked in here already married to my daughter."

Hendrick frowned down at the contract, making a show of flipping through the pages. "Nope. Says nothing like that in here. I thought you wanted your daughter's husband to take over for you when you retire? Wasn't that the point of this arranged marriage?"

"I didn't know Kit Pierce was one of King's Mercenaries."

"Why would that matter? I would think that would only make me over qualified."

"You had my daughter days ago and refused to give her back. Killed one of my men in the fight."

"I had conflicting information at the time. All good now."

"Son." His father leaned forward. "It's important this alliance goes smoothly. People are circling and business is waning with the absence of a rational leader. This is about protection for both families. For your mother. Your men. You. And your wife."

"Well. It doesn't sound like the two of you are in any position to argue." Hendrick pulled out the pen, made the changes and initialed beside them. At the bottom, he crossed out his father's name and signed his own.

He knew he was charging in here and making enemies from the start. But that served his purpose. Piss them all off until they exploded with the truth. His father knew what happened to Shane. He'd seen it in his eyes the other night, and he saw it now.

Holding the papers over his shoulder, he passed the contract to Hudson. "As soon as I settle in here, I'll bring Kinley for a visit and we can talk further."

His father held his hand out to stop the tirade about to burst from Curry. They shared a look before standing.

"Welcome home, son."

Hendrick swallowed the lump those words caused. The door shut behind them. He sighed, the pain that he'd buried walking in here burst forth. Fuck, he hadn't expected this.

"It's hard to be in here," Hudson murmured.

"Yeah." He stood and turned around to sit on the desk rather than stay seated where he didn't belong. "I want to meet with everyone who was loyal to Shane. But not at once and not only them. Set rounds of interviews with every one of the men here. Tell me where their loyalties lie before."

Using his foot, he kicked open the drawers of the desk.

"And we need to find where my father has hidden everything."

The door opened. They all tensed until they saw Kinley. Cole walked in behind her.

"Thanks for sticking around. But you two should get back."

Cole nodded. "Dak and King put us on assignment." He grinned.

"Those assholes." But he didn't say it with any heat. He hoped nothing major came up while they were here. Three mercenaries were a tight crew to work with. "All right. Let's make the most of it then. One of us is with Kinley at all times."

"How did it go with our fathers?" Kinley put herself in front of Hendrick, focusing his attention on her.

"About as well as I expected. Your father is pissed. Mine is trying to figure me out." He settled his hands on her hips. He didn't know if she wanted his touch or not, but he did what felt comfortable to him. "Are you okay?"

"Not really."

"Your mothers are passive aggressive as fuck. Everything out of their mouths was some sort of slight disguised as a compliment." Cole pushed off the wall before poking his head out to check in with Archer.

"I'll be fine. It was hard not to slip into old habits. I don't think I was very successful."

"It will get better." Hendrick hoped that wasn't a lie. They needed to settle in as if they intended to stay. Not everyone would be happy with the change and he doubted he'd get his father's trust soon, but he needed the respect and the fear of the men.

"And that's where we come in." Gear rolled his shoulders. "I'm doing rounds."

"Time for bed, pretty girl." It was the only thing left to do, even if he wouldn't be able to join her.

18

KINLEY WISHED HER SKIN WAS A LITTLE THICKER. The veiled insults from their mothers about the wedding bothered her. And she hated that. Hated that they tried to ruin what had been perfect.

The tension in her shoulders was becoming painful. She'd never felt this strained when living under her father's roof. But her life had been different then. She'd been the seemingly obedient daughter. Now she'd gone against him. Being on the wrong side of a crime boss was stressful. She may even be on the wrong side of two.

Hendrick led her through the house. They passed the odd guard stationed at different exits on the main level. Archer followed them and Cole kept a further distance behind.

Kinley held his hand behind his back going up the stairs. They'd updated the house over time, but the structure was similar to her father's. All separate rooms, brown-toned carpets and decorative pieces. And no family pictures on the wall except for perfectly posed portraits. It seemed they had similar upbringings.

He stopped at the end of the long hall, opening the last door. "This was my old room. The room we're in doesn't matter much, but we should make plans to renovate unless my parents leave."

"They won't do that for a long time, will they?"

"No." Hendrick pulled her inside, then said something to Archer on the other side of the door before shutting them in.

"Has this room changed at all?"

Hendrick looked around the room, from one side to the other. "Yes, and no. They gutted it the week after I left, all but the outside walls, only to put it back exactly as it was, but with a guest bathroom. They destroyed my bed, other furniture, anything I left behind."

"I'm sorry." She hadn't formed an attachment to most of her things, but the destruction of everything of hers would hurt.

"Don't be. If I'd wanted to keep anything, I wouldn't have left it here."

"It's not about the stuff. I don't care about any of my stuff left at my parents, but that doesn't mean its destruction wouldn't hurt."

He gave her a sad smile while tucking her hair behind her ear. "I'll wait here while you shower. Cole is bringing up our bags."

Even though he touched her with his hands and with his gaze, his mind was elsewhere. Not that she blamed him. Kinley nodded and stepped away, letting the distance exist.

The bathroom was stocked and bright white. Everything gleamed with an opalescent shine. Stripping, she watched herself in the mirror and tried to see how she'd changed in the past few days. She couldn't see it, because it was still happening. Unfastening the sheaths and holsters on her thighs, she set the weapons on the bathroom counter, except for one knife. She set one knife inside the shower with her. Maybe it was overkill, but she didn't trust anyone here other than the mercenaries.

Hendrick was here for his mission. She needed to focus on hers.

Unsure how secure it was here, she rushed her shower. Wrapped in towels, she poked her head out of the bathroom door. Only Hendrick was there with their suitcases.

He unpacked while she pulled out a small silk pajama set she'd never seen before. Ember and King had walked into the apartment, both with arm loads of bags. The other two women had helped her pack, moving clothes from the bags to the suitcase.

"Where are your weapons?" Hendrick's gaze draped down her body. Kinley looked over her left shoulder, holding up her right hand beside her cheek. The back of the knife she'd kept in the shower sat along her forearm, just like Gear had taught her after their shooting lesson. "Good girl."

Kinley let the towel drop to the floor. "The rest are still in the bathroom."

"Keep them beside you while you sleep."

"Won't you be here?"

"Eventually."

Kinley set the knife down long enough to get dressed. She pulled the towel from her hair. Picking the one up from the floor, she took them to the bathroom. The sounds of Hendrick continuing to unpack followed her.

She strapped one sheath back to her thigh for the knife she held while she finished getting ready for bed. Drying her hair, brushing her teeth. Her routine didn't settle right. Not with a threat looming near. They didn't even know if a threat here existed. This was what they'd wanted, the alliance they made. It just hadn't happened on their terms.

Gathering the rest of her weapons, she went back into the bedroom. Hendrick had finished and was leaning against the closet door.

He watched her, and Kinley slowed her steps. His focus gave her something else to think about. She stood next to the closest side of the bed.

"No. Other side."

"Why?"

"I'm the one closest to the door."

Kinley liked the warmth that hit her chest. There was something about someone who sought to protect her. It sure as hell hadn't been her father. Or Cassius. Not for the same reasons. Couldn't damage a pawn. But she wasn't a pawn to Hendrick.

"One under the bed. One under the mattress. And one on the nightstand." He stalked toward her, watching how she placed each weapon.

She put the gun on the nightstand and two of the knives in the other two places he'd told her.

"Good. Cole, Archer, or Gear will always be outside the door." He cupped her cheek. "Get some rest."

"There's no way I can sleep, Hendrick." Her blood pumped sluggishly, as if frozen between fight or flight. "I don't like this feeling."

"What feeling is that?"

"Powerless, but I know I'm not. I'm stuck, like in a

nightmare where you need to scream, but your voice won't work."

"There's no threat tonight." He settled his hands on her shoulders and turned her around. Digging his thumbs into the muscles of her shoulders, he worked at the tension. "Fuck, Kinley. You're tight."

She chuckled, because there was a better time to say those words.

A sharp sting on the shell of her ear made her gasp. "That too, pretty girl." His breath heated her skin. He followed it with his lips. "On the bed." He held out his hand and helped her up, but pulled her to stay sitting in the middle. Crawling up behind her, he resumed working on her shoulders.

With slow pressure, Hendrick forced her to relax. She shouldn't like how much his hands could do to her. He never said a word while he moved further down her back and back up. She'd barely noticed when he pulled her back to his chest and worked her upper arms.

"I could make some joke about how your hands are lethal, but it wouldn't be a joke."

"No, it wouldn't. But they'll always do your bidding." Hendrick slid his hand to her chest, still massaging, but gentle as he kneaded her breasts under the silk tank top. "What is your bidding now, pretty girl?"

Her only response was a deep breath. She'd relaxed, but didn't think it possible to let go enough for him to take this further. "It's not the right time."

"Yes, it is. You're going to come for me, then you're going to sleep. I'm giving you a chance to tell me how."

Like a whip, his words lashed away her uncertainty. She whimpered and arched, pushing her breasts into his hands.

"You want my hands, Kinley? Or should I tongue fuck you until you pass out?"

"Hendrick." She whispered his name like a plea.

He took one hand out of her shirt and slid it beneath her bottoms. "Or do you want me to decide, pretty girl? Do you want to take what I can give you?"

"Yes. Please."

His finger tapped at her clit. "You will not make a sound."

"Okay," she whispered, and nodded her head against his chest.

"Good girl." Thick fingers slid through her folds. He circled her entrance and set his thumb against her clit to do the same.

Kinley had to pinch her lips between her teeth to keep quiet. Lifting her hips, she tried to impale herself on his teasing fingers.

"Greedy." He pulled them away, and she choked on her own whimper. They sat there frozen. This was all up to him. In that moment, she vowed retribution. But Hendrick always seemed to have full control before she gained any for herself. "Ready?"

"Yes," she growled.

He chuckled low and slammed his fingers into her. He worked her hard and fast, kneading her breast at the same time. "You're soaked for me, Kinley." The sound of his finger fucking was loud in the room without either of them making any more noise than a whisper.

Changing his hold on her breast, he pinched her nipple between his thumb and finger.

"Such a good girl, keeping quiet." He pinched harder, trying to pull a sound from her. Revenge would be sweet.

But she'd forgotten all about where they were, or any threat that might appear. She forgot about the reasons they came here. The only thought in her mind was the climax forcing itself over her body.

"Come, Kinley. Make a mess on my fingers so I can clean them off."

Such filthy words, but they made her orgasm burst free. He curled his fingers and made his thrusts shallow. When he pulled free, he kept them curled as if to scoop her climax from her. Her body still quivered as he lifted his hand to his lips. Her eyes were closed, but she heard him sucking his fingers clean.

He'd sapped the energy from her, leaving her mind numb. Sliding from behind her, he pulled the blanket from beneath her and tucked her in. Warm, wet lips covered hers. His tongue dove inside and ran over hers, feeding her her own taste.

"Sleep, pretty girl."

And she did with her arm outreached to bring him to bed with her.

IT JUST ABOUT killed him to leave her. The way she felt was an exact mirror image of his own. Stuck in a nightmare and unable to defend himself. Every word from his lips whispered. Every hit and strike lacked the power to do damage. Sleuthing wasn't his favourite part of his job. Torture, hiding in the shadows and attacking for the fun of it. Those he enjoyed. Playing a part to gain answers terrified him.

He wondered if he'd snap at some point and torture his own father for the answers.

But there was more involved. Kinley was tied up in this alliance and secrets and him. The original marriage was supposed to be with Shane, and Hendrick couldn't help the instinct tethering that to his death. The timing was too convenient.

He couldn't afford to get lost in Kinley's body this first night. It had been obvious Curry's and Cassius's thoughts on their return, but his own father's hadn't been so clear. Suspicion and glee had taken turns crossing the old man's eyes.

Time—the only weapon available to him for this. They had to make it look like they were here to stay.

Kinley's eyes drifted closed as her arm fell to her side when she tried to reach for him. One forced orgasm wasn't enough to make her pass out, but she'd zapped her own energy holding herself so tense. She'd feared making the wrong move since they'd picked her up before coming here.

He shut her door silently. "No one goes in this room except for us." The us he referred to were any of the mercenaries, but that went without explaining. Archer was new to the group, but he'd settled in well.

"Of course. She asleep?" He lifted an eyebrow.

"Yes."

"You should get some, too." The man moved to stand like a fucking tank, blocking the entire door.

"I will at some point. We all will." Hendrick slapped Archer on the shoulder. "I'll be in the office with Hudson."

Archer started to speak, but Hendrick cut him off.

"I trust him explicitly. He was the closest thing to another brother we had. He was as much Shane's best friend as he was his second in command. That position is his."

"Be careful." His warning made Hendrick pause.

"Why?"

"Your father demoted him for a reason. If the point is to gain his trust, replacing everything to the way your brother had won't do you any good."

"Or the point is to piss him off enough to make him snap."

Archer scoffed. "Only a crazy man like you would choose that route."

Hendrick gave a single finger salute and left, but a grin still played at his lips. He liked the man he was. He hadn't apologized for it growing up and hadn't since.

Cole stationed himself at the bottom of the stairs, having a staring contest with his father's guard. Every twitch from Cole made the other man flinch. Hendrick would replace all of his father's men. Until then, having Cole and Archer around would be a good thing.

Hudson waited for him outside the office. Hendrick gestured for him to join him. As soon as the door closed, Hudson pointed at him. "You have some explaining to do."

"I didn't want to tell you before we came." He shook his head and leaned against the front of the massive desk.

"In case I gave it away?" Hurt pinched Hudson's tone.

"You wouldn't have." Hendrick sighed. He should have given Hudson a heads up.

"You didn't want to do it." The man understood too much. The three of them grew up together. He hadn't exaggerated when he'd told Archer Hudson was like another brother.

"No. But this is the only way to get the truth."

"It isn't the only way." Hudson moved to the back corner of the room. "I've heard you have an effective option you use all the time." Lifting his leg, he hit one of the floorboards with his heel. The wood popped up for him to catch.

"As little as I care about my father, torturing him doesn't do any good in the end. Shane cared about what he'd built here." Hendrick frowned as Hudson bent to pull something out of the floor.

"So, you're back for Shane's legacy?" He pulled out a glass bottle half full with Shane's favourite blended whiskey. "His secret stash."

Hendrick pushed back tears. "I'm not staying. But everything he did shouldn't crumble."

"I agree."

"So tell me everything I don't already know."

Hudson poured two glasses and passed one to Hendrick. The scent forced his eyes closed. The only time he'd drank this with Shane had been when they'd meet in a bar. Shane would order the bottle, they'd both drink two glasses, then he'd tell the bartender to give the rest away. Ladies first, of course.

Realizing Hudson stayed silent, Hendrick lifted his glass. "To Shane."

"To Shane," Hudson repeated, his voice as torn as Hendrick's. They downed the glasses and poured a second while Hudson started talking about Shane and the business, most he already knew. Hendrick focused on every word. And with each one, he grew more proud of the man his younger brother had been.

KINLEY STIRRED WHEN a heavy body moved the bed. She gasped and reached for the knife under the mattress. A large hand grabbed her wrist.

"Shh. It's me." Hendrick pulled her arm back and tucked her against his chest.

Her heart still pounded from the scare. She'd been so sound asleep since he'd left, it terrified her.

"I told you. You're safe for tonight."

"You don't know that." She sighed, because at least with him next to her, she was safe. At least her body told her she was. "What time is it?"

"Five."

"You've been up all night."

He nodded against the pillow and pulled her tighter. She'd slept more than enough. It was his turn.

"Is someone outside the door?" He seemed ready to sleep, and she doubted he'd allow them to be unguarded during that time.

"Gear."

"Good. Now, hush." This was her small taste of revenge. Kinley wiggled down the bed. She intended to give him the pleasure he'd given her.

"What do you think you're doing?" He held the blankets up out of her way.

"If I have to explain, then you aren't as smart as I thought you were." She wrapped her hand around his already hard cock.

"Kinley."

"Don't make a sound." She nipped at his stomach, then traced one side of the V downward with her tongue. Thankfully, he'd stripped before coming to bed.

She held his cock out for herself and swirled her tongue around the head. His taste was clean and the head of his cock was still a little damp from a shower.

He groaned.

"Shh."

He chuckled, and it was the first free laugh she'd heard since their wedding night.

Kinley opened and relaxed her throat. She worked him to the back, driving their need high from the start. His cock twitched each time she swiped her tongue along the underside.

Before Hendrick, sucking a cock had been prominent in all her fantasies, but she'd never been sure if the reality would live up to what she'd imagined. But Hendrick was like a drug for her. She popped off and looked up at him. The blankets sat around her shoulders. Licking her lips, she held his gaze.

"Take me deep, pretty girl." His voice was harsh, raw.

Kinley set herself up to do just that. His fingers speared into her hair and moved with her, letting her set the pace. But only until his cock expanded, and she tasted the first drop on her tongue.

"Drink it down." He thrust his hips forward and pulled her onto his cock until he settled down her throat. Kinley struggled to breathe through her nose, tears leaking from her eyes.

Hendrick came, his body rumbling with whatever growl he let loose. Kinley's ears were ringing and her core clenched. But this wasn't about her right now.

He coated her throat and flooded her mouth. Pulling her head back, he looked down at her and watched her swallow. He used his thumb to wipe away the wetness on her cheeks. Moving herself back up the bed.

"Your turn to rest." She kissed him and slipped from the bed, but he grabbed her hand before she got out of reach.

"Not yet. Show me your cunt."

"What?"

"You heard me, pretty girl. I want to see what sucking me off did to you. Put your foot on the bed."

Because she needed release and had intended to go to the bathroom to take care of it herself while he slept, she obeyed. He let go of her hand and she lifted her foot, setting her knee wide so he could see everything.

"Put some on your fingers and feed it to me."

Kinley blinked. The request was so dirty in his raspy, exhausted voice. But the Hendrick she'd gotten to know over the past few days was still there in his eyes.

"Now."

Sliding her fingers down her body, she moved them to her entrance. She had to hold her breath to keep herself from making any noise. When she pulled her hand back up, Hendrick grabbed her wrist and pulled her forward to suck on her fingers.

"Come, Kinley. Let me watch you."

Kinley moved back into position and set her fingers on her clit, desperate to explode. She tightened the muscles in her legs and worked the over sensitive nerves.

"I love that sucking my cock does this to you. It could be the most excruciating torture."

Kinley threw her head back, a whisper of a breath escaping her lungs. He would do exactly as he said.

Withhold her release as torture and all he'd have to do to get her there is fuck her mouth.

"Tilt your hips. I want to see it all."

She angled herself and instantly exploded. Moving her fingers up ever so slightly, she moved with the rhythm of her body to extend the pleasure as long as possible.

"My pretty girl." Hendrick reached out and gripped her ankle before she backed away. "Don't leave the room."

"I won't. Just the bathroom."

He nodded and rolled onto his back, closing his eyes. She feared he had enraptured her. Which would only make their job harder. They both had goals and then needed to go their separate ways. He'd promised her freedom.

19

HENDRICK HAD LISTENED to Kinley shower, then dig through her suitcases while he slept. He didn't allow his body to fall into a deep sleep, but pulled on practice to put himself at a level of consciousness that gave him rest.

Two hours later, he forced himself awake.

"That wasn't long." Kinley closed the open suitcase and pushed it against the wall inside the closet.

"That's all I have time for right now. I'll get more tonight." And there was still more for him and Hudson to go through. Since his father had banned Hudson from the house since Shane died, he couldn't tell Hendrick anything current. Only how Shane had managed people and who they were. The first thing Hendrick needed to do was thin out his father's guards, replacing some of them with Shane's, now his.

His mind was already on the upcoming meetings as he stood and stalked into the closet, passing Kinley. He eyed his clothes, knowing what his father would say the moment he walked down the stairs. A man in his position wore suits.

He pulled on jeans and a T-shirt, adding his weapons to their customary places. Hiding them wasn't necessary this time, but he always had some hidden.

"What's my role here?" Kinley sat on the end of the bed, her legs crossed and her palms holding her weight. She wore another dress. Glancing at the nightstand, he noticed the holsters and sheaths were missing.

Hendrick quirked a brow at her legs. Kinley pulled the hem of the dress up just enough for him to catch sight of the leather strapped to her thighs. "Good girl."

"I don't want to be locked away in a bedroom."

"You won't. You are free to do whatever you want. Whatever you think is your job as the wife of a crime boss."

She blinked at him.

"As long as you have one of the mercenaries with you, you are free to go anywhere inside the house. We'll visit your parents in a few days."

"Do I try to talk to your mother?"

Hendrick paused while fastening his belt. "Yeah. That's a good idea. If nothing else, you won't be bored. Even extend an invitation to only your mother if you want."

She curled her nose and shook her head. "I've had enough of her backhanded compliments last night."

"I'm busy all day, but I'll be in the office for most of it. You don't need permission to walk in. It doesn't matter who says otherwise. If you need me, you come find me."

"I will."

His first meeting was with the other men closest to

Shane. He wanted to shore up those defenses before moving people around. Hendrick placed a quick kiss on Kinley's forehead and left. Gear still waited outside the door. "You're with Kinley for the morning."

Gear nodded and held the door open for Kinley. Hendrick had already turned away and darted down the stairs. Hudson and Archer waited for him at the bottom.

"Let's get this over with."

His father sat at the dining table at the head seat. Hendrick held back his laugh at the pompous move. Whatever made his father feel better about himself. His mother sat on his right, sipping coffee from a tiny, flower-painted cup. They set two other places across from her.

"Good morning, son."

Hendrick only raised his brow and continued toward the office.

"Take time for breakfast." Condescension coated his aged voice. "There's no need to rush into duties you know nothing about." He flicked the newspaper he read, dropping his eyes to the words rather than keeping them on Hendrick. It was a power move. A way to make him feel insignificant. At least, that's how it had made him feel as a child.

But Hendrick needed his father to gain at least some trust in him. He had to play along for now. He leaned toward Hudson. "Tell them to wait."

Hudson nodded and left toward the office. His father frowned. "Where is he going?"

"Doing his job."

"I already have men placed in that position. Astin here is more than happy to stand at your shoulder." He

hiked his thumb at a man standing several feet
behind him.

Hendrick ignored him and poured himself coffee,
taking the seat beside his father..

"Where's your wife?" His mother tilted her head, her
cup clinked lightly against the small saucer.

"I'm right here." Kinley's voice rang with confidence.
The small smile on her lips wasn't only friendly, but
held her own threat. She walked in, owning the room as
much as Hendrick had done the night before.

Fucking gorgeous.

She took a seat next to him. "Good morning," she
chimed and started dishing up breakfast onto the
waiting plate. Turning her smile toward Hendrick, she
placed food on the empty plate in front of him.

"Kinley, dear. I thought I could give you a tour of the
house and introduce you to the staff this morning."

"That would be lovely, Mrs. Pierce."

"Please. Call me Charlotte."

"Kinley has a meeting at eleven this morning." Gear
grabbed a pastry off one tray and sat at the other end of
the table, biting into the flaky crust. Crumbs spilled
over the table. Both of his parents looked disgusted,
making it all the better.

Hendrick didn't know what meeting Gear referred
to, and he didn't think Kinley did either, but she didn't
miss a beat.

"Yes. There's enough time before then to have a
tour."

"Wonderful," his mother said with a tight smile.

"It's been a long time since you've been gone, Kit. I
doubt you remember all the players." The players were
the dealers and buyers.

"I know more about the players than you." He'd been more immersed in this world than ever before by working for King and Dak. They knew the major names in the city. And the not so major names.

His father scoffed and set his paper down. "I'd like to host a party. A chance to re-introduce you. Once everyone is used to your face, I'll step back again and hand everything over."

"Whatever you want to do. But I'm not taking over when people are comfortable with my face. I'm taking over now." Hendrick stood, leaving the food untouched. Hudson waited in the doorway of the office.

"Kit." His father's voice boomed like talking to a teenager.

Hendrick paused and looked over his shoulder. "I have meetings. I'll be in the office for the day. Why don't you come in later and we discuss your plans for a party? You're right. I should start a relationship of my own with the people I'll be dealing with."

He watched his father's face turn a satisfying red, then left.

KINLEY PREFERRED THE deadly man who'd threatened to choke her in his pain than the lifeless man that walked out of the bedroom that morning.

It wasn't as if she had known what to expect out of their marriage. They'd had a few days of scorching sex, hard training, and a beautiful wedding. This was territory neither of them were familiar with. But she hadn't expected the way he'd closed off from her the moment he woke.

There wasn't anything for her to do about it now. She had to follow along as if she expected his behaviour. She refused to let any of them believe he'd forced her into this. Not knowing how long they'd be here, Kinley wanted at least some authority. Enough to give her the freedom to say or do as she pleased.

She finished eating with Hendrick's parents. Gear's presence at the table created enough awkwardness to keep the older couple from asking her questions. What they found awkward and disturbing, Kinley found comforting.

"A tour of the house before a tour of the grounds, yes?"

"Sounds like a great plan." Kinley stood and followed Charlotte toward the kitchen. Gear scraped his chair across the floor as he stood. The sound was loud enough to make them all pause. Charlotte curled her nose before straightening into a smile.

"It's just a kitchen, young man. Your presence isn't needed."

Gear ignored her and stood behind Kinley.

"Do you do all the cooking, Charlotte, or do you have a hired chef?" Kinley changed the subject.

"I cook unless we're hosting an event. I have those catered. We've had a chef on staff in the past. But I missed the kitchen too much to keep them." Something about the different embellishments had Kinley thinking that wasn't the real reason. She'd bet it had been a drop in income that put Hendrick's mother back in the kitchen.

Kinley didn't give Charlotte a chance to direct any conversation. With each room they entered, Kinley asked questions of her own, drawing on how her own household had run. By the time eleven rolled around and Gear cleared his throat, Charlotte looked confused.

"Oh, well. Uh, we'll pick up where we left off this afternoon." She stuttered out her farewell.

"Of course." Kinley looked to Gear, and he gestured toward the stairs.

He closed them in the bedroom. "You're good at this."

Kinley let out a long breath. She might be good at it, but it was exhausting staying one step ahead of someone. "What meeting do I have?"

"With me."

Kinley narrowed her eyes.

"We're taking time each day to train. Until we can leave the house, we'll do it here." He pointed to the floor of the bedroom.

"Won't people think we're having an affair right under Hendrick's nose?"

Gear shrugged. "That's a problem for him to handle."

Kinley laughed, covering it with her fingers. "Did he ask you to do this?"

"No. It's become an unwritten rule that you'll all go through the same training as us."

"*You'll all*? Who does that entail?"

"You, Ember, Sophie, and any other woman one of us brings home." He made it sound like they were all children bringing home stray kittens, but there was the affection glinting in his eyes as when he'd talked to Nana Marie. Gear liked the strays, even if he wouldn't admit it.

He gave her time to change out of the dress, then worked her hard for the next two hours. She was heaving and sweating by the end, but held close the feeling of achievement.

"Cole will be outside when you're done showering. He'll be here to switch with me in five minutes."

"Okay." And she laughed as she walked toward the bathroom to shower. People really would think they were having an affair. She wasn't sure what anyone would have heard while they sparred and then coming out of the bedroom freshly showered. The question was, did she warn Hendrick of the potential problem or let it catch him by surprise?

She made it quick and dressed back in the same dress and blow dried her hair to flow down her back. It lacked the waves she'd put into it that morning, but Kinley decided she didn't care about what any of them thought.

When she opened the bedroom door, Cole turned and stepped back. "Did you have fun with Gear?"

"I did."

"When do I get a turn?"

Kinley laughed, holding a hand to her stomach. Cole seemed to catch onto her thoughts.

"I can't wait."

Clearing her throat, she started walking toward the stairs. "I believe my mother-in-law is waiting for me."

"She is. And has been since you left her. She hasn't left the bottom of the stairs."

The idea of the rumour she was having an affair wasn't so funny anymore.

"Don't get scared now." Cole ushered her forward. He was right. Taking a moment for a full breath, she made her way down the stairs.

"I hope you didn't wait all this time for my meeting to finish."

Charlotte took several steps back. "You're playing a dangerous game."

"I'm no good at games. I tend not to play them. Where were we?" Kinley blinked at the older woman, waiting to see what she'd say next. She seemed to think better of questioning Kinley again and motioned them toward the glass doors in the living room.

"The grounds."

Kinley followed as a dutiful daughter-in-law would.

After leading the rest of the day with Charlotte, controlling every turn of the conversation, Kinley was even more exhausted than she'd been before sparring with Gear. But she helped Charlotte make dinner.

With Cole hovering, and then Archer, Charlotte didn't keep up anymore conversation while they cooked. At least there was wine while they worked. The alcohol helped calm her.

She hadn't had the same tense nerves as the night before. Putting herself in a position of power had settled them for the time being.

Hendrick emerged from the office, rolling his neck back and forth, with Hudson in tow. She hoped he'd talk to her when they went to bed tonight. Kinley craved the information of how things worked here.

Cassius might have only given her what he'd wanted her to know, but Kinley enjoyed working through the business and issues with the employees in her mind. She wanted to do that with Hendrick.

Having toured with his mother, it had been obvious she had a similar role to her own mother. A pretty face and a housewife. No mind of her own. Kinley didn't want that for her time here.

———

HE'D SCARED OVER half of the men that had walked into the office on sight. After an hour, he'd already gone through all the men Hudson guaranteed were still loyal to Shane. And at that point, he'd pulled out his knives to play with. The first thing he was doing in the morning was putting a target board in the office.

His mother's chicken and dumplings drew him from the office with the memories the scent invoked. Memories of a time when he and Shane had been too young to see the future forced upon them. Two little boys who looked up to their mother for all that she could give them. A time when she had.

Kinley sipped from a glass of red wine before setting the glass aside to pull rolls from the oven. His mother had never made homemade rolls or bread before. But apparently his wife could.

His breath caught when she turned and captured his gaze. Cole slid in behind her and reached for the steaming rolls. Kinley whirled on him, slapping his arm. She froze as if realizing what she'd done.

His mother gasped, pulling Kinley away from Cole.

"What the fuck?" Cole snapped, staring at the women. He wasn't mad at Kinley, Hendrick knew that, but it appeared that way to his mother. She set Kinley beside her and lifted her chin at Cole.

"She's learning. But please leave the kitchen until we are done cooking. Simon likes things to look a certain way."

Another memory filtered its way into his mind. His father towering over his mother, berating her for the appearance of dinner. He and Shane had just looked at the food, not understanding. They'd shrugged and stayed quiet so their father didn't turn his anger on them.

"I don't give a fuck how the food looks." Hendrick moved in on the other side of Cole and stole a roll for himself. Cole's was gone, having shoved it in his mouth after cursing at the women. "Is dinner ready?"

"Not yet. We need to serve it to the table."

"No, you don't." The smells left him ravenous, and he wasn't about to wait for the sight of perfection.

"Kit. No." Panic rushed through his mother as she physically tried to remove him from the kitchen. He wondered if things had gotten worse for her over the years. Shane had never mentioned it. It's possible there'd only been changes since Shane's death.

Hendrick sighed and instead of reaching for the plates and bowls, he reached for the serving dishes. Setting them on the counter, he spread his hands to allow his mother to do as she wished.

She still seemed flustered as she slid the rolls onto a cooling rack as they were, rather than separating them. Kinley stepped back for all of it, frowning as hard as Cole beside her. She didn't notice as they all backed from the kitchen. Once she placed the food in the serving dishes and covered them , Kinley moved in beside her to help carry it all to the table.

Hendrick and Cole gathered the plates, bowls, and silverware. His mother's surprise stopped her as she went back to the kitchen. He'd never seen this side of her. Or had, but not the effect on her.

Hudson hovered in the dining room. Hendrick raised a brow in question and nodded at his mother, hoping the other man understood what he was asking.

He frowned as hard as the rest of them and shook his head. This urgency was new. Hendrick needed to keep an eye on his father. Pushing him away today had felt good, but may not have been the best decision overall.

Seeing more of her back than her affection, Hendrick held little love for his mother, but he wouldn't have her treated as it seemed she was. Shane wouldn't have stood for it either if he'd known.

His father walked into the dining room when they set the last dish on the table as if he'd choreographed the whole scene. His strut held him high like a fucking king. Before the old man took the seat at the head of the table again, Hendrick held out Kinley's chair for her, then took his.

"That was *cute* last night, Kit. Quit pushing your luck."

"I've been told I have an adorable appeal." He uncovered the dish closest to him and offered it to Kinley first. Cole coughed, covering the *bullshit* with his fist.

As they all started to eat, his father had no choice but to take a seat at the other end of the table. His mother didn't sit until he did.

"It's a shame you were so busy today, Kit. Tomorrow will be different." Hendrick let his father prattle on about his plans for the party he wanted to host. As much as it grated, he'd stick closer to his father for the next few days. He'd gotten what he could out of all the men on the grounds today. Hudson had the new rotation and positions for each. In fact, Hendrick had told him to create it himself, spreading the men he trusted out from the house to the end of the grounds. They'd have eyes at all stations.

"I'll plan the menu for this Friday." His mother broke his concentration. A party on Friday with all the players.

"We'll extend the invitations tomorrow." His father pointed his fork at Hendrick.

"Sure. A party sounds fun." Glancing back at Hudson, he exchanged a look. Hudson would extend invites to anyone that Shane dealt with without their father.

"Kinley. I know your mother hosted similar parties. I'm sure you know what to do for this."

Kinley smiled down the table. "I'm more than capable. I'd be happy to help."

They finished eating with veiled threats passing in smiles around the table. It was fucking irritating and exhausting.

"Time for bed, wife." Hendrick took Kinley's hand and pulled her from the table.

"We haven't had dessert or drinks. It's only eight." His mother gripped the table in a panic.

Hendrick motioned for Archer to come over. "Watch my parents tonight." Then, raising his voice, he turned back to his mother. "Dinner was delicious. But I'm more than full enough to skip dessert and drinks."

Gear and Cole followed them to the stairs. Cole remained at the bottom and Gear stayed outside the bedroom.

Kinley sighed and flopped onto the bed. "That was exhausting."

"Very."

She closed her eyes with a sigh while Hendrick took a shower. By the time he returned to the bedroom to lose himself in Kinley's body, she was fast asleep with her face smooshed into the pillow.

20

A FORMAL INVITATION ARRIVED FOR DINNER.
Kinley recognized her mother's handwriting on new
stationary. Two days passed of only seeing Hendrick in
passing or when they went to bed and one or the other
of them was asleep in seconds, drained.

Once, she'd woken to Hendrick's tongue on her clit.
They'd both frantically chased pleasure without a
single word. And that had left her more emotionally
raw than any time before. Even in the dark, his eyes
penetrated hers. Piercing heat sparked a passion for
him in her heart. But Hendrick wasn't what needed to
be in her sights.

Kinley turned the invitation over and over at the
table. Hendrick sat there grudgingly, like every morning, all to appease his father. That first day, he'd kept his
distance, but since, he'd tagged along with his father to
get closer, to gain trust.

We wish for Kit and Kinley to attend dinner this evening.
That was all it said. So many things could hide in those
words.

Congratulations on your marriage. Let's celebrate.
We need to discuss your marriage.
Here's some bait. Come step into my trap.

Kinley didn't trust them, but she'd never get her money back if they didn't find out what he'd done with it.

Looking up from the fancy scrawl, she met Hendrick's gaze as he sipped coffee. He nodded.

Her training session a few hours later consisted of counter attacks for anything her father might try. If they had an opportunity to get her money tonight, they would, but the only priority was finding out where it was and how to access it.

Both Cole and Gear worked with her, going through moves to break someone's hold and practiced reaching for her weapons.

Charlotte stood, disapproving, at the bottom of the stairs. The rumours of an affair spread. Hendrick laughed every single one off, then claimed her mouth in a brutal kiss that left her dizzy for everyone to see.

Choosing an outfit for this dinner stressed her out. Hendrick had told her she didn't need to hide her weapons, or hide her thoughts. But she just didn't know how to handle her father anymore. She'd defied him in the biggest way possible. There'd be no way to regain trust with him. She might as well walk in there with her true soul on display.

The information about her money was key and he may be more cautious about letting information slip if she walked in there like she was Hendrick's equal. One last time. One last dinner in that house pretending to be the amiable daughter. Only to get what she wanted and then her father would see the real daughter he'd r*aised*.

Settling on a dress similar to the red one she'd worn when they'd first arrived, Kinley pulled it up her body so as not to mess with her hair or make-up. She'd added a harsher red to her lips rather than the neutral colours that helped her blend in, and her hair was in an updo to keep it out of her face and out of her way if the environment of the night became anything but dinner.

She zipped the back of the dress as far as she could up her back. A click behind her had her whirling toward the door.

Hendrick strolled in, dressed in his usual. And she loved him even more for being unapologetically him.

She gasped and blinked as he strolled across the room. She loved him.

He nudged her shoulder for her to give him her back, allowing her to breathe through her revelation without him seeing it. Rough knuckles brushed her skin as he dragged the zipper all the way up. She shivered as his lips skimmed the column of her neck.

"You ready?"

"As I'll ever be." There was no more preparation to do. "Gear and Cole went over everything. Stay close, information first. Don't let any of them get me alone."

"Good girl." He nipped her ear, and she tilted her head to give him whatever access he wanted. She was powerless with him now. The moments of pretending she was still mad at him weren't worth it. There were bigger enemies under their nose than fearing the emotions between them. And Hendrick seemed to let go of whatever had spooked him that first night together.

He slid his hands down her body until he reached the hem of her dress. Kinley held her breath, not daring

SARAH URQUHART

to do anything to stop him. With so much distance since they'd arrived, she was dying for anything he could give her.

His fingers trailed up her thighs, stopping at the weapons strapped there. He checked the tightness before moving past them.

"You should breathe, pretty girl."

Kinley let the air out in a whoosh, but held in the next pull the moment his fingers tapped against her clit.

"All mine, Kinley." He stroked over the hood. "I won't let anything happen to you."

It was an impossible promise. There were too many unknowns, but he'd do everything he could and more.

A knock on the door stopped the steady circle he'd started around the sensitive bud. He sighed and licked her pulse at the base of her neck. Letting her skirt fall, he took her hand and led her to the door.

Gear stood on the other side, decked out as usual except for his chain hanging over his shoulder. But he had it on him somewhere and Kinley looked forward to when it made an appearance.

The drive was similar to the drive to Hendrick's father's. Silent, foreboding, but Kinley had a new perspective of herself. Everything looked so familiar. Every guard was in the same place along the driveway and at the front of the house. It seemed odd seeing the same shrubs and flowers blooming, every lawn decoration in the exact same place despite only being gone for days. She'd had the experiences of a lifetime in those days. A lifetime should have passed here, too.

No one tried to stop them as they parked and got out of the SUV. Gear stepped out of the back seat and held his hand back for her. Hendrick and Archer got out of the front. They'd left Cole behind at the house with Hudson.

The doors swung open with a single word from the man standing in front of them. It was a fucking show. She'd seen her father do it before with someone he was trying to impress. Or to impress upon someone his importance.

He stood with his arm around her mother's waist in the foyer. His smile was like a sneer in sheep's clothing. Kinley had never been on this side of her father's ire before, and she hated the sickening feeling that coiled in her veins.

"Wonderful to see you again. Daughter."

ALL OF HENDRICK'S senses fired the moment they walked in the door. A trap lingered in the air. Kinley's father had a smirk on his face that reeked of deception.

Hendrick skated his hand up Kinley's spine and settled it at the base of her neck, his fingers draping over her shoulder. It was a warning and one that didn't go unnoticed. Curry's smirk twitched. Cassius stood behind the couple, his shoulders tensing.

And he didn't miss what Kinley's body did under his touch. Instead of shying away from the control, she leaned into it.

His crazy crawled under his skin. The atmosphere was like a room full of flammable gases and Hendrick was the match. Kinley was the catalyst. The words had escaped earlier, and they did two things to him. Calmed him and made him as insane as ever, because he would do anything for this woman.

Putting her in danger now made Hendrick question this entire plan. But to abandon it would be to abandon Shane. His entire body was at war.

"Drinks first, shall we?" Curry swung an arm toward his left. A sunken living room glowed with an already roaring fire. An unnecessary fire considering the season. Curry liked the show, the appearance of being important.

A drink cart sat behind one of the two couches, five drinks already poured. Hendrick kept a hold of Kinley as they followed. Gear and Archer kept pace behind them.

Curry stopped, his hand up flat. "Your dogs can stay at the door."

"They follow us or we leave." Kinley snapped before Hendrick could answer. Her father laughed. Her mother had wide eyes, and a smile wavered on her lips as if she was unsure what reaction she was supposed to have.

"Your shoes are too big for you, Kinley. I'm sure your husband understands. You will soon, too. They wait at the door."

"You heard my wife, Curry. They follow or we leave."

The older man puffed his chest. Cassius changed positions to put himself opposite Gear and Archer. Kinley's mother passed the drinks as they sat, then hovered at the cart.

The only ones left without drinks were Gear and Archer, who stood at different positions. One beside the couch they sat on and one behind it.

"Sit down, Luann. They aren't thirsty."

Luann perched on the edge of the coach next to

Curry. Knees together primly, and her drink almost floating between her fingers.

"Sudden career change, Kit. Or Hendrick. What am I supposed to call you?"

"That depends on the conversation we're having."

"How about the conversation where I convince you to divorce my daughter and hand her over to me?"

"That conversation won't end the way you hope." Hendrick had to fight the urge to pull Kinley closer to him. Instead, he stayed where he was, relaxed against the overly large cushions.

"We'll see. The adjustment must be difficult for you. Assassin to businessman in a day." Curry was playing to a script. And they had no choice but to play along.

"Not as difficult as you'd think." Because he'd been going along with whatever Hudson suggested. The real boss behind his father's business the past several days had been Hudson. And who better than to carry on Shane's legacy? "Tell me about your business, Curry?"

His eyes narrowed. "Genius, really. Everyone needs a secure place to conduct their unsavory business. I saw a hole in the market and I filled it."

"Genius." Hendrick echoed dryly enough he needed to drain his glass. Even his own father wasn't this arrogant.

Curry took that as an invitation to give tips on how to manage employees. He talked for a solid fifteen minutes like he was a king.

At the first lull, Kinley's mother spoke to her daughter. "Interesting dress, Kinley. It..." she paused. "It has a delicate frame to it."

Hendrick tilted his head to regard his wife when she didn't bother to answer. Kinley blinked at her mother.

The dress Kinley wore was the complete opposite of the skin tight skirt and blouse. Hendrick would rather his wife in a matching outfit to his, weapons and all. But they may not have made it in the door.

"Another drink, He... Ki..." her mother stalled, her hand still reaching for his empty glass while she tried to figure out what to call.

"Please." Hendrick passed her the glass. Kinley had barely touched hers.

"It's a desired business I've built here."

"Is that so?" Hendrick hadn't been prepared for the amount of bragging. He'd been prepared for an attack on himself and an instant attempt at taking Kinley.

"It is. I've had multiple offers to buy it over the years. Ever since Kinley was born, and we weren't able to have another child." Because in his mind, he'd needed a son.

"Why have you never considered selling?"

"This is mine and if I can't pass it down to Kinley, I intended to pass it to the next best thing. Her husband."

Hendrick didn't miss the past tense. Curry didn't plan on following through with the alliance and the contract. Hendrick didn't give a shit what he did with his business. "I think that's an emotional decision. Were none of those offers worth considering?"

"People like Sterne, Kipling, and Wilder don't have the amount of money this business is worth to buy it, let alone the capabilities. This is all mine. It can't be learned anywhere else."

Hendrick blinked and held his expression frozen. He tried not to look at Kinley, asking silently if her father had always been this out to lunch.

"Even you, as a mercenary, aren't capable of managing this."

"I thought that was what the apprenticeship in the contract was for?"

Curry gave a tight smile.

"Have any of those making offers turned persistent?"

"Sabotage doesn't scare me."

"Sabotage?" Kinley straightened, leaning forward. "What sabotage?" She drew her father's attention, but he changed. The arrogance darkened into anger.

"Cassius told me what happened when he first found you two."

"I'm sure he did. What sabotage?" Kinley waved her hand in a circle, telling him to answer her.

"I'm disappointed in you, Kinley. You knew you shouldn't have gone against Cassius then."

"I didn't want to be traded in a transaction." By the end of her words, Kinley had clenched her teeth.

Curry laughed. "Yet, here you are. Seems you're right where you're supposed to be."

"Then why do you want the divorce?" Agitation spiked Kinley's tone. The wine in her glass moved, as if she jerked while tightening her grip.

"Because you weren't supposed to marry a mercenary." Curry's eyes dropped onto Hendrick.

"I don't understand what people have against us." Hendrick shook his head, then leaned it back to look at Archer. "Do you?"

Archer only smirked, knowing he didn't need to answer.

"We had a deal. I return and you give me my money back. Where is it?"

"A place that is and always has been out of your reach." Curry slid his attention to Hendrick. "The contract is null and void. Just as your marriage will be the moment you sign the divorce papers." He signaled with a finger over his shoulder, and one guard pulled a manila envelope from behind his back and set it down on the coffee table between them. How the man had them drawn in their stead, Hendrick didn't know. And he didn't care.

"I'm not signing any divorce papers." Now he allowed his body to tense and ready itself for a fight. He felt the change in the air as the bodies hiding toward the back made themselves known. The words had been a cue from Curry. The man knew Hendrick wouldn't sign them.

Luann adjusted in her seat for the first time, angling herself away from her husband. Curry smiled at Kinley like he just watched the trap spring on a mouse. "Sign the papers, Kinley. And I'll consider giving you your money back."

"*Consider* giving it back?"

Curry waited with the same look on his face.

"I'm not signing the papers."

Curry made another signal over his shoulder. "You're both signing." Four men, one in each corner of the room, drew their guns and pointed them not only at Hendrick, but at Kinley, too.

The man was a fucking idiot and couldn't see three feet in front of his own face.

Hendrick had thought the biggest danger would come from his own father. He hadn't expected the blind hostility that put Kinley in danger.

ADRENALINE PUMPED. TWO of them pointed their guns at her and the other two pointed theirs at Hendrick. Gear and Archer set themselves into defensive positions, weapons drawn, but there were too many places they needed to direct their attention. Gear's chain hung in a loose grip from his hands, and Archer's gun pointed at the closest target.

And Cassius only stepped closer to Kinley, his sights set on her. He was going to grab her. She felt his grip through his gaze.

The entire dinner invitation had been a trap.

Hendrick leaned toward her, his lips brushing her ear. "Stay calm. You can do this." He squeezed her wrist and stood, pulling her with him. His full height was powerful, even against the weapons pointed at him. He stood between her and Cassius.

"I expected more time to pass until someone grew balls enough to make threats against some of King's mercenaries."

"You're outnumbered and out-gunned. Sit back down. Kinley. Be smart. Step away from your soon to be ex-husband or you'll soon be a widow."

"You know what to do, pretty girl." His hand that hung between them nudged her in the direction of the guard past her mother's shoulder. Their bodies blocked the slight movement. For all her father knew, Hendrick told her to do what she needed to survive.

Kinley didn't answer her father, but tried to keep her body from giving away their plan.

"Curry, I think you'll find you're the one out-gunned." Hendrick lunged toward Cassius, setting them all in motion.

Kinley watched Cassius fall forward, his face

smashing on the glass coffee table. Gear's chain sounded off behind her and shots popped off.

She tucked and rolled away from Hendrick and past the other couch, pulling knives from her thigh as she stood. She tried not to think about what she was about to do. Her only aim was to disable the guy in front of her with a gun.

The gun wavered. He didn't know where he should point it. Her father hadn't ordered them to shoot her. Or she'd already have a bullet wound.

As she stood, she struck his inner elbow with the back of one knife, collapsing the arm that held the gun. Swiping up with the other knife, Kinley sliced the tendon at his shoulder. The gun fell to the floor with a clang.

He bent forward enough to elbow him in the temple, disorienting him enough to assess the rest of the room, but she didn't turn her back on him. Instead, she stepped back and to the side.

Gear dropped a potentially dead body at his feet and Archer was in a physical battle with the one that had been closest to him, both their guns out of their hands.

Cassius was coming to, blinking heavily, and pushing himself up from the floor. Hendrick disarmed the fourth and grinned while spinning knives.

Whipping his arm backward, he slung a small blade into Cassius's arm without turning around.

Kinley's mother huddled herself into a ball on the floor between the couch and coffee table. A mottled red face replaced her father's arrogance. He scrambled toward Cassius, pulling the blade from his arm.

His arm reaching out toward a discarded gun launched Kinley into motion.

Hendrick had only given her one knife throwing lesson. And she needed to sink it into her father. In a matter of seconds, Kinley had to decide how much she cared for her father. A father that she had thought cared for her in some way of his own. And when she'd been a little girl, she'd loved him like any child. But she wasn't sure when that love died.

Throwing the knife, and hoping she did it correctly, she held her breath while it flew through the air. It didn't stick, but sliced his shoulder.

It was enough to get Hendrick's attention and bring Gear closer to help. Hendrick glanced over his shoulder, then put his energy into one motion that finished the guy in front of him with a knife in the gut.

Kinley hated that she flinched. She looked away while the man fell.

Hendrick stepped around Cassius and her father on the floor. "I'd *love* nothing more than to stay and have more fun. But we'll leave you to clean up your mess. It's a shame we didn't get to eat dinner. Maybe next time." He wrapped his arm around Kinley's waist and pulled her along with him, backing her to the door while she met her father's gaze. Then Cassius's. Then her mother's. The woman turned away from her daughter and crawled to her husband.

She'd made her bed and kept it.

Kinley still gripped her knives, and she noticed they all had a firm handle on theirs as they made their way to the front door, ready for another attack as they left.

Coldness seeped into her skin, and they moved out of the door and down the driveway in a blur. The night air was sharp against her, and a harsh contrast to Hendrick's touch. It was her only focus.

Hendrick didn't let her go until she was in the back of the SUV. This time, Gear took the front seat and Hendrick sat in the back with her.

"You did good, pretty girl." He set his hand on her thigh and squeezed, but his eyes were searching out the windows.

Kinley focused on her breathing, bringing herself back to the present on her own. As she blinked, their deep voices filtered in.

"I knew it was a trap before we even stepped through the door." Hendrick shook his head.

"We'll get your money back another way, Kinley." Gear growled over his shoulder.

Her money. This had all been for her money and had almost cost her Hendrick. She could live without money. She couldn't live without Hendrick.

But...

"I know where it is."

21

KINLEY WAS COLD. Once they were far from Curry's house, Hendrick let his guard down, trusting the other two to keep watch for followers, and pulled Kinley onto his lap.

"You know where your money is?"

"Yes. But..." she trailed off, swallowing audibly.

"But what, pretty girl?" Hendrick ran his hands down her bare arms, ignoring the blood drying on her skin. He'd never considered her fragile until this moment.

"It's not worth it." Kinley slumped against him, burying her face in his neck. She shivered, prompting Hendrick to wrap his arms around her.

She was right. It wasn't worth it. None of this was worth her life. Not her money and not revenge over Shane.

But he had one thing to do before getting them free.

He couldn't avenge Shane, but he could protect his legacy. And Hudson was the key.

They made it back with no incidents. Bruises,

bumps, and cuts marred each of them, except for Kinley. She had blood along her arms, chest, and the front of her dress.

The house was settled for the night, everyone in their place watching from the shadows. Hudson and Cole emerged from the office as they came in. Hendrick nodded to the stairs. He needed somewhere Kinley could be as comfortable as possible, but they needed to deal with all of this now.

They crowded into the not quite large bedroom. He set Kinley down against the pile of pillows. Gear tossed him a throw blanket to wrap around her shoulders.

"Kinley." Lifting her chin with his thumb and finger, he forced her to look at him. The others towered around the room behind him.

She blinked and pulled in a breath. Touches of shock tried to pull her under, but she only looked tired.

"How do you know where your money is?"

"A place that is and always has been out of your reach." She quoted her father's words. "Cassius talked about it all the time when I was younger. There's a separate set of accounts. The only place anyone ever accesses them from is a separate office in the house. It's the only locked door I ever found, other than my bedroom. He has several safety nets of finances to fall back on. I'd always thought it was one of the smartest things my father did. But I don't have any details about those accounts or how to access them."

"Leave that to Roen." Cole pulled out his phone and started typing.

"What happened?" Hudson asked low.

"It was a trap. They tried to force us to sign divorce papers and take Kinley." Hendrick didn't turn away from his wife. "Two dead." Neither of those two were Cassius or Curry. But Hendrick kept those words to himself for now. They may have betrayed her, but he couldn't be sure how Kinley would feel about their deaths.

Kinley's eyes cleared the longer they stared at each other while Gear summed up the events for Cole and Hudson.

Once they'd caught everyone up and there was nothing more to do about her money until they heard from Roen, Hendrick spoke.

"Everyone out."

Cole reached down and squeezed Kinley's shoulder, but it was Gear that crouched beside the bed and pulled her hand free from under the blanket.

"Good job." He placed a kiss on her forehead as he stood. Hendrick had never seen Gear get emotional with anyone. It was enough to make him pause.

They were alone. Hendrick pulled Kinley from the bed. "Let's get cleaned up, pretty girl."

She left the blanket sprawled on the bed. He led her into the bathroom with her hand in his.

He put them in the shower, clothes and all. As the water soaked their clothes, they didn't break the hold their gazes had on each other. Kinley looked up at him with trust and an emotion he'd only recently recognized he had for her.

Hendrick dragged the zipped down the back of her dress. The water was pink swirling down the drain, rinsing from their skin and their clothes. He peeled the heavy fabric from her shoulders and forced it down her body. Kicking it to the corner, he did the same with his. Her small hands moved with his, but didn't have any strength to help him out of the clothes.

He added to the pile in the corner and then took her hands and set them at her sides. Then, gripping her chin, he forced her head up.

"You're mine, Kinley." The words were simple, possessive, and matter of fact.

"Yes. I am." She licked her lips. "Hendrick?" She tried to pull her head free.

"No. Talk later, pretty girl." He sealed their lips and moved over hers, capturing her in a hold. Reaching for the bar of soap, he rubbed it over her body. Down her back, around her hips and ass. Up and down her arms that she'd kept where he'd put them. Slipping her under the water washed away the suds on her back. And only then did he break the kiss.

Kinley pulled in a breath with a long, loud gasp. Turning her around, he repeated his thorough washing on her front and soaped up himself at the same time. His focus was on the blood, but he wanted her distracted while he washed away the evening.

Latching onto her neck, he nipped and sucked.

"Hendrick." Her chest rose. "You... you said..."

He knew what he'd said, and he was glad she hadn't forgotten or missed it. "Yeah, pretty girl. I said it."

"And you meant it." It wasn't a question.

"Always."

The water washed the soap and the last of the blood down the drain.

"Are you okay after what happened tonight, Kinley?" With the evidence gone, he turned her around and searched her eyes.

"It was hard, but I'm okay."

The shock had cleared from her eyes. Hazy lust coated the deep colour instead.

"I could have lost you tonight." She moved her hands, setting them on his chest. "It didn't take even a full second for me to choose you over my father. I saw him reach for the gun and I had to do something. That something wasn't as effective, but it stopped him and gave you the advantage again. Seeing him reach for that gun and knowing your back was to him... I didn't want to do anything from that moment on unless you were with me."

"I wanted to turn away before we ever stepped through the door. No revenge holds as much worth as you, Kinley."

Her lips parted, and her eyes turned glassy for another reason other than lust. She blinked away tears. "What are you saying?"

"I'm keeping you by my side for the rest of my life, pretty girl. I won't put that life in danger again."

"We're leaving?"

"Almost. I'm ousting my father and giving it all to Hudson. Then we're out. We'll get your money back, but you won't have anything to do with it."

"No."

He frowned.

"Not no to your plan about ousting your father. But if I'm getting *my* money back, then I'm doing it. Otherwise, I don't want it. I'll earn it again another way."

"You don't have to be part of it."

"I know." She wrapped her arms around his neck. "Thank you for that. But that isn't who I want to be."

Hendrick speared his fingers into her wet hair. "Okay, pretty girl. You can do it your way." He tightened his hold in her hair, fisting at the back of her head. "But right now, we're doing things my way." He put pressure on her, urging her to her knees.

Kinley's lips parted and her lips lifted in a soft smile. Her body conceded to his demands, and she set her knees on the tile floor. She didn't need any further demands.

Hendrick had to fight his eyes closing as the heat of her mouth covered him. The water cascaded over his chest and down to run over her face. She closed her eyes and stroked her tongue in circles along the underside.

She was a vision at his feet. And precious. He doubted she'd let him send her back to Dak and King to keep her safe while he finished business here.

The resulting battle would make it fun to try.

His balls drew tight. He had to stop her. With the hold in her hair, he pulled her up and pinned her to the wall. He pulled her up on her toes and hooked one leg over his hips.

"Look at me." The demand hurt rushing out of his throat. He pushed into her the moment her eyes locked on his. "I love you, pretty girl."

She cried out and clutched at his shoulders. Once the shock was over, she gasped out her reply. "I love you too, Hendrick."

He brought them both to blinding orgasms, chasing that emotion like it was the only air he needed to survive.

WHEN HENDRICK SUGGESTED she go back to King Security, Kinley had laughed and shoved him off the bed. She'd whispered, "No fucking way," once he crawled back in beside her.

Now they went about their mornings as if last night hadn't happened. The house was a flurry from the moment Kinley stepped foot outside of the bedroom.

Hendrick's father had scheduled the party for that evening. They'd moved and rearranged the furniture to allow both space and seats for several guests. The kitchen was full with a cooking staff, one yelling fast paced orders as if the guests were about to arrive any minute.

Charlotte caught her at the bottom of the stairs. "Thank God you're up." She lowered her voice. "There's so much to do."

Stress wrung from the other woman as if she'd had an entire pot of coffee to herself, and Kinley wondered if that might be the case. Her eyes bulged over deep circles. The party was hours away and, from the looks of things, they were half ready before nine in the morning.

This wasn't the first time Kinley noticed a vehement reaction to having everything perfect from Hendrick's mother. Taking Charlotte's hands, Kinley tugged her along to the kitchen.

"Excuse me." Kinley called out to the head chef. "I don't believe we've met. I'm Kinley Pierce." She stuck her hand out and waited for the other man to shake it. She glared when he took too long. "It's very early and there is more than enough time to make everything just right. Do you mind quieting things down for the next few hours while you prepare? Also, we'd love some tea and anything you might whip up for a quick brunch. I'll compensate you for the extra small efforts, I promise." Kinley topped it all off with her sweetest smile, but she was proud of the steel in her voice. It was new and tasted divine.

The chef frowned. Instead of answering, he only gave a single firm nod.

"Thank you." Retaking Charlotte's hands, Kinley led her out to the back patio.

"We don't have time for this." Charlotte tried to pull her hands free, but Kinley tightened her grip.

"We do." This was the kind of thing Kinley wished she could have done for her own mother. But her own mother was as addicted to the success as her father.

"But it must... It has to be... I have to make..."

"It will be... And we will make it happen."

A server followed them out with a tray. Tea steamed from a fancy teapot and two omelettes filled two plates.

"Thank you." Kinley spoke directly to the server and waited for him to leave. She set the tray on the table and placed a plate in front of Charlotte. Kinley poured the tea and took her own seat.

"You're so calm."

"Because it's barely nine and I need time to wake up. We have all day, Charlotte, and you already have half of everything done."

"I do?" The other woman blinked and looked through the glass doors leading back into the house.

"Yes, you do."

"Oh." Charlotte fell into silence and Kinley let her. They both needed the calm of the morning air and the birds singing. For once, Kinley didn't control the situation with her mother-in-law. She just let them be.

It wasn't until the commotion inside rose did they

lift their heads from resting against the back of the chairs.

"I didn't used to take events like these so seriously." Charlotte stood and helped Kinley set the dishes back on the tray.

"Your world hasn't been the same. That affects you in ways you can never predict."

Charlotte nodded, moving the items around on the tray.

Kinley touched her wrist, making her pause. "I'm sorry for your loss."

A small gasp slipped between her lips and her eyes glassed over. "Thank you." Charlotte choked down the tears before they could make an appearance.

Kinley didn't push, but she wondered if she was the first to say it.

Inside the house, Hendrick and his father were setting security place for the party. The heat from Hendrick's eyes drew her attention in a second. They locked gazes over the crowd. Soon, they would be out of here. She knew what he wanted to do, but not the execution.

But one look shared so much. Everything they'd said in the shower the night before, and every hope for the future.

Charlotte seemed to snap out of her calm at the sight of her husband. And that was the last full breath Kinley had until it was time to dress for the party.

HENDRICK MOVED AMONG the guests as if he was one rather than fluffing his feathers like a peacock at the head of the room. He recognized faces from his past and his current life. The shock on the ones that recognized him as one of King's mercenaries was worth the time spent in the crowd.

He hadn't been at Kinley's side since they came down the stairs. She stuck close to his mother until his father demanded his wife stand beside him. Since then, guests had stopped Kinley for conversation every few steps. Gear trailed close behind her the entire evening.

And Hendrick had her position locked for hours.

Without his father knowing, Hendrick invited anyone Hudson suggested. The people Shane had dealt with that their father refused to speak to. They had spread out each of their arrivals, so his father had yet to notice the increased number of guests. But an inch crawled up his skin, waiting for an explosion that he looked forward to.

He'd made Hudson head of security for the night, knowing his father put his own man in place. A quick conversation with him cleared him of any such notions. His father's choice of men were too easy to scare.

A sharp clinking rose above the voices. "Could I have your attention?" His father smiled across the room, but it slipped. Hendrick saw the force it took to keep a face in place.

The room was full of dealers, money men, and low-level mercenaries. Even Kinley's parents were around here somewhere, although they steered clear of both him and Kinley. Hudson escorted Cassius from the property himself while Hendrick had stood on the front stairs and watched.

This wasn't a crowd he wanted his wife mingling in, but as most men brought dates or wives, the chances of the environment being dangerous were slim. Not impossible, but slim.

"My oldest has returned home." He pinned his gaze on Hendrick in the crowd. "Come on up, son."

As Hendrick moved through the parting crowd, his father didn't offer any explanation as to where he'd been. But soon the whole room would know he'd become far more dangerous than he ever could as his father's son.

"As you all know, I've already retired. Shane, God rest his soul, had graciously taken over so this old man could enjoy time with his wife." He squeezed Hendrick's mother to his side. "With Shane's passing, Kit has returned to take his rightful place. This is the last party I'll throw."

As if he'd given them a cue, the applause rose around the room.

"Let me reintroduce my eldest. Kit." Hendrick stepped up beside his father. The applause wasn't as enthusiastic as a moment ago. As the echo of hands died, his father spoke up again. "And his new bride, Kinley Curry."

Hendrick gritted his teeth. He'd warned his father against pulling Kinley into this. But his father was out to suit himself. And pointing out the alliance with the Curry family did exactly that.

Kinley's father was in the centre of the room, fuming as he glared at Hendrick. Gear led Kinley toward Hendrick, but the look on his face matched Hendrick's thoughts. She settled against him with a placating smile for the crowd of criminals.

"Alliances can be bumpy, but this one is smoothing out and our two families will be stronger for it." His father made the veiled threat sound like exciting news for everyone. But Hendrick marked every frown and glare directed toward them. "Please take the time to introduce yourself to my son. It's been a long time since he's been amongst us. Enjoy the party, everyone."

The only people that bothered to find Hendrick to talk to him were the ones he'd invited. Each of them hoped to renew contracts that Shane had put in place. Hendrick promised them big changes.

"Let me make one thing clear."

Hendrick spun around, towing Kinley with him. Curry's red face only reached his chin.

"There is no alliance."

"Curry." An unfamiliar voice came from the other side of Kinley. Hendrick never met Rhys Wilder before, but he knew who he was, son of syndicate leader Greyson Wilder. "Nice to see you again."

Curry's demeanor changed. He covered his blustering with false confidence.

"I don't suppose you've decided to sell?" Rhys waved his hand, brushing off any answer from Curry. "Of course not. I'm sure you need more time to consider my offer."

Curry had boasted about people wishing to buy his business. He'd dropped Wilder's name.

"Hendrick." Rhys stuck his hand out. He was the first guest that night to call him by the name he preferred rather than Kit. "I knew your brother. I'm sorry he's gone."

"Thank you." Hendrick couldn't remember Shane ever mentioning Rhys.

Rhys looked between Curry and Hendrick, his brow quirked up. Then he turned to Kinley. He held out his

hand until Kinley politely set hers in his. Gently squeezing, Rhys smiled. "Pleasure to meet you, darling. I hope
we'll see each other again soon."

Rhys parted with a nod for each of them. Hendrick
expected Curry to return to his tirade over the alliance,
but with stiff shoulders, he turned away.

Something nagged at Hendrick, but he couldn't grab
hold of it. Shane. It had something to do with Shane.

Sighing, he let it go. Vengeance wasn't his goal
anymore. Ousting his father and getting them the fuck
out of there was.

Both Curry and Rhys left the party only minutes
after speaking with Hendrick and Kinley. And the rest
of the party lasted until three in the morning.

Hendrick had sent Kinley up to bed soon after
midnight with Cole outside the bedroom door. From
that moment on, the event had digressed into drunken
gambling and brawling. Only a few had hidden
weapons they'd tried to wield. Being drunk, they were
easy to disarm and kick out.

Hendrick didn't climb the stairs until the last guest
was off the property. The conversation with Rhys still
clung to him as he settled behind a sleeping Kinley.

She'd insisted she'd never fall asleep with the party
still going on, but she'd worked hard alongside his
mother.

Kinley curled into his chest, still sound asleep.
Hendrick needed to let go of Shane and focus on who
he had here in his arms.

22

LIGHT TAPPING ON THE BEDROOM DOOR WOKE Hendrick from an odd sleep. He'd been reliving the party in his dream, but with eerily clear detail.

Blinking, he shook his head and slid his arm out from under Kinley. She let out a small whimper but didn't wake, curling onto her opposite side. He didn't care about his nudity as he slipped out of the bedroom.

Hudson, Gear, and Cole stood shoulder to shoulder. The house carried a quietness that only occurred after an event like the party. They were always Hendrick's favourite, an easy time to move around the house and to sneak out. Even the guards were exhausted.

Except the mercenaries. Tiredness pulled on each of them, but they all knew better than to leave this house vulnerable. They'd all catch up on their rest over the next day or two.

"What is it?" Despite knowing that no one would wake, he kept his voice low so as not to disturb Kinley.

"A letter. Came with strict instructions. They could only give it to one of King's mercenaries and had to be delivered to you immediately." Cole held out an unmarked white envelope.

Sliding his finger under the corner, he tore the paper. Hendrick pulled out the small piece of paper with a single fold over a hotel keycard.

I'd like to meet with you. Keep it to yourself. 8108 Stock Road. Room 422.

Wilder

Hendrick pocketed the keycard and passed the paper back to Cole. "Burn that."

Cole frowned at the note. "He doesn't say when."

"Now. We leave in five minutes. Gear, I want you and Archer to stay here with Kinley." Hendrick slipped back into the room. He debated waking Kinley, but why bother when he hoped to be back before she woke for the day. According to the clock on the nightstand, he'd only been in bed for an hour and a half, and the rest of the house wouldn't stir until mid morning.

He dressed and strapped his weapons to their comfortable homes. One more look at his wife to see she still slept peacefully with the covers past her chin, and he left. Gear was leaning against the wall next to the door, and Hudson and Cole looked ready to hit the road.

The hotel was only ten minutes away, and the streets were as quiet as the house. No one saw them leave, and no one followed them. The hotel was a luxurious one. Gleaming tile and fireplaces in the lobby.

But the night shift behind the front desk didn't bat an eye at the likes of the three of them stalking toward the elevator. That spoke volumes about the owner and the clientèle.

They needed the keycard to start the elevator.

Curiosity burned Hendrick's gut. Thoughts had raced during the silent drive and knowing he'd find out what this was about in a minute didn't slow them.

The elevator dinged and room 422 was only three doors down on the right. He didn't hesitate or stop to knock. Hendrick slid the plastic card over the lock scanner and pulled down the handle. Why knock when he had the key?

"Your brother used to enter the same way. Like he owned the place." Rhys sat in an armchair, two guards behind him, one at each shoulder. Another armchair sat angled beside him. The small table between them had a bottle and two empty glasses.

"I'm not here to sit and chat. I'd rather you get to the point." Hendrick sat, but refrained from pouring a drink.

"All right." Rhys leaned forward, resting his elbows on his knees. "I was in the middle of a business deal with your brother." Rhys looked over at Hudson, apology pinching his lips. "Maybe keeping it secret hadn't been the best plan, but neither of us could afford for the details to get out."

"What deal?"

"A partnership. And I want to make you the same offer. We both run similar businesses. I have the same vision as Shane did. Corruption shouldn't exist here. I'd rather only deal with an elite clientèle. We'd be able to exist with more security, more time, and more money."

Hurt lanced through Hendrick. Why wouldn't Shane have told him about this? Despite the secrecy, he'd thought Shane had told him everything. And with that, doubt crept in. "How do I know you're telling the truth?"

"Shane said if I ever had to deal with you, you might be skeptical. He said if I told you a story about two boys by the river, you'd believe me."

As Hendrick recalled the story, Rhys spoke it word for word as he and Shane had so many times.

"Two boys about twelve and ten left their house in the middle of a summer night, their pockets full of their father's coin collection. Deep in the woods, they found a river. They'd heard the water rushing many times, but never ventured that far. This night they did."

Their father was still looking for that coin collection to this day. Only Hudson was the other person who knew this story. And now the other men in the room. But that didn't matter anymore.

"They tossed each coin into the rushing water with a curse and wish. Then sat on the bank for hours until the stars faded."

If Shane used the story with Rhys as a way to get to Hendrick if needed, then he'd trusted him. There were so many other things Shane could have used rather than that story. It was too personal for both of them, and they only ever recounted it when they'd had too much to drink. They'd list off the wishes and curses, counting which came true.

Hendrick pulled the top off the bottle on the table and poured the two drinks. With a small salute, he downed the whiskey. Rhys did the same.

"For what it's worth, I considered Shane a friend. I really am sorry he's gone."

Hendrick nodded, unable to voice anything with the emotion clogging his throat. After pouring a second drink and taking a sip, he looked up at Hudson. "You didn't know about this deal?"

"No. Seems Shane stuck to that promise. But I knew who he was meeting. I never understood why, but Shane insisted it was just a friendship over mutual interests."

"Maybe the secrecy wasn't the best decision."

"Why do you say that?"

Rhys didn't answer.

"You think his death had something to do with your partnership?"

"I don't know how anyone would have found out about the partnership. He met with me the night he died. Before he went home. I have nothing to say it's connected except instinct."

Hendrick lived on instinct.

"I want to offer you the same deal. I want a partnership. Providing all of Shane's contracts and stipulations are put back in place."

He didn't plan on being around much longer to put all of Shane's work in the right order. But Hudson would. This seemed like the best place to start putting Hudson in charge.

"I understand you need to think about it." Rhys slid a card across the small table. The only thing written on it was a phone number. "Call anytime."

"Neither of you kept any records of the deal, did you?"

"No. It was all verbal."

"Only in person?"

"A few occasions over the phone. But we were careful with those conversations."

"Now that you know, what would you have said to Shane if he'd told you about the deal?" Hendrick leaned back in the chair and pointed at one of the hard chairs around the table for Hudson to sit.

"I should have figured it out. Rhys and Shane make a good business match." He set his gaze on Rhys. "I would have told him that the partnership would need to happen slowly so as not to trigger your father. But ultimately, it would be the best decision to secure power."

Hendrick's initial thoughts after listening to Rhys were the same. "We'll be in touch."

Rhys lifted his glass in farewell.

The dark sky was turning grey as they exited the hotel. Kinley would wake soon, and Hendrick wanted time alone with her before the rest of the house demanded attention.

⸻

SHE'D TWISTED THE sheets into knot after knot in the past hour. Kinley had sworn she'd felt Hendrick beside her while she'd slept, but the bed was cold and there was no sign he'd been there. Gear stood outside the bedroom door and he'd assured her that nothing had gone wrong. Hendrick had been called out, but that was all he'd dare say.

The house had a quietness she used to love. These were the kind of nights Kinley felt what it was like to be free. Until Cassius caught on and started sleeping outside her bedroom door once she hit her later teen years. About the time she'd started talking about her first boyfriend at school.

But when she still had a touch of innocence, Kinley had explored the night as if she'd owned it. Eating ice-cream from the container while sitting on the kitchen counter. Having her first taste of alcohol on her bedroom balcony. Hiding from Cassius and his men in the bushes and trees on the property. Stealing her mother's car to teach herself how to drive.

But the quietness of this night, in this house, carried secrets. The air was thick with tension. Kinley tried to shake off the feeling while waiting for Hendrick to return.

The door made the barest sound as he opened it. Kinley lurched from the bed. "Is everything okay?"

"Yeah, pretty girl. Everything is fine." He wrapped his arms around her, giving her the comfort she needed. It hadn't occurred to her to hide that, to ease off the bed and give the appearance of curiosity rather than worry. It showed her how much she trusted Hendrick.

"Where were you?"

"A meeting. I just found out my brother had bigger plans than I realized."

"Do those plans change yours?"

"No. It gives them a better chance."

They don't get back to sleep. Slow and steady, the house awoke, pushing the tension of secrecy in the air to the shadows. Because they'd rather see things move quicker now and get out of there, they don't dally with showers or getting downstairs for breakfast.

Charlotte practically shook at the table, eating each bite with caution, and Hendrick's father brooded through his meal after being relegated to the opposite end of the table once again by Hendrick.

But Hendrick ran his fingers up and down her thigh beneath the table, keeping Kinley distracted from the thoughts of others.

His father finished with a clang of his silverware

against his plate. "I'm meeting with Curry in a few hours to smooth things over. I intend for us all to have dinner there tonight. This alliance must stand and we don't have the time to wait out the petty feelings of old men. Last night made it clear there are many still circling since Shane's death. We can't afford to be weak. Both families are strong on their own. Together, we could be unstoppable." He scraped his chair on the floor as he stood. Charlotte winced as he stormed from the room before Hendrick could protest.

Kinley looked at her husband. He hadn't been about to protest. He leaned back in his chair and watched his father's retreating back with a tilting head.

Charlotte cleaned up her dishes and took them to the kitchen, never making a sound and never once lifting her head to look at them.

"You're not going." Hendrick lowered his chin, pinning her to the chair with his gaze.

"Yes, I am." Kinley was quick to answer. She'd expected him to say neither of them was going, but his declaration of only her didn't change what she was going to say next. "One last chance and one last opportunity. But we go in differently this time. Your father has a single-minded focus on an alliance. He won't try the same thing twice, especially with more security there."

"I thought you'd given up on getting your money back?"

Pinching her lips between her teeth, Kinley sighed through her nose. It hadn't been worth the risk to actively chase her money. But this wasn't the same scenario. And Hendrick wasn't ready for them to pull out yet. Kinley already made it clear she wouldn't abandon him until this was finished. So why not gain everything they could if given the opportunity? Giving up her money and letting it go due to risk were two different things.

"Kinley?"

"I'm not willing to charge in there for it. But why not take advantage of this opportunity?"

Hendrick rubbed a hand over his face. "I don't want you anywhere near there. We'll…"

She cut him off. "No. Either I do it or I don't want it." Stupid, petty, and stubborn. But Hendrick had made her believe she was a warrior princess in disguise. She wanted to be the one to succeed for herself.

The others had moved to take seats at the table as soon as Hendrick's parents left. Gear leaned on his elbows, bringing himself closer to Hendrick.

"Don't tell me you'd bring her." Hendrick lifted his hand to stop Gear from speaking. "If you were in my seat, I'd bet you'd have already forced her back with King and Dak."

"I wouldn't have brought her here to begin with, but we aren't talking about me and my hypothetical relationship. We're talking about yours. I don't like it, but she isn't wrong when she says this is a good opportunity and we'll have the most security there that we can." Gear leaned back. "Just playing devil's advocate."

"Sometimes, I think you are the devil's advocate," Hendrick grumbled. He looked at Kinley, reaching over and grasping her chin in a punishing hold. She allowed him to tilt her head back. Inside, she did a little dance. He was going to let her go. She saw it in his eyes, despite the tightness of his jaw.

Shaking his head, he pressed his lips to hers, ending the kiss with a bite to her bottom lip.

"Thank you, Hendrick."

"THIS IS MUCH better." Kinley strapped her last weapon to her thigh and faced Hendrick, her hip cocked and a smile on her face to match his.

She looked damn good. Shiny leggings tightly formed to her legs and ass. A glittery tank top worthy of an evening out. And every weapon he'd given her on display and within easy reach. Kinley was his match.

Hendrick closed the distance and slid his hands around her ribs. "I wish I had time to fuck you right now." He bent his head and nipped along her jaw. "You look delicious."

Kinley arched her back and tilted her head, giving him access to swirl his tongue in the hollow below her ear. "I'd have to take all these weapons off."

"No, you wouldn't. I want to fuck you with them on."

Kinley's breath hitched inward and froze. Tapping on the door stalled the progress of Hendrick's fingers under her shirt.

"Something to look forward to later." He straightened and looked at her. "Do you have everything Roen gave you?" The moment Hendrick agreed to let her come, he'd called Roen. She knew where her money was and Roen provided the flash drive she'd need that would hack into her father's system to get her money. They each carried a copy and directions to that room in her father's house. But Kinley made it clear she wanted to be the one to do it.

Kinley patted her left breast. "All bras should have an inside pocket like this. Ember could make a fortune."

SARAH URQUHART

"Mercenary bras. That's terrifying." He kissed her nose and turned them toward the door. Cole waited outside the bedroom, and Gear and Archer stationed themselves at the bottom of the stairs.

His father was dressed in a suit and had his men do the same. With Hendrick's mother on his arm, they filled the living room while waiting for Hendrick and Kinley to come down. His mother wore a simple dress, but the jewelry around her neck and hanging from her ears made a loud statement.

His parents gasped when Hendrick and Kinley stepped into the room.

"Go change." It wasn't the first time his father had said those words in that tone. Hendrick hadn't listened then, and he wouldn't listen now.

"Kinley, you can't wear..." his mother looked her up and down, "all of that."

"The last time we went over there, they tried to take Kinley. The alliance won't go through if that happens. I won't give them a chance to try again tonight." Hendrick didn't bother addressing his choice of attire.

"Going in there on the offensive won't do any good for the alliance, either."

"That's for you to figure out." Hendrick walked away before he responded. He took Kinley to the front door and left, Hudson and Gear following close behind. Cole and Archer would be behind his parents.

Usually, the thought of chaos calmed him, but not this time. Walking into her parents' home again, no matter how they'd dressed, was guaranteed chaos. Hendrick promised himself that he was getting Kinley out of here tomorrow. This was the last chance for her to get her money back, and that was it. Pain grew in his chest with even the possibility of her getting hurt tonight. Unfortunately, a takeover of his father's company and passing it all off to Hudson would take more time, but Kinley didn't need to be in the middle of that. He still hadn't discussed it with Hudson.

Security around Curry's place was a little thicker than last time, but so was Hendrick's. Not only the mercenaries and Hudson were with him, but also any man Hudson trusted cased the property and would slip inside Curry's house the moment they served drinks.

Curry and his wife had the same reaction to their appearance as Hendrick's parents. He looked down at his wife to see a smug smile on her soft features. They were seeing their true daughter in this moment and it seemed they didn't care much for it.

His parents filtered in after them, filling the foyer by standing next to Hendrick.

"Maybe this time, we'll make it to dinner." Hendrick leaned down as if speaking to Kinley, but kept his gaze on Curry. The words didn't hold a direct threat, but Curry understood.

It was Hendrick's father that broke the tension and led them into the living room for drinks.

"I'm sure we can all behave ourselves for a few hours. Long enough to come to equal ground." His father motions for the man standing next to the drink cart to pour.

"Hard to relax with a threat staring you in the face." Curry glared at Hendrick and Kinley, keeping them in his sight as they all filed into the living room.

"Kit has a particular personality. Don't let it get to you. He isn't stupid enough to attack when he knows the alliance is best for everyone."

Hendrick knew no such thing.

"His *personality* is rubbing off on my daughter."

"You and Cassius created this." Kinley pointed to herself, letting the gesture drop down her body. "My husband perfected it."

Her father's chest and cheeks puffed out. "You're walking on thin..."

"Curry." Hendrick's father cut him off. "You said yourself this afternoon you'd consider allowing this alliance and marriage to stand. Remember what's at stake."

Hendrick watched the reminder click in place in Curry's eyes. His blustering over his daughter settled. Accepting the drink his man passed, he sat, pulling his wife with him.

Why hadn't he considered it before? They have a mutual enemy. Not just a need to be stronger due to unbalance. His father acted as if vultures were swarming, but since Hendrick took over, there'd been no sign of anyone. Curry only mentioned potential buyers. And inconsequential sabotage. But the man wouldn't admit to significant sabotage to Hendrick. From the beginning, Hendrick wanted to know the reason behind this alliance. Why wouldn't Curry just let his daughter go when he had no proper plans for her future? This was why. A mutual enemy. Curry gains protection now and his father got Hendrick back. And they both get protection in the future. But from who?

23

——————

THE DISCUSSIONS WERE MEANINGLESS. VEILED
insults behind sour smiles while discussing business,
but never going into any detail to determine what they
were talking about. Both Charlotte and Kinley's mother
blinked often to keep themselves awake and alert.
Hendrick rolled his neck often, offering grunts every so
often to the conversation.

Her father seemed to have relaxed and forgotten
about her slight with her choice of attire. But Kinley had
to admit, she felt more in control and more capable with
her weapons known. And several of them.

A petite woman with hair wrapped tightly in a bun
announced that dinner was ready. She didn't wait for a
response, but hurried back to the kitchen. Kinley and
Hendrick stayed seated until everyone else had taken
several steps toward the dining table.

"Now," Hendrick whispered. "Follow her, Cole."

Kinley trailed behind Hendrick as he followed the
others toward the dining room, but she ducked out the
patio doors, Cole on her heels. She'd already given each

of them the layout, so Cole knew where he was going when he led her through the shadows to avoid her father's guards and the cameras. The fewer people they encountered, the better. Until she secured her money.

Only two rooms in the house had doors leading out to a patio—the living room and her father's office. But not the one they needed to access. Cole knelt next to the other set of doors and had them unlocked in seconds. No one stood inside the dark room, but her father kept someone stationed outside the door.

"Ready?" Cole stood in a ready stance where the door would open.

Kinley reached for the door—one hand on the handle, the other on the lock. "Ready." Slow breath in and out. She turned the lock and pushed down on the handle almost simultaneously.

Cole reached out and grabbed the guy standing there, pulling him into the office by his collar. Kinley chanced a quick look to see if he was the only one there. But he wouldn't be the only one around. Having someone over for dinner that her father considered an enemy would force him to up his security, taking some guards away from this wing of the house. While there may have only been one stationed at this door, another would be scouting the halls.

Kinley shut them back in the office. Cole had an arm around the guard's neck. Marcus. He was one of Cassius's favourites. His eyes flared when they landed on her, but consciousness didn't hold him for much longer.

Cole held him a few more minutes after he stopped struggling. Sliding him to the floor so as not to make a thump, Cole pulled zip ties from his back pocket. The quick work he made of securing his hands and feet and shoving him behind the corner armchair was impressive.

They took the same stance at the door and nodded when they were both ready to do it again. But when they opened, no one new was there.

A small relief, but this wasn't over yet.

Cole once again took the lead down the hall. Kinley worked hard to follow his every footstep.

Around the corner stood another guard, this one she didn't know. The door behind him was the one they needed to get through. Cole didn't give a signal. The first moment the guard turned his back, he slid along the wall. Silent and fast, Cole had a grip around his neck, but he didn't wait for him to pass out this time. Pulling back, he slammed into his temple.

"Can you pick up a lock?"

"I've picked every lock in this house hundreds of times. I'm not as fast as you, but I can do it."

"Good." Cole set the body against the wall and stepped back. His gaze wasn't on Kinley as she knelt in front of the door. He watched both ends of the hall, ready to act quick upon discovery.

The second the door clicked open, Cole hauled the guard over his shoulder and brought him into the room with them. He slumped the guy in the corner, securing him with more zip ties from his pocket.

This office was more like a large closet than a full room. It had always seemed redundant to her to have two offices with similar security. The technological security might be more advanced in here, but getting inside was never a problem.

The small row of computer screens hummed. At

least they wouldn't have to wait for any systems to boot. She nudged the mouse and the black screens lit up, prompting for a password.

"Just stick the drive in the computer. Roen's systems will do the rest." Cole pulled out his phone and swiped before holding it to his ear. It must have vibrated in his pocket. "Stop calling while I'm taking out guards. It's distracting." He spoke with an exasperated drawl that carried humour in spades.

Kinley snorted. Cole hadn't looked the least bit distracted. She'd never known someone was calling him.

She turned away from Cole and searched the side of the computer monitor. No ports. Looking under the desk, she found the tower. There in the front were at least three ports. Perfect.

Reaching into the slim pouch inside the padding of her bra, Kinley pulled out the flash drive and inserted it into the computer.

"Yeah, she just put it in."

Seconds later, the password boxes started flashing with disguised symbols until one worked and the screens came to life.

One screen had the files and programs on the desktop, the other two screens had security footage. The first screen flipped through files automatically.

One video feed showed the dining room with everyone there and the other flipped through the empty house like a slow-moving picture book.

A steady thump echoed from the hall, getting closer with each one. The sound was enough to make them both pause and look toward the door, but it was the distinctive sound of a slumping body that made Cole tense even further.

"Gotta go." Cole slipped his phone back in his pocket. "Stay here. That should be done soon." He pointed at the computer. Whatever genius Roen had cooked up in that small device would search the computer for every financial transaction and transfer the ones matching Kinley's accounts to a secured account of her own. Part of her wished she'd asked for more. To take more from her father and cripple him a bit. Enough for her to build on top of his foundation. Or even enough to give him too much work to follow her as she escaped.

Cole left the small office. Kinley breathed through her worry and focused on the video feed. She wished there was sound. Lips moved, but she couldn't make out the words as most of them mumbled. Running the mouse along the bottom of the screen, she looked for a way to turn on the sound.

There. She clicked and leaned in close to catch every word. No one yet sat at the table. They seemed to have stalled in the open space between the kitchen and dining room. Her father and mother were on one side, flanked by only two guards. Hendrick, his parents, Gear, and Hudson stood on the other.

But not Cassius. He'd been absent since they walked in the door. That was unlike him. He was almost always at his father's right hand. Especially when an appearance was important.

The entire evening had distracted Kinley too much to worry about why he wasn't there, but now that it clicked, a sharp prickle ran down her spine. She turned toward the door to check on Hendrick, but voices kept her attention on the screen.

"See Curry? This alliance can work out just fine." Hendrick's father reached for a chair at the table.

Her father scoffed. "Fine? This hasn't solved your problem like you think. I saw the guests at your party. And so did you."

"Do you have another way to solve your problem?" Crossing his arms, he stepped back up next to his son. Hendrick was focused on the conversation—standing still as if he was loath to disturb them.

"A different alliance. Adding to my own forces. I have a few. Not just taking out one obstacle and replacing it with the same." Her father didn't hide his glance at Hendrick.

Hendrick replaced his brother. And they took his brother out. But those words didn't necessarily mean what they sounded like. His own father didn't have him killed. Why would he?

But Hendrick had picked up on the hidden meaning and the look. His eyes changed. Nothing else on his body did, but the only other time Kinley had seen that shine in his eyes had been when they'd been here the last time. There's always a glint, but this was different. This burned bright and the pixelation of the video had no power to distort it.

"We created this plan together, Curry. Don't act like you had nothing to do with it and weren't all in joining the families with my other son from the beginning."

Emotions were high between them all, otherwise there's no way any of them would let these words free in front of Hendrick.

She had to get out there. Hendrick heaved. Gear and

Hudson looked at him with worry, tense and ready to act, but whether it would be in his defense to hold him back, Kinley didn't know.

The other screen had stopped flashing. Yanking out the drive, she slid back into its pocket while she reached for the door, but it swung inward before she could grab it.

Cassius blocked the way out. Dressed not in a suit for entertaining as he should be, but in full gear and ready to attack. He'd been waiting this entire evening.

"Hey, kiddo."

***

TAKING OUT AN obstacle and replacing it with the same.

Don't act like you had nothing to do with it and weren't all in joining the families with my other son from the beginning.

No. His father wouldn't have gone that far. Shane differed from him with the business in so many ways. But money was money. What the hell did the old man care as long as he had the funds to stay retired?

They couldn't be referring to Shane as the *obstacle*. But a cautious side glance from both his father and Curry told Hendrick the truth. They realized they were running their mouths when they shouldn't, but both were angry enough not to stop.

The fake facade of the night disappeared before they even reached the table. No one noticed Kinley's absence. All it had taken was a too sharp veiled barb to poke through their barrier. The two older men seemed to have some history beyond this alliance alone.

A fiery haze filled his lungs. And his vision.

He racked his brain to figure out who was a threat to his father. The business had been running smoothly, according to Hudson. His father spoke of people circling, unrest among the players, but there had been no evidence.

The only player that came out of the woodwork was Rhys Wilder.

Curry had shut down at the party when Rhys approached.

"Who?" The word dropped like a bomb between the two men and they stopped bickering. They blinked at Hendrick. "Who are you both up against?"

Stuttering escaped their lips, but neither answered. His father recognized the danger in Hendrick. He'd never shown self preservation before, but he saw the need for it now. And that told Hendrick how terrified he was of his actions.

"Wilder." Hudson spoke the name with quiet realization. He put it all together, the same as Hendrick. Curry and his father flinched. Not enough for most people to notice, but Hendrick's focus tightened on the two of them. The two that orchestrated everything.

"You assured me you could control him." Curry shook as he pointed at Hendrick and accused his father.

Hendrick laughed. The bubble grew into an uncontrollable rage inside him. The more the two of them spoke, the more certain Hendrick understood what happened to his brother.

"All you had to do was be patient and accept the

alliance." His own father took a step toward Curry. "We're in this mess right now because of you."

"I wasn't the one to suggest killing your son to cut ties with his supply chains and clients."

"That didn't stop you from tagging along to watch.

"And to get Wilder out of the way." Curry kept going, ignoring the interruption. "It might have stopped his involvement with your business, but he hasn't stopped sabotaging mine. You haven't held up your end of the bargain with protection."

"You refused the alliance to get the protection."

The words slid into Hendrick's mind. And when this night was over, they'd all make sense. But right now, he couldn't get past his father killing Shane.

Everything happened too fast after that. Hendrick roared with fury. Guards moved away from walls, but no one laid a hand on him. He heard the women screaming and their smaller feet scuffling away.

Gear's chain clinked in the air and the steel he heard could have been his or Hudson's

Hendrick's hand wrapped around his father's throat and lifted him off the floor with ease, his anger giving him a power he'd never registered before.

His favourite blade felt smooth in his hand as he held the tip at his father's centre, pointing up between the ribs.

"You killed him."

His father didn't struggle, but his face changed colour and his eyes narrowed.

"Say it."

"Why? You need words to clear your conscious of what you're about to do? Shane brought in the wrong kind of money and working with Wilder would only make things worse." He choked around every few words as Hendrick's grip tightened.

A battle cry erupted, but the body already went limp in his hold as his mother charged from the side.

"You fucking monster!" She screamed and Hendrick expected her to grab his arm, though he didn't loosen his hold.

Hendrick didn't even feel the knife penetrating his father's body, but warm blood trickled over his hand, making him blink. The mild sensation wasn't enough to pull him from this red hot path.

Hendrick's mother passed him and followed her husband to the ground, beating on his chest as she cursed him to the depths of hell for killing her son. He turned away from her while she relived her grief.

He assumed the others secured all of Curry's guards because Curry stood wide open. His hands shook at his sides.

"We couldn't let Wilder get that kind of control. We can't let him. He isn't who we want running this industry."

"*We?*" That single word was the other man's death sentence. They'd spoken as if it had been a joint plan, but that didn't mean joint execution. No matter, Curry wouldn't live past the next few minutes, anyway.

"Don't get distracted from what's important."

Hendrick chuckled. "Important? None of this is important to me. I was only here to find out who killed my brother." He twirled his knife. "Mission accomplished."

He grabbed Curry by the collar and pulled him forward to land on the blade, not quite with the angle he wanted. Hendrick twisted his wrist to ensure he hit and destroyed something vital.

A small gasp preceded Curry slumping to the floor.

Fuck. He'd just killed his wife's father. His rage still simmered on his skin when he looked up. But the sight set everything into a fresh blaze.

Cassius held Kinley in a tight hold with a knife to her neck. She was missing most of her weapons, but some were still in their place. Cassius couldn't fully disarm her without letting her go and she couldn't attack without getting her throat cut.

Every breath hurt, but he forced the air inside his body to calm him. He didn't have the upper hand in this, and charging over with a crazy rage would kill Kinley.

Not. Fucking. Happening.

MAYBE LATER SHE could be proud of the fight she gave Cassius. Maybe. If she got out of here. The only thing keeping his knife off her neck was her hands. If she let one out from under his arm, he'd cut her with the amount of pressure he was putting against her.

Hendrick looked like a bloodied warrior, his eyes showing another world. It had been shock that made her gasp. Not sadness or fear.

He'd killed both of their fathers. She hadn't seen or heard anything on the security feed since the moment Cassius showed. Cole wasn't there and his body hadn't been outside the office. She didn't know where he was and could only pray he was still alive. Cassius, not looking like he had a scratch on him, didn't bode well.

Hendrick stepped over her father, and Cassius tightened his arm, bending back her fingers.

"Don't come closer."

"Let her go."

"No. But I'll tell you what you're going to do. You're going to sign the divorce papers Curry has stashed in his office, and then you're all going to walk out of here."

Hendrick didn't move. She watched the physical change in him, the moment the rage hardened into something controllable but no less dangerous.

"Stop!" Cassius lifted his chin away from the side of her face and growled. "Call them off."

Kinley darted her eyes sideways and saw Gear moving in, his chain dangling from his hands. She tried to understand what was going through Cassius's mind. If he needed her, why was he threatening to kill her? Using her to get through Hendrick wouldn't work. One or both of them would end up dead. She'd never taken Cassius as reckless.

Hendrick cocked his head at Gear, but Kinley knew better. The communication between them had nothing to do with backing off. She wondered if there was ever a time the mercenaries backed off.

Then his eyes settled on her. Not Cassius. Not the threat. Her. And he stepped backward, putting her father's body between them again.

Her core hollowed and froze, like ice crystallizing on glass. But he wasn't abandoning her. The instant shock of him backing away hurt, but if she searched his gaze, she saw his true intention. He was here if he needed her, but he saw a way for her to get out of this herself. He'd never step away if there wasn't.

Cassius hadn't rid her of all her weapons. She still had a few knives—one of them at her thigh.

"Curry was going to change it all and give me everything. He didn't finish." He turned his head. "Go get the papers."

Footsteps sounded behind them. He'd sent someone to her father's office. She had noticed no one behind them. Damn it.

"Everything belongs to Kinley's husband. And that is going to be me."

"Not in a million years, Cass." The sound of her voice surprised her. It was difficult to speak and her words came out in a harsh whisper.

"There are worse things that will happen to you if you don't. You can play dress up all you like, but you're still no match."

"The bruise forming on your jaw and the blood dripping from your ribs would say otherwise." He may have gotten a hold of her, but she'd hurt him more than he thought possible. There'd been a moment of shock that she'd relished.

Cassius growled and used his other hand to grip her chin, forcing her to look at him. "You'll soon regret it."

But she didn't hear him. His change in position gave her the opportunity she needed, giving her enough slack to drop one hand. Kinley didn't bother with words or another threat. She focused only on striking before he knew what was happening.

She pulled the knife from its sheath on her thigh and shoved it back into his. He pushed her hand against the arm around her neck with all her might.

Cassius cried out, but his hold didn't waver enough for her to get away. Bringing the knife up, she sliced the back of his forearm. Blood poured from the cut and the muscle gave out.

Pushing his arm away, she hit his wrist to force him to drop the knife. She spun and kicked the centre of the large circle of blood coating his pants. He screamed and dropped to the floor.

Adrenaline surged inside her. She'd beat him. On her own.

"I made you a promise, pretty girl." The words sounded so far away. Like a dream. And she was helpless to stop herself. Kinley swung her leg around into a perfect roundhouse. Cassius didn't have the forethought past his pain to catch her leg before it hit the side of his head.

He went down, and the adrenaline pushed her to follow him. She knelt with one knee on his wrist as he reached toward his side and the other knee on his chest. She set her knife against his throat. The side of the blade pushed up under his chin and the edge dented his skin, a thin cut forming under the pressure.

The pause was enough for the moment to fade, for her to take in her position. She was where Hendrick promised she'd be. Cassius had manipulated her for her entire life. But when she'd been a little girl, she saw a friend. That was what hurt the most—the trust she'd had in this man.

Heat engulfed her back, fighting away the cold forming from the adrenaline crash.

"Don't fuck with *my* wife." Hendrick's breath brushed her cheek. "I didn't have to do a thing. But I am going to do this for her."

His hand slid along her arm, his own knife in his grasp. He nudged her arm out of the way, his blade replacing hers.

"You're not killing him, Kinley. You don't need that on your shoulders."

With him there to take on the burden, she lost all strength. Gear was there to pull her away while Hendrick took her place. He held her face against his chest, his arm muffling any sound.

After all she'd done, she still appreciated the shelter.

When he let her go, the room was too quiet except for faint sobbing. Kinley pushed away from Gear. Hendrick was there to hold her, but she held up her hand.

Following the cries, she found her mother on the kitchen floor.

"He killed my husband." Hatred and despair filled her voice.

"And your husband killed his brother. You know how this works." Kinley's sympathy didn't reach far. "You were willing to sell me off to whoever he chose without concern if they'd be good to me. That's how you work."

"Are they going to kill me, too?"

"No." Hendrick moved up behind Kinley, setting his large hands at her hips. She tried to hold in her wince. Cassius wasn't the only one that came out of their fight hurt. But every knick and blow had been numb until now.

"You're free to do as you wish." Kinley couldn't say she didn't want to see her mother ever again, but for now, everything was still too raw to repair any bond between them.

"But if you cause problems…"

"I won't." Her mother threw her hands up and practically yelled to cut Hendrick off from his threats.

"Well, shit." A groan-filled voice came from the hall. "I missed all the fun." Blood dripped down Cole's head and he held an arm across his ribs.

Kinley let out a shaky breath. "Thank God you're okay."

"I can't believe he caught me off guard." His gaze was on Cassius. Kinley hadn't let herself look at him yet, and doubted she would. She didn't need to see the body to know he was dead. There was too much death in the room.

"Do you want to keep this house, Kinley?" Hendrick turned her away from her mother.

"No. I want the business. Not the house."

"Your mother?"

Kinley turned around and held out her hand. Her mother took it and stood. "You can keep the house. Or you can sell it and keep the money. Either way, the house is yours."

"I'm not sure what I'm supposed to do."

Kinley sighed, but Hendrick answered for her.

"Just take some time. I'll set you up in a safehouse for now."

Kinley saw the wisdom of the decision. It gave her space from her mother, kept her safe in case anyone thought to use her, and it helped them monitor her to make sure she wasn't a threat to any of them.

"We need clean up." Hendrick kept her next to him as he turned toward the others.

"Already called." Gear settled against the untouched table.

Charlotte stood from her husband's body. A fierce look in her eyes that made Kinley tense. She'd been so small and cautious.

"Kit." Charlotte let out a breath. "Hendrick. I'm sorry."

Hendrick tilted his head, regarding his mother as if seeing her for the first time. "Me too."

It seemed to be all the words they needed.

"You get Kinley out of here. We'll handle clean up." Gear nodded toward the door.

"No. I need to be here for this. Cole, do you have someone else with you for protection, or can you take Kinley back to King Security?"

"I shouldn't drive."

"I'll drive them, then come back and help." Archer stepped forward.

"If you need to be here, then I should be here too." Kinley gripped his arm."

He smiled down at her, cupping her jaw. "No, pretty girl. This will take a while." He kissed her, soft and possessive. "Go."

She wanted to argue, but she didn't have the strength. Her lips moved to say something, anything that didn't sound like something final.

Hendrick didn't wait for her to find her words. He kissed her again and nudged her toward Cole and Archer.

Her life had taken a tailspin once already, and it was about to take another. Kinley didn't know where she would end up when this night was over.

24

CLEAN UP WAS a mess. They could hide all the deaths if they wanted businesses to change hands. It was easy enough to find everything they needed from Curry's office. Roen's focus once he'd arrived had been going through his computers and files. Kinley would own it all by morning with a simple signature from her mother, who didn't put up a fight over it. The woman was angry, but still in shock.

Hendrick pulled Hudson aside as the others finished. "I'm handing everything over to you."

"You're what?"

"I don't want any of this. Never have. You know that. And you always have and still have Shane's dreams at heart."

Hudson frowned.

"It's all yours, Hudson."

He lifted his chin. "Thank you."

Hendrick smiled and wrapped the other man in a half hug. "You deserve it, brother." They separated, and

Hendrick looked around the room. "This was easier than the hostile takeover I was planning."

"Hostile takeover?"

"Yeah. To give it to you." Hendrick slapped Hudson on the shoulder and joined the others in the room. They already had Kinley's mother taken to a safehouse, and his mother had gone home with select men they trusted. Handing everything over to Hudson would take a bit more paperwork than Kinley's, but he'd have it done as soon as possible and would help with getting rid of the men loyal to his father and who stayed loyal to the dead man.

"We'll finish up here. There's nothing more for you." Gear blocked Hendrick's path further into the mess. Archer stood beside him.

"You need to go back to Kinley." Archer spoke low. They were right and Archer's words made him wonder if Kinley's adrenaline crash had hit her full force.

"Okay." Hendrick nodded to each of them, giving Hudson free rein on any more decision that might rise, and left.

He found Cole on Kinley's couch, getting treated by Thane.

"Hey, Doc."

"Your woman won't let me look at her." Thane growled, but didn't look away from Cole's head as he stitched.

"Blows to the head. I don't recommend them." Cole quirked his brow. But he hitched his thumb over his shoulder toward the bedroom.

"Bring her out here or I'm coming in there. She was too pale." Thane pinned him with a glare this time. He wasn't usually so demanding about treating someone, so his insistence worried Hendrick.

"Got it." He slipped into the bedroom and found Kinley standing naked in the bathroom in front of the mirror, the door wide open and the bright lights glaring off every bruise.

Hendrick locked his jaw as he stepped up behind her.

"I'm fine." She met his eyes for only a moment in the mirror.

"Lie to me again, pretty girl." Hendrick had to lock his jaw and form fists at his side to keep from grabbing her. A bruise bloomed on her shoulder. Dried blood covered several cuts over her arms, ribs, and legs. And how she stood straight on her swollen ankle, he didn't know.

He took his time looking down her body, noting every injury. Fresh blood dripped on the tile. That was all he could take until he grabbed her hips. He turned her around and set her on the counter.

Kneeling on the floor, he lifted her leg, the one not swollen. She had a gash in the back of her calf. How had he missed this before sending her back here? But there was dried blood surrounding this cut like the others. It wasn't so deep that it hadn't stopped bleeding, but whatever she'd done in here and broken it open.

"Doc threatened to barge in here if I didn't get you out there."

"He's already been banging on the door once."

"Kinley."

"I really am fine. But okay, I'll go out."

Hendrick led her to the bedroom and grabbed one

of his T-shirts to slip over her head before opening the door.

Doc was finished with Cole by the time they got out there and he pinned Kinley with a dark look. But he was gentle when checking and cleaning every scrape and bruise.

"Ice. For the ankle and the shoulder. And I'll send something to help the cuts heal and avoid scarring." He stood with a squeeze to Kinley's wrist and a nod to Hendrick.

"I'll go, too." Cole stood steadier than Hendrick would think after the blow to the head, but Thane wasn't far from him.

They were alone. Hendrick sat on the couch and pulled Kinley to him, draping her legs over his lap. "I promised you freedom."

"You did."

"What are you going to do with it?" The pain stalled in his chest so as not to appear in his voice. He'd let her go if that's what she wanted. Hendrick wanted a future with her. But now that everything was over, Kinley might not want the same thing anymore.

"Is the only way to have freedom without you?"

"I wouldn't say being with a mercenary is freedom."

"Neither is running my father's business. But freedom is the life I want."

"Yeah, pretty girl. It is."

"I want you, Hendrick. I'm not running away with my freedom. I'm staying with you."

"Thank fuck." Hendrick pulled her close and devoured her lips. "You're mine, pretty girl. And I'm yours."

"I love you."

"Mmm, say it again."

Kinley smiled against him. "Make me."

Hendrick laughed, every emotion of the night releasing in that sound. His rage, his grief, his happiness, sorrow, and love.

"Pick a number, pretty girl."

SHE WOULD HAVE loved to spend the next several days in bed, but the consequences of that night made their appearance only hours later.

The others returned with all of her father's files and everything they needed to prove she had ownership of the businesses. Even the house, as it seemed. He really had intended for everything to go to her husband, but Hendrick, being Hendrick, refused and soon had papers signed to make it all hers. Where he had those contacts to make that happen in a single night, she didn't know. But she wanted them for herself.

Both of their mothers were in safe houses. Charlotte said she wanted to travel—to get as far away from her husband's filth as she could. Her words. But for now, Hendrick wanted to keep her safe and out of trouble. He didn't know his mother anymore.

Hudson showed up not long after the others with similar files and paperwork. Everything was happening so fast it made Kinley dizzy. Hendrick let every detail roll off him.

But there was still a line of tension in his shoulders. Kinley didn't have the chance to pull him aside for several hours. Talking, signing, planning, debriefing, and more with each person involved. Hudson didn't expect too much difficulty in taking over, but he had Hendrick to back him up when needed. With the mercenaries behind Hudson, people would either fall in line or leave.

The same applied to her. All of her father's employees were now hers. This would be a much bigger mess to go through than Hudson's.

They were alone hours later. Kinley hopped onto the table and slid along it until she was in front of Hendrick's chair.

"Are you all right?" She set one hand on his cheek and the other on the arm that moved up her thigh.

"I'm all right. Are you?"

"I'm overwhelmed. Hendrick?" She waited a beat before continuing. "I'm sorry about my father's role in Shane's death."

"Don't. You didn't know, and there was nothing you could have done if you had."

"All the same."

"Thank you, pretty girl." He sighed and leaned his forehead against her stomach. "I was ready to let it go to protect you. I never expected my father. I knew he was capable, but I didn't think he'd ever kill his own son. He hadn't killed me growing up, or even after I abandoned my place and the family." He continued to speak against her, his breath warming her. "I don't regret it."

Kinley ran her fingers through his hair, soothing the big man as much as she could. The big man that she needed by her side to be the next crime boss in a long line. She didn't need him because he was one of King's mercenaries. No. Kinley needed him because he was her match, the other half to her heart.

A throat clearing tore their attention away from

each other, but they didn't rush. Hendrick only turned his head while keeping it against her and Kinley didn't remove her fingers from his hair.

"You two have a visitor." Gear quirked an eyebrow, then took a stance near the door, his chain visible over his shoulders.

Hendrick straightened and set Kinley on her feet.

Rhys Wilder walked in. She remembered him from the party and the centre of all of this, although not intentionally.

"Word travels fast." Hendrick relaxed, but only a little.

"Indeed."

"Maybe not fast enough. I can't offer any deal or partnership."

That made Rhys pause in his next step, but he caught up to himself and his expression cleared. "Hudson."

Hendrick nodded.

"Good. Shane spoke highly of him. But I came here to talk to you anyway." Rhys tilted his head to look at Kinley with a charming smile she knew better than to trust at face value.

Hendrick gestured for Rhys to sit and nudged her back into her chair before reclaiming his.

"I want to make you an offer. To buy each establishment and other business assets from you."

This was what he'd been trying to do with her father. When her father refused, Rhys had attacked the business. Sabotage, her father had called it. So what was the difference between offering a partnership to Shane, but wanting to buy from her father? They were two very different people. If Kinley looked for a partnership, she'd look for someone like-minded. And that wouldn't be her father.

"The amount I'm offering is more than generous." He pulled a piece of paper from his suit jacket pocket and slid it across the table. Kinley picked it up and unfolded it. It took effort to school her features, but she made sure not a single muscle twitched on her face.

"And if I say no?"

"Then I'll try to convince you."

"The same way you tried to convince my father?"

"No." Rhys spared a glance at Hendrick.

Kinley stared at Rhys. She concentrated on her breathing and kept the same expressionless face as the others in the room. Although, she was certain Hendrick's eyes would give him away if she spared him a look. But this was her business now, and her decision.

She'd hoped the other man would flinch or even blink. But at least his lips twitched ever so slightly.

"I have to decline your offer." Kinley tried not to grin as the shock registered on his face. It was the first change in emotion he'd shown, and she was the cause. "But I have a counteroffer."

Rhys didn't hide his amusement. "I'm all ears."

"A partnership. I'm not giving up my father's business. I have plans to change it. When I'm finished, it won't resemble anything my father created, except for its main purpose."

"I had similar plans once I acquired it." He leaned his elbows on the table. "I wonder if our visions align."

"I'm willing to find out. Are you?"

His lips lifted as he pulled in a slow, deep breath. "I am. It seems you have a deal." He held out his hand, crossing it in front of Hendrick toward her.

She shook it, feeling excitement and fear mingle together in her core.

"We'll talk soon." Gear led Rhys out. Dealing with her father's people would not be easy and if there were to be a big change like this, it's better for it to happen right away rather than later.

Hendrick lifted her hand, turning her palm to his lips. "For what it's worth, I think that was the right decision."

"It's worth a lot. My vision might be too big for me to handle. And dealing with all the employees will be a mess. I know you'd offer backup, but he has resources. I didn't agree with much of how my father managed things."

"I have something I need to show you." Hendrick pulled her from her chair and led her to the elevator.

"What's that?"

Hendrick pushed the button to take them down to the parking garage. "It isn't much, and we can move, but it's my home."

HIS APARTMENT WASN'T much more than a bachelor pad. But it had been his home for a long time, despite not spending much of his time here. It was safe, secure, and would fit the two of them for now.

Kinley walked in front of him, her head tilted as she took in the small open concept. She rubbed her hands up and down her arms. Hendrick moved to the thermostat and turned it up. He hadn't been in here since the day he packed to go to his father's. It wasn't the season for the heat, but for whatever reason, Kinley had a chill.

"We can move." Even if the two of them would be comfortable here, he imagined they would outgrow the space.

"We don't need to rush." She turned on him with a smile that melted his worries. He hadn't realized he'd needed her to like this place. She'd come from a small mansion. This was likely the size of her old bedroom.

Kinley closed the distance between them and wrapped her arms around his waist.

"Where we live doesn't matter just yet. We're both going to be busy soon. The only thing that matters..." she trailed off, tilting her head up to give him access.

"What matters to you, pretty girl?" Hendrick pulled her against him, pressing her body to his.

"You," she whispered.

"Even with all this crazy?" He nuzzled her neck.

"I wouldn't have you any other way."

"I'd ask if you think you can be the wife of a mercenary, but being a crime boss yourself puts you at a whole other level."

"Is that what I am now?"

"Basically." Hendrick peeled her shirt up her torso. "Let me give you the grand tour."

Kinley let him lead her backward to walk through the apartment. He pinched the back of her bra and let it fall in their wake. Through the kitchen, around the island, past the front door and into the living room.

They stalled when he pushed her legging down. With her thighs trapped, Hendrick slid his fingers to her centre.

"Looks nice," she gasped.

"You haven't seen the best part." Hendrick stroked her clit until she was panting.

"What a terrible line."

"It won't be so terrible when I have you laid out on the bed to do with as I please."

"What about what I please?"

"You'll get it all. Just as you get all of me."

"I like all of you."

"What was that? You *like* all of me."

A wicked grin split her lips. Her hazy eyes filled with a challenge. "Yeah. Like."

Hendrick let his own chuckle loose and got to work. Bending her over the back of the couch, he set his tongue to her entrance and swirled before moving through her folds to flick her clit. Squeezing both ass cheeks, he spread her wider to give him access.

With her leggings still tight around her thighs, she couldn't move, couldn't escape.

"Hendrick."

As much as he wanted to tease, her plea forced him to shove her leggings the rest of the way off. He didn't need to tease to play this game. Overwhelming instant pleasure would do the same.

He pulled her up and lifted her into a bridal carry to make their way to the bedroom.

"I want to hear every sound you make, pretty girl." Hendrick laid her out on the bed and set his tongue back on her clit. With two fingers, he worked her until he lost his own control, grinding his cock into the bed.

He felt the first flutters of her walls around his fingers, and he ripped himself away. He wanted to feel that first orgasm around his cock.

She whimpered as he moved up the bed, but he didn't give her time to protest. Hendrick sealed their bodies together. With a grip on the back of her neck, he kissed her, devouring everything she gave to him.

He chased the peak, knowing she was on the edge. Breaking the kiss, he roared into her neck as he filled her. Kinley bit down, muffling her cry as she came around him, her legs shaking.

"I was right the first night I met you." Hendrick set his forehead against hers while getting his breath under control.

"Right about what?" Kinley had the same problem catching her air, but she blinked up at him while tracing her fingers over the indent from her teeth.

"You're going to be chaos. Good thing I love chaos."

THE END

WANT MORE OF the mercenary world? Have you read my free novella, Breaking Away? To get the prequel to the King's Mercenaries series, join my newsletter with the link below. My newsletter is the best place to stay up to date on new releases, special events, and sneak peeks.

https://bit.ly/sarahurq

Also, visit my website at...

http://www.authorsarahurquhart.com

...to see my full book list.

KING'S MERCENARIES SERIES

Breaking Away, A Novella
Shades of Cruelty
Shades of Savage
Shades of Chaos

ACKNOWLEDGMENTS

You have to look at the little joys and appreciate the people in your life when you're on the struggle bus. The curve balls were flying hard and fast while I wrote this book, and even the one before this. And it's been the small things that kept my head up. They kept me from burying myself in unnecessary work. I may have taken longer to get this book out than planned, but I've come out on the other end hale and whole. I have a few people to thank for that.

Always first is my family. The support and excitement I have over my books from my siblings and parents is some of the biggest encouragement I could ever have. My husband supports every decision I make with my business and is always there with suggestions of his own, most of them good. As he likes to remind me often, he isn't just a pretty face.

I have great kids. While still young, they like that their mom is an author. Which would explain why my son announced to his entire grade three class last year that I was an author. Best kept secret, his teacher said. But they are as patient as little minds can be when I say I need to get some work done before we can do all the fun things.

The sprint group I am part of is amazing! Seeing each other almost every day has become part of my routine. We help each other with plot, characters, admin, and other times we have a blast laughing and joking. So to Ellie Pond, C.S. Berry, Holly Roberds, Ivy Nelson, Danielle Romero, and so many more of you; you're amazing and I couldn't do this without you.

This past year, I've expanded my team. I have the best PA ever. Leah, you're the best and I love how much you care about your work and all the authors who are smart enough to hire you. I can't imagine the struggles I'd have without you!

I started this by saying I appreciated not only the people, but the joys. Being able to take my kids to their sports every week—who am I kidding; it's daily—is a blessing and joy. I love watching them succeed in the things that makes them happy. I'm grateful for the local archery club. It's an activity I've wanted to learn since I was a child and now I enjoy it with my family. And to all the other authors out there that write books. This is a hard job, but so much fun. And I get to enjoy reading your books too. All of these things fill my well and make it so I can keep going forward.

FOLLOW SARAH ON HER SOCIAL MEDIA

https://www.instagram.com/authorsarahu/
https://www.facebook.com/groups/sarahswildones
https://www.facebook.com/authorsarahu
https://www.bookbub.com/profile/sarah-urquhart